Penny,
I can't wa
can send me a copy
of your first book.
I know it will be
just fabulous!
Lots of love,

xxxxx

SIREN STORIES

Presents

LILLY PROSPERO
AND THE MAGIC RABBIT

Book One in the Lilly Prospero Series

J.J. Barnes

My first book is dedicated to my first child, Rose.
My two biggest goals in life were motherhood and to be a writer.
Both have brought me joy, but Rose brought me true love.

Chapter One

"We've found her. We've found the Life Giver!"

Keren Archer looked up from her desk, calm and poised, not betraying the all-consuming excitement that was surging inside her. The pale skinned assistant in front of her was practically vibrating, her translucent blue eyes full of triumph. "And the bracelet?"

"Still on. The curse holds."

Keren Archer nodded thoughtfully, considering the next step in this longed for development. "Thank you, Fawn, bring me everything you have and I'll start the process for bringing her home."

~ƸӜƷ~

Lilly Prospero stood outside the gates of her new school and nervously twiddled the crystal on her charm bracelet. Nerves bubbled in her chest but she tried to push them down as she scolded herself, rubbing her wet palms on her new green school jumper. If she behaved in the right way, spoke to the right people and liked the right things, she could actually become one of the popular kids. She could have friends and fun for the first time in her life. She could be the person she had always wanted to be, instead of the lonely loser she had always felt like. If she didn't screw it up, and she knew how big an if that was.

Fixing a confident smile to her face, and wishing she was anybody else but her, Lilly stepped inside the school grounds and headed through the crowds of fellow green and grey clad pupils towards the imposing building at the end of the path.

Rifling through her bag, she looked for her welcome sheet, hoping to find the map of the school so she could get to her new form room without making a fool of herself. As she turned the corner onto the playground she walked smack into a red headed girl, knocking the bottle of lemonade the girl was drinking down her front.

"Oh my god," gasped Lilly, staring in horror at what she had just done. "I am so sorry."

"What the hell are you thinking?" screeched the girl, her green eyes flashing with fury as she plucked at her now soaking wet sweater. "Are you blind?"

"No, I'm new. I'm sorry. I'm Lilly." Lilly stuttered, hating herself for talking like an inarticulate fool.

The girl tossed her mane of red curls back over her shoulders and glared at Lilly with eyes heavily adorned with mascara. "Get. Out. Of. My. Way." She spat venomously.

Lilly stumbled backwards and let the girl pass, watching as she stalked away towards a group of girls who stood watching, open mouthed. Scurrying away and starting across the playground towards the cloakroom, Lilly gave herself a little pep talk. She tried to reassure herself that even a poor start didn't mean hope was lost, she could still get her act together and start her new life with style… If she didn't screw it up any more. Big if.

As she approached the doors she felt someone tug at her arm. She turned, expecting to see the red haired girl ready to give her some abuse, but nobody was there. She looked around for a moment, confused, then went to keep going before a more violent tug wrenched at her, dragging her to the ground. She cried out in pain and shock as her knees scraped across the tarmac, clutching at her arm where her shoulder had been pulled, a strange feeling of fear creeping through her. She looked around wide eyed, desperately searching for her attacker, but still nobody. She tried not to cry, blinking frantically, her grazed knees stinging and her pride destroyed.

Around her, faces laughed and fingers pointed. The red haired girl was approaching, flanked by her friends, a smirk of glee splashed across her face as she took in Lilly's sprawled form. They walked past her, stepping over her bag and the scattered debris that had fallen, and walked into the school, laughing.

Lilly sighed in despair. All hope was lost. She would forever be Lilly. Lilly the clutz. Lilly the loser. Lilly the terminal failure. She wanted to cry, but knew that crying on her first day of school in front of everyone would be tantamount to a death knoll for her.

Picking everything up and stuffing it into her bag, Lilly hurried into the school and away from the cackling audience. She rubbed at her eyes with the sleeve of her jumper as she sniffed fruitily, and then went to twiddle at the crystal on her charm bracelet but found her arm bare; the bracelet was gone. Cursing her luck, she looked around the floor, felt up inside her sleeve and hunted through the things in her bag, but there was no sign of it. Her heart broke and she felt fresh tears begin to creep their way into her eyes.

"Are you okay?"

Lilly looked up and saw a good looking sixth form boy with thick dark curls and dark brown eyes leaning on the door with his arms crossed, watching her.

"I lost my bracelet," she spluttered, sniffling in embarrassment. "I'm new."

"I guessed that. I'd have noticed you before otherwise." He spoke with an easy confidence, his eyes fixed to hers.

Lilly's mouth went dry and her heart raced as she tried to find something interesting or witty to say. She failed. Her mind was blank. She wasn't sure she knew English anymore. Her tongue felt fat. "Do you know where 10D's form room is?" she asked eventually, then put her face in her hands as she realised she was officially a lost cause.

"Down the corridor," he said smiling, dimples framing his mouth in an amused smile. He seemed very aware of the effect he was having on her, and he seemed to be enjoying it too. "To the left. Mrs Robinson's room."

"Thanks," Lilly said awkwardly and went to step forward. He didn't move from where he was leaning and Lilly wondered if she was supposed to wriggle past him or wait for him to leave. She looked at her feet shyly, tucking her bobbed brown hair behind one ear, and when she looked up again he had disappeared. She looked around, wondering where he had gone and feeling both relief and disappointment, then hurried down the corridor and found the form room just before the start of school bell rang.

Pushing open the door, Lilly stepped into the room and was confronted with the red haired girl she had bumped into earlier sitting on a desk, surrounded by her friends.

"You," she spat, looking her up and down in disgust. "What are you doing in here?"

"10D. My form." Lilly stuttered as she tried to gather her words and force her hands to stop shaking. "I'm new."

"You said," she snarled, rolling her eyes at one of the girl next to her. "Right before tipping lemonade all over me."

Lilly was aware that all eyes were on her, and none of them held kindness. She hesitated, unsure what she was supposed to do and feeling like an idiot, when behind her the door opened again and a woman bustled in carrying a stack of folders and a hot mug of coffee.

"Look out, look out," she said, ushering Lilly out of the way, dropping everything except the coffee onto her desk. "You must be Lilly, I'm Mrs Robinson, your new form tutor. If you'd like to take a seat by the window, across from Saffron there," she said, gesturing to where the red haired girl was sitting, glaring. "We can get started."

Lilly shuffled towards the desk and sat down awkwardly, determined to keep her head down and avoid too much unwanted attention. Blending into the background was her preferred state, especially when things were already going so badly wrong.

Around her there was chatter and busy movement as her classmates sat in their seats and exchanged gossip with their friends. She heard the words "new girl" far too often for her liking and she sunk lower in her seat, keeping her grey eyes firmly on the desk in front of her.

"We have a new pupil today, ladies and gents," Mrs Robinson announced, clapping her hands together to summons the attention of the masses. Lilly felt her gut tighten. No, why, no. Please no. "So even though there's only a few weeks left until the summer, let's all try and make sure she feels like this is her home. Why don't you stand up and tell us a bit about yourself, Lilly?"

Around the room faces spun to stare at Lilly. This was it. This was how she was going to die.

"Erm, hi. I'm Lilly Prospero." She said as she stood and held up a hand in an awkward wave and wished she was anywhere else but there. "Erm… I'm fifteen and we moved here because my mum got a new job. Well it's not a new job, it's the same job, just for a new person. Erm, she's an accountant, she was working for a big company in the city but then got cherry picked by some rich client who wanted a private accountant, so we moved here so she could work just for him. So, that's why I'm here. Now. Not there. And erm, I like painting and drawing, love it really, it's my favourite thing in the world. I'm not really good at much else to be honest. So, yeah. Hi. I'm Lilly." She heard muffled chuckles around the room and quickly dropped to the seat to bury her face in her hands for the second time already that morning.

"How lovely," said Mrs Robinson brightly. "I'm sure everyone will make you feel very welcome, and you'll soon feel like you've always been here."

Lilly realised she already did. Another school, another group of people who had either no interest in her or an active dislike. More classes she knew she would be rubbish in and more drudgery she was fed up of before it had even begun. Same reality, new location.

After register was taken, Lilly, trying to memorise her surroundings, started following the crowd towards their first class of the day. Something she was dreading. Maths.

Walking down one of the corridors, Lilly felt her skin prickle, and quickly turned back. Standing in the doorway of a classroom she'd just passed was the curly haired sixth former, a smile playing over his lips as he watched her intently. He flashed her a quick grin and she turned away feeling embarrassed. He must have been smiling in a laughing way, her obvious inadequacy giving him amusement, but something about that natural assumption didn't sit quite right with her. Shyly, she looked back over her shoulder for a second look, but he had already gone.

In maths she was shown to her new seat, next to a boy named Jake who smiled at her indifferently and started chatting about football to the boy on the desk behind them. One of Saffron's friends was on the seat across from hers, and she narrowed her eyes at Lilly as she sat down. Lilly looked quickly away and stared at her hands, accepting the sheets of fractions that landed in front of her from Mr Tristan, and tried to focus her mind on the task at hand.

Lilly's mum was amazing at maths, an excelled in her accountancy work because of it. Her father, the manager of a cleaning products company, spent all day looking at spreadsheets and numbers. For them maths was as simple as speaking English, but for Lilly it was like trying to learn Portuguese. She frowned and started scratching at the paper with her pencil, trying to force the numbers to obey her will, and failing.

After ten minutes she began to look around as boredom started to take over. She let her eyes wander over the display boards and book cases, and check out her new classmates, distracting herself from the painful work she was supposed to be doing. Saffron was tapping away rapidly on her calculator, scribbling answers down, working down the third page of work as though it were no challenge at all. Suddenly, as Lilly watched her enviously, Saffron turned and caught Lilly's eye.

Without hesitating, Saffron shoved her hand straight in the air and called out, "Mr Tristan!"

"Yes, Saffron?"

"The new girl was just trying to copy from Maisie's page," she said, pointing an accusatory finger towards Lilly.

On the desk across from her, Saffron's friend looked aghast. Lilly's mouth fell open and she tried to protest her innocence, but found just a strangely strangled squeaking is all that came out.

Mr Tristan came over, looking at Maisie's page and then at Lilly's. "Well she's not making a very good job of it," he said with a condescending tone as her classmates began to laugh behind their hands. "It looks like you'll have some catching up to do, Miss Prospero."

Lilly felt her face redden and she stared down at the work she was doing feeling utterly mortified. She hated Saffron. Hated her. Her confidence, her beauty, the obvious popularity she courted with ease. Saffron had everything Lilly had ever wanted and how she loathed her for it. She wished Saffron could feel a shred of the embarrassment she had been feeling since she arrived at that school. Just once. Just to take her down a peg or two.

Staring at a particularly difficult question, Lilly idly began doodling on the edge of her worksheet. She drew a fluffy round body, beady eyes, and eight long, spindly legs. She smiled at the little cartoon spider momentarily, then forced herself to concentrate back on her work, staring at the calculator and trying to figure out if any of the symbols on it matched those on the question.

"AAAAARGH!" came a scream from across the room. "Help me!"

Saffron fell from her chair, scrambling backwards, panic on her face and her chest heaving as she panted in horror.

"Saffron?" asked Mr Tristan, hurrying over. "What on earth is the matter?"

"Spider! A huge spider!" she howled, ignoring the laughter that was resonating around the room as she thrashed around on her bum, wildly rubbing at her hair in case the offending creature had nested in the curls. "It looked poisonous!"

"Don't be ridiculous, there are no poisonous spiders in England!" Mr Tristan said dismissively, carefully lifting things from Saffron's desk and peering around on the floor nervously. "Are you sure you saw one? There's nothing there now."

"Certain," she said, dragging herself to her feet and trying to regain some dignity, smoothing down her skirt and fluffing her hair. "It was there. I saw it."

As Saffron hesitantly lowered herself back into her seat, Lilly caught sight of a large, black spider scurrying across the floor and out under the door. She grinned to herself, a peculiar sense of vindication filling her, and moved some of the papers on her desk around looking for the spider she had sketched before, but it was gone.

After maths they moved onto history, where Mr Stubbs, who smelled strongly of coffee, reeled off information as though he were a human text book. Then to Geography, where Dr Murray got excited talking about a mountain in Peru. Lilly sat through each class listening and making notes, but struggling to care about the information she was trying to process.

At lunch time, Lilly decided to take herself for a walk around the school grounds, partly to familiarise herself with the place, and partly to avoid confrontation or humiliation. She wandered along, chewing on her egg sandwich and watching the groups of friends chatting and playing ball games. Finishing her sandwich, she shoved the box back into her bag and her sleeve pulled up revealing her bare arm. She looked sadly at the spot where her bracelet should have been and wondered if it might have been handed in at the school office, deciding to go and ask.

As she walked around the building towards the office, balancing precariously on the narrow curb, she spotted the curly haired sixth former leaning against a tree, chatting idly to Saffron who was gazing at him in adoration. He spotted her, stopped speaking to Saffron, and held eye contact with her. She wobbled and lost her balance, stepping heavily onto the road. Saffron turned to see what had stolen the object of her desire's attention and Lilly darted away in panic, dropping the boy's gaze and disappearing around a corner. The last thing she needed was to enrage Saffron further, and she had a suspicion that attention being stolen from her would certainly do that.

Panting, Lilly hurried to the school office to enquire about her lost bracelet, but was disappointed to learn it had not been handed in. Sighing she turned away, dully accepting the bracelet was lost and feeling her chest tighten in grief.

"A charm bracelet?" she heard a voice, and looked up to see the history teacher, Mr Stubbs, standing nearby.

"Yeah, it was special," she said sadly, her fingers plucking at the cuff of her jumper where she would have felt the bracelet sitting. "I've had it since I was a baby."

"I see," he said, a serious look on his face. "And it fell off?"

Lilly hesitated, not wanting to tell the man about whatever had dragged at her arm moments before the bracelet went missing, knowing that a jewellery thieving poltergeist theory was not likely to improve her first day of school impression. "I think so."

"How unlucky," he said, shaking his head then looking at her intently, a curious expression on his face that made the hairs on Lilly's neck stand on end. "Well I'll make sure to keep my eyes peeled for you, Lilly Prospero. It sounds like it was of great importance."

Lilly began to feel a little freaked out, and nodded gratitude before hurrying away and round the corner. Once out of sight, she stopped and leaned against the wall of the corridor and closed her eyes for a moment. Even for Lilly, things seemed to be getting weird.

~ƐӁƷ~

Entering the art room that afternoon, Lilly smelled the paints, chalks and inks, took in the wash of coloured papers and fabrics, the splattered work tables and clunky sculptures, and felt herself relax for the first time that day. Being surrounded by art supplies was her natural state and she couldn't wait to get started on the lesson, whatever it was it may hold. If every class could be an art class, Lilly would enjoy school more than anything in the world.

"Lilly Prospero?" called the teacher into the crowd of pupils that were swarming into his room. "There you are!" He approached her and held out a trunk like tattooed arm, extending his large hairy hand towards her and gripped her own, shaking it in a remarkably gentle way. "Hogg. Nice to meet you. Please take a seat anywhere, I am told art is your wheel house so I'm sure we'll get on just fine."

She nodded and mouthed a thank you that didn't quite make it out of her mouth. She slightly overwhelmed by the size and volume of the enormous, bald, leather waist coat wearing man that seemed to occupy half the room just by himself. He wasn't entirely what she had anticipated of a high school art teacher, but she liked him.

"Well, Miss Prospero here joins us on quite an important day," said Mr Hogg as he held a piece of paper aloft in front of him, peering at what was written there and reading aloud. "The opportunity of a lifetime has landed in our laps. Chief executive of Adamantine Power, Keren Archer, was a pupil at our school not so long ago. AP are having a big overhaul, going green, and looking for a new logo to represent this new start. Instead of hiring a professional from this highly competitive industry, Ms Archer is running a competition for year tens at this very school. The winner will not only get a chance to work with Ms Archer's outstanding team over the summer, but will be paid the industry standard for their final design." He stopped reading and peered around the room proudly. "Corporate jargon aside that seems like a pretty damn good opportunity to me."

Around the room ears were pricking up. Saffron appeared to be quivering in excitement. Lilly felt her heart begin to race. If she won she might get instant access to popularity. Instant respect. Instant acceptance.

"As this is only available to year tens," Mr Hogg flourished the paper and went on, "you are in a very privileged position. The competition will be run in three stages. The first stage is open to anybody who wishes to enter and will be a landscape picture. From these entries, just three will be selected to move on. The second round is abstract, and two will progress. The third round is a portrait of a person or animal, and from these two pictures a winner will be selected. It is not mandatory, but should anyone wish to enter they can sign their names here." He held a form aloft. "The landscape entry is due in on Friday."

Saffron and Lilly were the first two on their feet, and Saffron snatched the pen up before Lilly had even got to the front of the room.

"Think you can win, do you?" she laughed in Lilly's face.

"Yes actually," Lilly said, nodding. She wasn't confident about many things in life, and was miserably aware of each and every one of her flaws, but art was her confidence and art, she knew, could be the key to changing her life.

Saffron looked taken aback by Lilly's uncharacteristic display of confidence, chucked the pen back on the desk, then stalked back to her seat. Lilly picked it up and wrote in clear, solid letters, 'LILLY ELIZABETH PROSPERO.'

For the rest of the lesson, she practiced with charcoal sticks, making notes as Mr Hogg spoke, dreaming about landscape ideas for the competition. Something striking, something different. Something that would make her stand out.

When the bell rang for the end of the day, Lilly shoved everything in her bag and made a break for freedom when she noticed the curly haired sixth former leaning against a tree watching her again. She frowned, it was starting to get a little creepy.

"Hey, new girl," he said, catching her eye and grinning.

"Lilly," she said, stepping forward hesitantly. "My name's Lilly."

"Alex," he said, offering her his hand, which she accepted and he shook. It was warm and soft. When he let go she felt her skin tingling where his touch had been.

Over his shoulder she became aware of two girls and a boy stood staring at the two of them, whispering rapidly with angry looks on their faces. She frowned in confusion, certain she didn't recognise them and not able to figure out how she'd already managed to piss off yet more people.

"So, Lilly, meet me tomorrow?" asked Alex, the corner of his mouth creeping up in a funny half smile. Lilly wasn't sure whether it was a request or a command.

"Why?" she asked. It didn't make sense that a handsome sixth former would be seeking her company. Of all the girls in the school, why her?

"It'll be worth your while." He said confidently.

"But…" she said nervously, it felt like a trap. Or a mistake. Why her? It was weird and made no sense at all, but she decided that even a friend as mysterious and peculiar as this one was better than no friend at all and nodded in agreement. "Okay. Where?"

"By the field. Where I saw you earlier. Lunch time."

"Okay. I'll see you tomorrow."

He waved, a mischievous look on his face. Then he turned and winked at the three who were watching from behind him, and walked away. As Lilly went to leave too, she felt a burning on the back of her neck as three pairs of eyes watched her leave. She tried to walk away slowly and calmly, but as she heard footsteps approach from behind, she dropped all pretence and ran.

Chapter Two

"That's a rabbit!" exclaimed Lilly in surprise when she stepped in the front door.

Her mum was sitting at the kitchen table working on her laptop, as per usual, except this time in her lap was a large, fluffy, brown rabbit. Lilly dropped to the floor and peered at the rabbit. The rabbit peered back.

"Your father and I thought you could use a nice surprise after your first day," her mum said, stroking the rabbit's head and smiling. "We know you were nervous and thought this could help. Isn't he a handsome boy? He's a house rabbit and he's already litter trained and very tame, so he can live in the house with us and sleep in your bedroom!"

"What's his name?"

"I don't know you'll have to ask him!" she said with a laugh. "But he's all yours. Do you want to take him?"

"Cool," Lilly whispered, holding out her hands to the rabbit who eyed her suspiciously. Carefully, and gently, she took the rabbit from her mums lap and held him against her body. He was warm and solid, with a white stripe down his nose and large brown eyes. He smelled of hay and she could feel his heart fluttering rapidly against her chest.

"Can I take him upstairs?" Lilly asked, unsure what the right thing to do is when you're presented with a surprise new pet.

"Of course," said her mum with a chuckle. "He's yours remember?"

"Cool, thanks mum," Lilly whispered again, so overwhelmed by the surprise of this new pet that the horrors and confusion of the day seemed to fade away. Carefully and slowly she carried the rabbit up the stairs and placed him gently on her bed. "So, what's your name?" she wondered out loud, looking him in the eyes with curiosity.

"Jeffrey," said the rabbit.

Lilly blinked. She looked around then looked back at the rabbit. "What?"

He cocked his head to the side and said, very slowly and clearly, "My name… is… Jeffrey."

"That's a weird name for a rabbit," she said, crossing her arms and frowning.

"That's what you're noticing?"

"No, but it seemed like a good place to start," said Lilly, feeling a little too shocked to find anything sensible to say.

"So anyway, Lilly Prospero, what do you like to do?" asked Jeffrey, peering around her room and assessing his surroundings with a pensive look on his furry face. "Any hobbies? Skills?"

Slightly taken aback by the rabbit's quizzical approach, Lilly said, "Well I like to draw and paint, why?"

"Show me."

"What, now?" asked Lilly, completely thrown by this strange development.

"No, next week! Of course now," he said, rolling his eyes.

"You're bossy for a rodent, you know?" said Lilly folding her arms.

He nodded. He knew.

Lilly fetched a sketch pad and pencils from her desk, and set them on the floor in front of the observing rabbit. She pulled out some colours and started to draw. Soon the page was filled with butterflies swooping across the page, their turquoise wings trimmed in pinks and golds, swirling patterns and shimmering edges. Sitting back to admire her work, Lilly felt her eyes go funny. She rubbed them then looked back at the page again, but it wasn't her eyes. The butterflies were actually starting to quiver, to move.

"What?" she gasped, staring in shock.

Jeffrey jumped down and sat beside her, watching. Soon, wings were starting to pull away from the page; translucent, silken colours glowing in the light. The butterflies launched themselves from the page, more and more flying out until soon her room was filled with shimmering wings.

"What the…" she said, ducking as a cloud of butterflies swooped down and whizzed over her head.

"The window!" called Jeffrey from under his paws. "Open the window!"

Lilly scurried over, worked the catch and flung open the window letting the breeze drift in and catch the butterflies. Soon the swarm was swirling across the breeze and out into the warm air of the June afternoon. As the last fluttered through, Lilly reached up and closed it again with a clunk.

"What the hell?" she demanded, turning on the rabbit.

"Impressive work," the rabbit said, nodding with a pleased smile on his face.

"I didn't do that!"

"Well I didn't," he said.

Lilly heard a knock on her bedroom door and jumped as her mum poked her head round, a big smile on her face.

"How's it going in here?"

"Oh! Fine! Just fine!" said Lilly, her voice far too high and her eyes far too wide.

Lilly tried to look innocent, as her mum looked puzzled and stepped into the room.

"Does he have a name?" she asked, fondling the rabbit's head.

"Jeffrey."

"Interesting choice," her mum said, laughing in surprise and sitting on the edge of the bed. "So, tell me about your first day at school."

"It sucked," Lilly said as she sighed and rested her head against the wall, closing her eyes as the memories of the day crept back in. "There's this girl, Saffron. She's evil and she hates me." Jeffrey sat by her feet, watching her, listening. "And I lost my charm bracelet," she said, holding up her bare arm.

"Oh no!" her mum took her wrist. "What a shame! It's not left your wrist since you were tiny."

"I know," Lilly agreed. She felt tears in her eyes and wiped them away with her sleeve. Jeffrey jumped up beside her and placed a soft brown paw tenderly on her leg. "I'm so sorry mum."

"Oh sweetheart, you don't have to apologise. Maybe it'll get handed in," suggested her mum, reaching over and giving Lilly's hand a reassuring squeeze. "It's not the end of the world, darling."

"Yeah maybe." Lilly said, sniffing. "There was one good thing. I'm entering an art competition. If I win I get to work at this power company over the summer, *and* design their new logo, *and* get paid for it. I've got to hand in a landscape painting on Friday." Jeffrey shuffled on the spot.

"That sounds brilliant," enthused her mum, clearly relieved that her daughter had some positives in the sea of misery she usually associated with education. "Do you have any ideas?"

"After school tomorrow can we go to that big industrial plant over on the other side of town? I want to paint the cooling towers but in pretty colours instead of greys and browns," said Lilly. "Make something beautiful out of something ugly."

"That sounds like a wonderful idea, honey. I'll pick you up." She said cheerfully and kissed her daughter's head as she got up. "School will get better, sweetheart. It just takes time. You'll see."

Once her mum was back downstairs, Jeffrey said to Lilly, "What power company?"

"Adamantine Power, apparently the lady who runs it went to our school or something," she said as Jeffrey's nose wiffled thoughtfully. "What's going on with the butterflies? How did that happen?"

"We'll figure it out, just don't tell anyone yet, okay?" he said. "We need to work out what's going on so we can make sure everything's safe."

"What's not safe?" asked Lilly, frowning. "It was some butterflies. It's hardly life or death."

"Well, it *is* life."

~ƐЖƺ~

When Lilly got up the next morning, she felt a surge of excitement mixed with a fog of dread. There seemed to suddenly be a lot more things she needed to deal with beside the ordinary school survival plans. She wanted to find out about Alex, she wanted to win the art contest, and she wanted to find out what her new talking rabbit had done to her drawing. Mostly she just wanted to avoid Saffron at all costs, but realised with a grim acceptance that that would be the hardest of her desires to actually achieve.

Walking to school she let her brain try to process everything that was going on, when suddenly a car screeched across and pulled up roughly onto the pavement in front of her, driven by a cross faced young woman with a cigarette between her fingers. The roadside door swung open and a shock of flaming red hair came into view as Saffron stepped out into traffic, jumping in panic as a bus went trundling past her. As she stepped onto the pavement, the car shot back out into traffic leaving Saffron alone and looking shaken in its wake.

"Are you okay?" Lilly asked her, before she could stop herself.

"Of course I am!" Saffron said indignantly, spinning to shoot Lilly a look of fury and embarrassment, before storming off towards the school.

Lilly followed at a distance and became aware she was being watched. The girl with long black braids who had been standing with her friends and staring at Alex and herself the day before was standing on the other side of the road, watching her, a fiery look on her face. Lilly gulped and hurried past, the girls stare searing into the back of her neck.

"That was Ashya Patel," came Alex's voice as he appeared next to her, startling her. "Just ignore her. She's a freak. Don't forget lunch time, okay?"

Lilly was about to ask him why Ashya had a problem with her, but before she could he had gone again. She looked around in confusion but he had disappeared into the crowd.

Keeping her head down and trying to avoid confrontation, Lilly settled into her classes quietly and managed to avoid making anybody angry. During Geography as she vaguely listened to Dr Murray rattle on endlessly about Peru, she absentmindedly doodled some bumble bees on the edge of her exercise book. Soon she had soon filled the margin of her page, the notes she had half-heartedly been making were dwarfed by her artistic efforts as large, stripy bees swirled across the page.

"Oh god," she whispered as suddenly the bees were beginning to quiver and their wings were beginning to flutter. Around the room people were looking around, looking to see where the buzzing sound that was gradually becoming more audible was coming from. Lilly stared in horror as suddenly, a swarm of enormous, brightly coloured bees shot into the air out of the page, flitting around the room in a haze of stripes and a high pitched buzz. Everyone started screaming, ducking for cover as the enormous insects whizzed around in a frenzied panic.

"Help!" screamed Adele as a swarm circled her.

"What's happening?" howled Lee, throwing himself to the ground and covering his head with his arms.

"One's on my head!" screeched Maisie, flapping wildly at her hair, panic on her face as a huge insect ripped itself free from her hair and zoomed off again.

"Get out!" shouted Dr Murray, racing to the door. "Quickly!"

"What the hell are they?" wailed Jake from beneath a table.

"Quickly! They look poisonous!" Dr Murray said, ducking as a bright orange bee shot at his face, cornering suddenly and shooting in the other direction.

Saffron screamed in horror, flapping above her head, her hair flying around her wildly as bees spun in the air by her head. Dr Murray pulled the door open, shouting for everyone to leave. Lilly ignored him, staring around the room, terrified that someone had seen where they had come from.

"Come on, Lilly!" shouted Dr Murray as Lilly remained rooted to her seat.

She remembered the butterflies from the day before and looked over at the windows. The swooping bees looked like they were starting to panic as they crashed around the top of the room looking for an escape route.

"Lilly! Out!" Dr Murray shouted from the door of the classroom, now empty of pupils

"Just a minute!" she called.

"No Lilly, now!" he insisted.

Ignoring him she got up and ran to the edge of the room to battle with the catch on the window before flinging it open.

"Go, go!" she urged the insects, desperate to free them before anything bad happened.

Lilly swore she heard a, "Thank you Lilly," whispered in her ear as the last one escaped, then Dr Murray appeared at her side and slammed the window shut.

"What were you thinking?" he shouted at her. "Come with me! Right now!"

Lilly looked up anxiously, and followed the furious teacher out of the room, the door slamming behind her. In the corridor outside stood her classmates, staring at her in bewilderment. A teasing smirk was playing across Saffron's face as Lilly walked passed.

She followed Dr Murray down through the corridors, across the entrance hall, and down the admin corridor.

"Sit," said Dr Murray, gesturing to a scratchy looking brown fabric chair that sat ominously outside one of the offices, then knocked on the door and disappeared inside.

Lilly sat, wishing herself anywhere but there, as the fabric chewed at the skin on her thighs.

A few minutes later, Dr Murray reappeared and gestured her inside, then walked away in silence. Lilly stood, took a deep breath, and stepped inside the office. Behind the desk was a sharp faced woman with short steel grey hair and half-moon glasses. She looked at Lilly with disdain for several moments as the room filled with uncomfortable silence.

"Sit," Lilly was instructed for the second time in five minutes as Mrs Krank pointed a manicured nail at one of the seats in front of her desk. Lilly sat. "Lilly Prospero, I am Mrs Krank, your head mistress. I assume you are ashamed that these are the circumstances in which we are first meeting."

"I… uh…" Lilly stuttered, but then realised it wasn't a question and quickly closed her mouth and started nervously picking at her thumb nail.

"Dr Murray just explained to me what happened. I now have phone calls to make to pest control, and, by the sounds of it, no evidence of the kind of potentially dangerous creature we are dealing with. I am told they were highly poisonous and foreign in appearance, and that you have released them into the community, completely ignoring instructions from your teacher."

"I…"

"You will report to your form room at the end of school for detention. I will require a letter of apology to Dr Murray, myself, and the pest control people whom you have thoughtlessly inconvenienced by your behaviour."

"I…"

"Go and collect your things." Said the teacher coolly, looking away from Lilly and shuffling some paperwork on her desk as though it were far more important than the child in front of her.

Lilly stood and shuffled her feet. "I'm sorry, I was just trying to help," she said woefully.

"Now," Mrs Krank said dismissively, flapping a hand at her and picking up the phone.

Lilly backed out then hurried back to the geography room as the lunch bell rang. The door had a 'Do Not Enter' sign stuck to it, and her belongings were piled outside. Dismally she wondered if her life could possibly get any worse as she picked everything up and headed out to meet Alex.

Chapter Three

Leaning on a tree, Alex was watching her approach with a teasing smile playing on his lips. Lilly felt her breath catch in her throat and wished she had more, or any, experience with boys. Anything that would stop her turning to a puddle every time Alex looked at her.

"Come with me," he said, holding out his hand as Lilly got close.

"Why?" she asked hesitantly.

"It's worth it," he said, grinning mischievously.

"Can't we talk here?" she asked, nervously looking around. Her mother's lingering rule of not going with strangers was sitting uncomfortably in her belly, although she felt a little silly for still heeding the childhood warning.

"It's about magic," he leaned forward and whispered in her ear. Holding out his hand again, he nodded earnestly with his eyes full of promise, and Lilly allowed herself to be lead away.

Lilly's pulse raced in trepidatious excitement as he took her around the back of the out buildings, across the fields, and into the wooded area at the back of the grounds. Then he vanished.

Lilly screamed. She could still feel his hand in hers, but he had disappeared.

Laughing, he reappeared as suddenly as he had gone.

"Magic!" he said in a jubilant voice, as she stared open mouthed at him. "See? Told you it was worth it."

Lilly didn't speak. Her mind had been hit by too big a cloud of wonderment to articulate any words.

"I know, you thought you were the only one, right?"

Lilly nodded mutely.

"So weird that your family don't have any power. I guess you're different to them."

"A bit," she agreed, though she hadn't really thought about whether they had magic before. She frowned. Did they?

"I can't imagine what that's like, not being able to escape back to reality after being in this place." He said sympathetically. "So, what can you do?"

"You don't know?" she asked. He shook his head. "Things I draw have started coming to life."

"That's cool. So, what have you drawn?"

"Butterflies and bees," she said sheepishly, for the first time feeling like it actually wasn't that impressive.

"I guess it's just because you're new to all this." He said thoughtfully, making Lilly feel even more inadequate than she already did. "Most people's powers are active from birth, at least in some way. It takes time to learn to control it. When I was little I'd turn invisible randomly and my parents were always losing me. The neighbours were convinced they were haunted because they kept hearing a child crying." He chuckled heartily. "Of course, when I learned to control it I still used to go and spook them, just for the fun of it. Eventually they moved."

"Were they okay?" Lilly asked, looking worried.

"I guess so, I never asked," he said. Lilly looked around, nervous. His tone unsettled her and she suddenly felt very isolated and vulnerable with the strange boy. Noticing, Alex put a hand on her arm and said reassuringly, "No, it's good, I promise. They were pathetic, mortal types. People with power moved in instead. Nobody wants to live next to mortals." He shuddered at the thought. Lilly gulped

"Oh, okay," she said, feeling completely overwhelmed and not convinced it was okay at all.

"So, drawing?" he said, changing the subject. "You're entering that art competition then?"

"Yeah, I am," she said.

"Good, you'll do well, I'm certain of it. So, how about tonight you do a bit of practice, then tomorrow I introduce you to a few more people?"

"People?"

"Yeah, our sort. Strong powers."

"More?"

He laughed again. "Yes, more! Oh Lilly, there's so much you don't know. What a good job I found you so quickly! You'd have been lost without me." Lilly realised he was right. She knew nothing. "Look, you need to take this seriously though," he said with a stern look on his face that made Lilly anxious. "There are some absolute hopeless cases who have powers but don't use them, don't develop them. They're a complete disgrace to the community, to be honest. If you're not going to use your power to its full potential then you don't deserve to have it. They end up either losing control of their magic and becoming dangerous, like that freak Ashya, or just having under developed rubbish powers that are no use to anybody, like this guy Billy who changes the colour of things like an absolute loser. Or, if they don't use it for long enough, their Powers just die." He looked pained at the idea. "If I had my way their powers would be removed and given to someone who deserves them. Someone who'd use them properly, you know?"

"Absolutely," she said earnestly. Despite the fact she wasn't certain she liked what he was saying, she was desperate to prove she wasn't one of those people. She deserved her power. She would use her power. They started walking back towards the school.

"So, tomorrow lunch time," he said authoritatively. "Come and meet some great people. And be ready, I don't want them thinking less of you because you're not very advanced. I understand, but they might not."

Lilly nodded frantically. She would definitely practice. Turning the corner around the outbuildings, Lilly and Alex nearly walked straight into Saffron who was talking on her phone, her eyes red with tears.

She spun round, hung up the phone, and looked in disgust at Lilly.

"Hey Saffron," said Alex, before winking at Lilly and walking away.

Lilly watched him leave, desperate for him to come back so she didn't have to face Saffron alone. As he disappeared into a crowd of pupils, she turned to look Saffron in the eye.

"What the hell does Alex Tomson want with you?" she spat at Lilly.

"We're just friends." Said Lilly, shuffling her feet and picking at her thumb nail. "Honest."

"You don't have any friends," she hissed, and stormed away, her long red curls flying behind her.

For the rest of the day, Saffron and her friends whispered about Lilly and sent her evil stares, but for the most part she was left alone. Gratefully she wallowed in the solitude. Her mind was racing, too occupied with the new world she was discovering to deal with the old one was stuck in. She wanted to practice her power and learn more about it, she wanted to impress the people Alex was introducing her to and not make a fool of herself for once, and she wanted to paint something amazing for the competition. But, first, she wanted to get through her after school detention.

Mrs Robinson greeted her sadly, "Sorry to see you here."

"Sorry to be here," Lilly said genuinely. Disappointing anybody weighed heavily on her, especially when it was one of the few people who actually seemed to like her.

"I'll be in and out," Mrs Robinson said, handing her a pad of lined paper, "but you can hand your letters to me when you finish at half past four, okay?"

Lilly agreed and started writing, but was distracted when the door was pushed open and Saffron slunk in looking miserable.

"I've got to wait in here again," she said to Mrs Robinson in a desolate voice, before she noticed Lilly watching her.

"Oh Saffron, not again." said Mrs Robinson, her voice heavy. "Okay pet, take a seat. I'll go see if I can find out what's happened this time."

The teacher stood sadly and stepped out into the corridor, shutting the door. Saffron swung her bag onto the desk with a thump and landed in the chair, resting her chin on her hands and avoiding looking at Lilly.

For the second time that day, Lilly found herself asking her, "Are you okay?"

This time, however, Saffron just shook her head sadly, and muttered, "Not really."

"What happened?"

"Stupid au pair forgot to pick me up again. She forgets all the time. She doesn't give a crap."

"I'm sorry."

"I could catch a bus, no problem," Saffron said grumpily, "but my mum's this total control freak and doesn't want me anywhere she doesn't know at any time. I'm fifteen, it's ridiculous."

"I'm sorry," said Lilly again. Despite everything she felt sorry for Saffron.

"I'm used to it." Saffron said dismissively, then turned to look at Lilly properly. "So, you're in for letting those freaky little bugs out, right?"

"Yeah," Lilly said awkwardly.

Saffron laughed. "You were crazy! We're all screaming and running for it and you're off to the window ignoring everyone. I bet Mrs Krank was furious."

"Yeah, she's a scary lady." Lilly agreed emphatically.

"Total bitch," agreed Saffron, smiling at her. Lilly wasn't sure she'd ever seen Saffron genuinely smile before. It was nice. It lit up her face and made her green eyes sparkle. Mrs Robinson came back in and they fell back into silence.

"Okay Saffron, Marika is stuck in Birmingham," the teacher said. "Apparently the M6 is snarled up. We're trying to get hold of your mother, but so far no luck. I'm so sorry."

Saffron sighed, giving Lilly a half smile of dull acceptance. Lilly went back to writing her letters, and when half four came she handed them to Mrs Robinson and picked up her bag. Hesitating, she turned to Saffron and said, "See you tomorrow."

"See you tomorrow," Saffron said, looking at her with kind eyes and a sad smile.

Heading down the corridor, preparing to see her mum and explain why she was in detention, Lilly heard someone say her name. She spun around and saw the other girl who had been stood with Ashya the day before, peering at her through dark almond eyes. She was tiny, not more than five feet tall, and very slim, but stared with an intensity which was fierce.

"You can't trust Alex."

"What?"

"He's dangerous. *They* are dangerous." Her voice was quiet but carried such ardour that Lilly felt every word resonate inside her. "You need to stay away from them."

Lilly took a step backwards, unsettled by the intense girl in front of her. "I don't know what you mean."

"You are going to hurt so many people!" she suddenly cried out, the stillness falling away and a wild look taking over her face.

"You don't know me!" protested Lilly stepped back again, shaking her head and feeling sick.

"I know you are going to be responsible for death." She said wept as tears starting to creep down her cheeks. Her eyes were fixed on Lilly and she looked in physical pain.

"Leave me alone," Lilly cried, then turned and ran.

From behind her, she heard the girl call out, "Drop out of the competition, Lilly!"

Breathing fast, she rushed out of the school wishing she could get straight home to talk to Jeffrey, needing the words of someone familiar with the magical world she had been suddenly thrust into. As she approached the school gates, wishing she could just escape, she saw her mother deep in conversation with Mrs Krank. Her heart dropped.

Getting closer she heard her mother say, "It sounds like she was the only one not to panic."

"I can assure you we are not in a state of panic!" protested Mrs Krank, her pitch increasing with her levels of frustration. "By all accounts those insects looked poisonous and we wanted to take appropriate precautions!"

"Do you expect a fifteen year old girl to have an encyclopaedic knowledge of the type of creatures that might infest a poorly maintained secondary school?" asked Lilly's mum, folding her arms. "You think that for protecting her class she should be punished, instead of admiring her for her fortitude?"

"I..." Mrs Krank said, looking nervous.

"My employer gave me a strong recommendation for this school when we moved to the area, Mrs Krank, and I don't want to regret following her advice." Said Lilly's mum with a sharp tone before they noticed Lilly watching them. "Lilly, have you finished the letters Mrs Krank asked you to write?"

"I gave them to Mrs Robinson."

"Then let's go."

Lilly followed her mother mutely, wishing she could talk to her with the kind of openness she was used to trusting her with. She was desperate to know if she knew Jeffrey was magic, and if she had any magic herself but had just stopped using it. She wanted to ask her about everything in her life that had changed in the past 48 hours and all the people who had given her reasons to be confused or scared. But, instead, she said, "Thanks mum."

"So, any run ins with Saffron today?" Lilly's mum asked, as they drove out of town towards the power station.

"Yeah, but we sort of made friends a bit later too." Lilly said vaguely. As she gazed out of the window she realised that Saffron was one of the few things she could be honest with her mum about and started talking rapidly. "So I was talking to this boy who she likes, Alex, and she saw us and got really bitchy about it. So then when I was in detention, right, she came in and she was dead upset because apparently her au pair keeps forgetting to pick her up and her parents won't do anything about it, and we chatted and stuff. It was nice. But now I don't know if she wants us to be friends?"

"Well, how things have changed!" she exclaimed. Lilly blinked, her mother's lack of understanding about just how right she was making her want to laugh out loud. "So Saffron sounds like she's a very unhappy young lady and could use a friend. Want to tell me about this Alex?"

"He's just a friend," Lilly said, blushing.

Her mum raised her eyebrows, but said nothing.

They pulled into the grounds of the power station, unloaded the car, and headed up the hill. Lilly set up her easel and paints in front of the huge cooling towers and her mum settled back on a camping chair with a book and a thermos of coffee.

Squishing paints out, Lilly allowed herself to relax. Painting was her safety, her calm. A space free from confusion. No animals to come alive and terrorise anybody. Just familiar and safe art. She breathed deeply and felt a calm wash over her that she hadn't felt since she had first stepped onto school grounds.

Soon the cooling towers were beautiful monoliths of lavender and mauve, turquoise and amaranth. The sky surrounding them glistened in cerulean and cornflower blue. Lilly smiled, lightly dabbing white flicks across the evening sky as a flock of seagulls drifted by on a warm breeze. She was pleased with her work, it made her proud.

"That's stunning, honey!" Said her mum behind her, but Lilly was too busy panicking to appreciate the compliment.

The white shapes, simple V's, were starting to quiver. Lilly watched in horror as they got larger and larger, flying through the painted sky and straight at her face. She hadn't painted birds! They had been just flicks of paint! How was this happening? She ducked as they launched themselves out of the canvas, feathers scattering everywhere as seagulls gushed from the paint and into reality. The canvas was knocked down and paint splattered across it as bird after bird gushed free from it.

The gulls circled around, gabbing away in funny, squawky voices, and whizzed off merrily into the sky in a swirl of white. After watching them leave, Lilly turned a worried face to her mother who had witnessed the entire event.

"Oh, darling! Your painting is ruined! Those wretched birds!"

Lilly wasn't sure how to react. Her mother wasn't mentioning the fact that a flock of seagulls had just flown straight out of the painting that was ruined. Was she not surprised? Did she know it would happen?

"Did you see where they came from?" Lilly asked.

Her mum shook her head. "No, but there are lots of birds flying around, it was pure dumb luck that one crazy group decided to sabotage you!"

Lilly frowned. Was her mother lying? Why would she do that?

"Can we go home?" Lilly asked, picking everything up. She needed to speak to Jeffrey. "I'll just do it again. It's fine. I have a pretty good memory."

Her mum gave her a sympathetic hug, and they headed home in silence.

~ƐЖƷ~

"Jeffrey, my mum saw seagulls fly out of my painting and she said nothing. Some weird girl told me I'm going to kill people. Alex is magic and says there's lots of people who are magic. What's happening? What's going on?" she asked, dropping her bags onto the carpet and rubbing her head, far too overwhelmed to think straight. "I'm so confused!"

The rabbit looked up from reading a copy of The Herald on the bed, and said, "Who's Alex?"

"He's just a boy. From school. He's my friend." Said Lilly defensively, not sure why she was irritated by the question. "That's not even the point!"

"Why was he telling you about magic? Did you tell him about yours?"

"No, he just knew," she said crossly. "Why does it matter? He said that loads of people have magic. Why didn't you tell me?"

"This is a lot of questions, Lilly," the rabbit sighed, scratching at his left ear with a long back foot.

"Please, Jeffrey," said Lilly miserably. "You're the only person I can trust. There's nobody else I can talk to."

"Okay, yes," he said honestly, "there are other people with magic. But that doesn't mean you should be using yours. Not until you have control; not until you understand it."

"Alex said people who don't use their powers don't deserve to keep them."

"That is one school of thought," said Jeffrey, slowly. "But personally I believe that power can be dangerous if you're not careful with it. If you don't respect it."

"Why didn't my mum react when she saw the birds fly out?"

"Maybe she didn't notice."

"I guess," said Lilly uncertainly, trying to remember whether her mum had been looking directly at the canvas or not. "Jeffrey, why does that girl think I'm going to kill people?"

"I don't know," he said sadly. "Do you think you are?"

"Unless I made a tiger come to life or something, I don't see how I could possibly kill people."

"To understand what potential you have we need to understand your magic," said Jeffrey assertively. "Until we do, make sure you only use it when absolutely necessary, and make sure you're always careful."

"Yeah, okay," Lilly said glumly. Not using her power wasn't the advice she had wanted, but the idea she was dangerous frightened her. Deep in thought, she restarted the painting that had been ruined before. Jeffrey went back to his paper, muttering incoherently about the articles he was reading. Lilly let her brain be still and put the craziness of the past two days out of her mind, but ensured she didn't paint anything so much as a fly that could come alive .

~ƐӜƷ~

Keren Archer held the phone to her ear.

"Has she used her power?" she asked into receiver. "Excellent. Show her more, make sure she understands reality. We can't lose her she's too important, but if they get their claws into her she could so easily be turned. She needs to trust us. She needs to understand her potential. She needs to use her power and see just how special she is for herself."

Chapter Four

Saffron didn't speak to Lilly the next morning. She chatted away to her friends as normal, much to Lilly's disappointment, but she also wasn't cruel to her which was nice. At break time she followed Lilly out of I.T and caught up to her.

"Was your mum mad at you for getting detention?" Saffron asked her, twisting nervously at one of her red ringlets.

"No," said Lilly shyly, then laughed. "She told Mrs Krank off."

"Awesome!" Saffron said, looking shocked. "She sounds cool."

"She is actually," Lilly said smiling proudly.

Saffron hesitated for a moment. "I was wondering if…"

"Hey!" came a voice from behind them, and both girls turned around to see Maisie, flanked by Georgina and Charlotte, looking cross. "What are you doing with *her?*

"Just chatting," said Saffron, a guilty tone to her voice.

"Let's go." Said Maisie, flicking her head to the side.

"Erm…" Saffron said, hesitantly, looking at Lilly with sad eyes. "I'm just…"

"Seriously?" spat Georgina. "Her?"

"Coming," said Saffron miserably. She followed them, throwing an apologetic look over her shoulder to Lilly, and disappearing around a corner.

A couple of times during maths, Maisie shot venomous looks at Lilly, but Saffron kept her eyes down and got on with her work. Lilly wished she'd look up, wished she'd give Lilly a sign that their potential friendship was real. When the lunchtime bell rang, Lilly put Saffron out of her mind, shoved everything into her bag and hurried away from the classroom. She felt sick with nerves about meeting more magical people, terrified she would look like a fool, but incredibly excited to discover about this new world she found intoxicating.

Where he had left her the other day, Alex was waiting again, playing on his phone with his sleeves rolled up and a tan on his strong arms. He looked up and spotted her as she approached, took her hand firmly in his with a confident smile, and led her away. Lilly followed him unquestioningly, completely unbalanced by his air of authority and assurance.

They took a different route this time and were soon in an alley between the kitchens and the art building. Lilly felt extremely apprehensive but glued a confident look on her face, determined to make a good first impression for once in her life.

Stepping out of the alley and into a quiet courtyard filled with bins and ladders, Alex greeted a group of people who were waiting and watching, inquisitive looks on their faces.

"This is Lilly, the Life Giver," he said, gesturing to Lilly who was trying to look inconspicuous behind him.

Faces smiled, and hands waved.

"Hey," she said shyly.

"She doesn't know much about anything," said Alex as Lilly cringed in humiliation. "But she is keen to learn and she's got some great power. Lil, these are my friends. This is Una." He gestured to a tall, slender girl with long blonde hair, liquid blue eyes, and a cold look on her face.

"I'm a Liquid Manipulator," she said disdainfully, offering no other greeting or information. Lilly felt her skin crawl under the girl's frosty glare, her insides squirmed.

"Yo, I'm Max," said a boy a lot younger than Lilly with freckles and a cocky grin. "I'm a Levitator." To demonstrate, he rose three feet in the air, spun in a circle, and lowered himself back down.

"Woah," said Lilly, genuinely amazed, which pleased the boy immensely.

"Don't be that impressed," said Alex with a laugh. "If he gets better he'll be able to actually fly. Levitation is the weak baby brother of flight."

Max shuffled and looked a bit embarrassed. Lilly gave him a sympathetic smile.

"I'm Sophia," said a girl next to Max warmly. "I'm a shape shifter."

"She's only mastered things the same size as her though," said Alex dismissively. "But she'll be able to change size one day with a bit of work, won't you?"

Sophia nodded mutely, looking ashamed.

"And this is Tereska. She's a Speaker." He pointed to a girl who stood silently at the end, her long, dark hair hanging limply over her coffee coloured skin. Her hazel eyes seemed full of thoughts her mouth wasn't sharing.

"What's a Speaker?" Lilly asked her, but she remained silent.

"Ironic, eh?" scoffed Alex, also offering no explanation.

"So, Life Giver, show us what you've got," instructed Una, hands on her hips and looking distinctly unimpressed.

"I dunno," Lilly said anxiously, remembering her promise to Jeffrey.

Alex leaned in and whispered in her ear, "Seriously? Come on, don't be a Billy. Don't waste this."

"Scared of your own power?" sneered Una.

"No, no of course not," Lilly said crossly, disliking Una more and more.

"Come on then," said Sophia. "She's not one of *them* is she, Alex?"

Alex shot Lilly a pointed look and she nodded hastily, rummaging in her bag for a notepad and pen, knowing she was about to ruin her chances of being accepted if she didn't perform well enough. Trying not to panic, she crouched down and rested the pad on her knees, not wanting to disappoint, not wanting to waste her gift. Carefully she drew the shape of a butterfly with spirals delicately decorating its wings, and a lithe body. Soon the now familiar quiver began and moments later the butterfly peeled its body from the page and spun up into the air and away into the light.

"Wow," exclaimed Max. "That was cool."

"It was a butterfly, it was hardly anything big," Una said snarkily much to Lilly's annoyance. "This is lame." She picked up her bag and went to leave.

"No, wait!" insisted Alex, appearing worried. "Hang on one second."

He pulled Lilly's arm and took her aside. "Lil, seriously. What's going on?"

"I want to be careful." She said sheepishly.

"Of what? What could go wrong? You're in control of this, it's your power! Waste it and you're going to lose control of it, and then what?"

"This Chinese girl yesterday told me I'm dangerous and I'm going to kill people if I use my power," Lilly said, looking nervously into his earnest eyes. She wished he would understand, longed for him to tell her everything would be alright.

"Amy!" he growled under his breath, then turned to his friends. "Amy Chan Li got to her. She's trying to destroy Lilly's power."

"Bitch!" spat Sophia. "Lilly, don't let them get to you, seriously. They're out to destroy us."

"Lilly, please, you can't deny this," said Alex, gripping her arms a little too tightly. "Your power is a huge part of you, if your Power dies, you die. Don't let them kill your true self."

"I can do it" she said, gritting her teeth with determination.

Crouching back down, Lilly took her pen in her hand. She felt the eyes of the group on her. Their desire to be impressed weighed heavily on her. She started to draw. She drew carefully and with consideration, putting thought and pride into her creation, willing what broke free from the page to be a reflection of her ability and worthiness for acceptance.

Sitting back, she watched. The quiver began and, moments later, a soft, grey paw poked free of the page, followed by a second and then two legs. A cat's face, large green eyes and straight black whiskers followed next and it scrabbled free, dragging it tail out last. Lilly grinned proudly.

Sophia breathed in.

"What are you staring at?" asked the cat haughtily, flicking her tail and sticking her nose in the air.

"It spoke!" gasped Max, sitting on the ground with a thud.

"Of course I spoke, you ridiculous boy," said the cat, fixing him with a steely glare. "It can't be that hard if you're accomplishing it."

"Now *that* is cool!" said Sophia with a laugh. "Can I touch it?"

"Don't even think about it," hissed the cat, her long tail flicking.

"Hi," said Lilly, dropping to her knees to be closer to the cat's height, her voice quiet and respectful. "I'm Lilly. I drew you."

The cat turned and looked at her, eyed her up and down then sat down.

"Priscilla," said the cat in a soft purr. "At last somebody worth speaking with!"

"What are you going to do with it now?" asked Una, jutting her hip out and raising an eyebrow. "Do you reckon they'll let you cart that thing around on the netball pitch?"

"That *thing* will not be carted anywhere, I'll have you know young lady," said Priscilla haughtily, turning to glare at Una through narrowed eyes. "And if you don't stop referring to me as 'it' I will give you the slashing of a lifetime!"

Una rolled her eyes but took a nervous step backwards.

"Erm, I actually don't know!" Lilly said, panicking. "I hadn't thought that far ahead."

"Release it into the wild?" suggested Max, then catching the look on Priscilla's face said quickly, "Her! Release *her* into the wild!"

"No!" said Lilly, aghast. "I can't do that to her! I made her! I'll phone my mum. I'm sure she'll take her home. She loves animals. She's always liked cats."

"I'll permit it," nodded Priscilla, licking a paw and washing her left ear.

Lilly carefully and gently lifted the cat into her arms. Priscilla cuddled into her and purred appreciatively.

"Well done," Alex said, smiling at her with a wink. "I'll see you soon, okay?"

"Thanks, bye then," said Lilly as she smiled with pride and held the cat close. She picked up her bag and carried the cat back down the alley, leaving the others whispering rapidly to one another.

"There's a party," Alex said, appearing beside her as she stepped out of the alley and making her jump again. "On the last day of school. Meet me there and we can celebrate your victory in the competition."

"I've not won yet!" said Lilly with a laugh, grateful for his confidence in her but scared of letting him down.

"Then we can celebrate your magnanimous defeat. But this is important, Lilly." He said and took her hand, pulling her close and looking into her eyes, his face close to hers. So close she could taste his breath. "Lilly, please, we need you. You're special. Please? Help us?"

"Yes, of course," she said in a quiet voice, her knees starting to wobble a little. She felt her breath start to speed up, losing her balance as her grey eyes fixated on his brown ones. Then she felt Priscilla's claws start to press sharply into her skin, and snapped back. "Help you do what?"

"They want to stop us using our powers," he said, shaking his head, a look of pain on his face. "They think using power is evil. That it should be stopped. They actually use their powers against us; use their powers to stop us using ours. It's twisted." Alex paused, and Lilly felt the pain in his heart. "This party, it's important. You could be the catalyst to end this. The one who ensures we are free to use our power freely and publicly. Think of the things we could do, the changes we could make to the world. Think of the lives we could save, Lilly, the good we could do. Because of you."

"Because of me?" Lilly asked, her eyes wide.

"I'm certain," he said, holding her gaze, his eyes full of promise. "I just need everyone else to see you, to appreciate you and how powerful you are. Like I do."

"Yes, of course." Lilly said, her voice barely audible as she forgot how to breathe.

"So, keep practicing?" He asked her and pointed at Priscilla, who narrowed her eyes and flicked her tail. "This was amazing. Nobody will be able to deny your talent if you do things like that."

"Yes, I will," Lilly breathed.

"See you soon, Lil." Said Alex. Then he vanished.

For a moment Lilly stood completely still, trying to take everything in, then Priscilla growled, "I don't like him."

"You just don't know him," Lilly said with a distant sigh. Then shook her head and forced herself to concentrate on the task at hand. "Right, let's go see if we can convince my mum to come and collect you without asking too many questions!"

Chapter Five

"WHAT DID YOU DO?" demanded Jeffrey when Lilly dropped her bags on her bed that afternoon, stamping his back foot and scowling at her.

"What?"

"That *thing* downstairs." Jeffrey said in disgust.

"Oh, *that.*" Lilly said with a sigh. She was so confused and her brain was exhausted.

When she had spoken on the phone to her mother, expecting at least a degree of shock, her mum had barely reacted at all, a strange glaze coming over her voice as she immediately agreed to come and collect Priscilla. When Lilly had arrived home that afternoon she had found Priscilla perched on a pink silk pillow on the table beside her mother's laptop, bedecked in a diamante collar, and licking daintily at a bowl of cream. Her mum acted as though Priscilla had always been there, giving not a single mention of this strange, new member of the Prospero family.

"I know I said I'd be careful and only use it when I had to, but I did have to!" Lilly insisted guiltily. "I needed to prove I was powerful enough."

"Powerful enough for what?" asked Jeffrey sternly, his ears twitching.

"To be accepted," she said earnestly, pleading at him with her eyes for approval and understanding." They need me, Jeffrey. People want to hurt them and Alex thinks I could really help. I could save lives. Amy thinks I'm going to take them, but if Alex is right and I could save them, I need to practice and prove to them what I can really do. I need them to see me."

"I understand. Come here," said Jeffrey gently. He nudged his head at the bed beside him and Lilly obediently sat. "You have a beautiful magic in you, honestly you do, and I definitely hope you use it for good and to help people. I don't know how yet, but I know that if we work together and learn enough about it then we can get the most out of you without risking anyone in the process. I believe in you."

"Thanks Jeffrey," she said, stroking his ears, finding comfort in the soft warmth.

"You're special, Lilly," he said, leaning against her affectionately. "I can see you."

"You're the best rabbit ever, Jeffrey." she said, kissing his fluffy head, grateful for his words but longing to achieve more despite his advice. "I just love escaping to reality, you know? They have such amazing powers!"

"You do know that *this* is reality, right?" he asked, putting a paw on her leg and looking up at her with concern in his eyes. "This, here, now. Your mum and dad, your home."

"Oh, I know," said Lilly vaguely. "But magic is the real world."

"What powers do they have?" asked the rabbit, frowning thoughtfully.

"Max can levitate, but Alex says if he works he'll be able to fly, and Una is a Liquid Manipulator, and there's Sophia who is a Shape Shifter, which is totally cool, and then Tereska. She's a Speaker, but I don't understand what that means."

"A Speaker?" Jeffrey mused. "Speaking is old magic. Very old."

"What does it mean?"

"Doesn't matter," he said dismissively. "So, how was the rest of your day?"

Lilly eyed him suspiciously, getting the distinct feeling he wasn't telling her something important. "Fine. My mum didn't react to Priscilla though. Sort of like with the seagulls. She just acted like nothing strange happened."

"It's certainly interesting," agreed Jeffrey, not meeting her eye.

"Come on, let's go and make friends with Priscilla," said Lilly. "She's new, we need to make her welcome."

Grumbling, Jeffrey allowed himself to be carried downstairs.

~ƐЖƷ~

The next morning, Lilly carried her painting into school carefully, excited to hand it in.

"Right, ladies and gents," announced Mr Hogg. "Let's see what we've got!"

He went around the room examining the offerings and commenting on each. Saffron's beach scene was beautiful, awash with rich colours, with a flock of white seagulls swooping through the cobalt sky.

Saffron smiled across the room at Lilly and mouthed, "Good luck."

Lilly nodded gratefully. She so wished Saffron would ignore her cruel, spiteful friends, and come over to her. As much as Alex's friendship in reality was exciting, and as much as Jeffrey's friendship at home was reassuring, she longed for a companion in the normality of day to day life that the solitude of unpopularity denied her. But Saffron didn't come over. She remained with her friends.

Sitting down in her history lesson, Lilly felt the skin on the back of her neck begin to prickle. When she looked up she realised Mr Stubbs was watching her, a peculiar expression on his face. He immediately looked away when she caught his eye and busied himself moving paperwork around his desk. Lilly squirmed uncomfortably in her seat. He seemed to be far too interested in her and she didn't understand why. It made her uncomfortable.

"Today, class, we are going to be applying the study of history to our own reality," Mr Stubbs said, standing once all the seats were filled. "You are going to be working on a family tree. Delve into your family, learn about your roots, your history. Work on it over the weekend and bring it in on Monday. Go back as far as you can, talk to everyone you can and learn about how your family have shaped *your* reality."

Maisie's hand stuck up in the air. "What does this have to do with World War One?"

"Well," said Mr Stubbs, pushing his hands into his pockets. "It's applying the techniques of learning about the past to our own pasts. History is full of scope for application in all areas of our world, Maisie."

Lilly pulled out her pad and started writing out the family she knew. Something was niggling at her but she couldn't work out what. Suddenly it hit her. Reality. Just the night before, she and Jeffrey had discussed reality and he had emphatically told her that her family was her reality. Was it a coincidence that suddenly she was being reminded of that again? It had to be, she decided, but an uneasy feeling remained with her.

Ten minutes later they heard the fire alarm suddenly blast out, its ring slamming around the room and startling everyone out of their History induced slumber.

"Right, everyone, down to the field," said Mr Stubbs with a dull sigh. "You know the drill. I do wish they'd tell me in advance when they're doing this."

They all picked up their bags and headed for the door, chatting as they went. Stepping outside, the atmosphere suddenly changed. Smoke was billowing from the back of the building and pupils were running away from it with panicked looks on their faces.

"Oh shit," muttered Mr Stubbs, hurrying the class away from the building. "Right, go, go, go!"

The field was soon full of excited chatter. The children lined up in their form groups and watched the black smoke violently attacking the white of the clouds.

"It was Ashya," came Alex's voice in Lilly's ear. She turned but he was still invisible.

"What?" she whispered out of the corner of her mouth, trying to be inconspicuous.

"She's a Firestarter. She was trying to overpower Una and set fire to the damn school." He sounded furious.

"What happened?" asked Lilly, but silence replied. He had gone.

Fire engines blasted into the school carpark. Firemen, kitted out in yellow, leapt from the engines and raced off to deal with the fire, Mrs Krank flapping around them like a pterodactyl.

"Right, everyone," announced Mrs Robinson, clapping her hands to get the attention of 10D. "Nobody is allowed to leave early without parental permission. However, nobody can go back in the building until the officials have given the all clear. We'll wait here until we know who's going where, but anybody permitted can leave early. Everyone else will wait until normal time in the mobile classrooms."

Lilly watched Saffron sighing a resigned sigh, and knew she wouldn't be granted the reprieve of an early finish.

As the office staff made calls, pupils were gradually either given the nod to leave of their own accord, or parents showed up to collect them. Ten minutes into waiting, Lilly's mum came walking over the field towards them. Lilly went to join her mother, who held up her hand for her to wait. Lilly watched as her mum took Mrs Robinson aside, speaking in a hushed voice.

"Saffron, Lilly," Mrs Robinson said, beckoning the girls over after a moment.

Hesitantly, with the eyes of Saffron's friends burning into their backs, Lilly and Saffron stepped out of line and walked to join Lilly's mum.

"It's nice to meet you, Saffron," said Lilly's mum kindly. "I've heard a lot about you. I was wondering if you'd like to come home with us today. Assuming your parents don't mind, of course."

Lilly looked open mouthed at her mother. She couldn't believe her mother was doing that to her. Now everyone would see Saffron publicly reject her and she could do nothing to stop it. It was like watching a slow motion car wreck.

"That'd be nice, thank you," said Saffron, looking at her feet.

Lilly stared at her, open mouthed. She couldn't believe what she had heard. It seemed even more shocking than when she first discovered magic. Saffron smiled at her shyly before looking back at her feet.

Mrs Robinson led them to the office staff, who had set up base in a mobile building, whilst behind them Saffron's friends talked loudly and in disgust about the situation. While one of the office ladies waited on the phone, the two girls stood in silence. After several attempts, she was able to reach Saffron's father, who immediately gave his permission.

"Wonderful," said Lilly's mum with an appreciative nod, and started out across the grounds towards the carpark. "Then let's head home. It's nearly lunch time so why don't we take Jeffrey and Priscilla outside and we can have a picnic!"

Lilly blushed. Her mum was obviously so excited that a friend was coming home that she was talking as though they were ten rather than fifteen, but Saffron seemed keen on the idea and was looking more and more relaxed the further they got from the school, so she didn't complain.

"Who are Jeffrey and Priscilla?" Saffron asked as they climbed into Lilly's mum's car.

"Jeffrey's a rabbit and Priscilla's a cat."

"That's nice," said Saffron with a disinterested smile. "I never had a pet, but I didn't really get the point anyway. It's just a rabbit, you know?"

"He is not *just* a rabbit," grumbled Lilly.

"Did you hand your painting in today as well, Saffron?" Lilly's mum asked before an awkward silence could descend.

"Yeah," said Saffron, fiddling with her hair. "I'm so nervous. I'll die if I don't go through!"

"Goodness! Well I'll keep everything crossed then!" Lilly's mum said with a hearty laugh.

When they pulled up at home, Lilly's mum ushered them upstairs, promising to call them when the picnic was ready.

Lilly pushed her bedroom door open and found Jeffrey and Priscilla deep in conversation. Jeffrey turned to Lilly and said, "You're home early!"

Then he spotted Saffron.

"The rabbit. It spoke." She breathed. And then she fainted.

"Saffron? Saffron?" Lilly said, shaking her friend's shoulders. "Oh god, she's dead!"

Jeffrey and Priscilla leaned over her. "She's not dead," said Priscilla, nudging Saffron's pale face with a paw. "I could slash her for you, that would shock her awake."

"Don't tell her about your magic, Lilly," said Jeffrey. "It's too soon, she won't handle it. We need to put protecting you before everything, alright? Talking animals is already too much for her. This isn't her world."

"Yeah, okay," Lilly agreed.

"Lilly?" Saffron said, as she opened her eyes.

"Oh well," sighed Priscilla, retracting her claws and inspecting her paw in a dissatisfied manner.

"Oh my god, the cat spoke too."

"Don't faint again!" Lilly said, scooping her hand under Saffron's head and sitting her upright.

"Saffron, you can't tell anyone," said Jeffrey, seriously. "This has to be our secret. Do you understand?"

Saffron gawped at him. "What is it?" she asked turning to Lilly, staring suspiciously at Jeffrey out of the corner of her eye.

"He's my rabbit."

"No, but, seriously."

"He's just my rabbit."

"Why can they talk?" Saffron asked.

"I don't actually know," Lilly admitted. "But please can it be our secret? Just ours?"

Saffron looked at the animals, who both gave her sweet, pleading smiles, and then back at Lilly. "Yeah. Our secret. Cool."

Lilly breathed a sigh of relief and helped Saffron to her feet.

"So, how long have you had talking animals?"

"Five days."

"Who knows about it?"

"Just you."

"Wow, that's pretty awesome," enthused Saffron with a huge smile. "Can I stroke them?"

"You'll have to ask them!" Lilly said, laughing.

"Oh yeah!" Saffron chuckled. "May I stroke you, please?"

"Please note, I prefer a firmer stroke on my neck, gradually lightening as you approach the tail, but do not *touch* the tail," instructed Priscilla strictly, approaching Saffron and standing before her with her head held high. Jeffrey rolled his eyes as Saffron obeyed the cat's instructions to the letter with joy on her face.

"This is so awesome," said Saffron breathily.

"Thanks!" said Lilly with proud delight.

"Girls!" came Lilly's mum's voice from downstairs. "Lunch is ready!"

"Do you want to carry Priscilla and I'll carry Jeffrey?" offered Lilly.

"Yeah!" she said excitedly. "Is that alright, Priscilla?"

"Certainly," nodded the cat.

Lilly gave Jeffrey a squeeze when she picked him up and buried her face in the soft fur on his neck. "I'm so glad Saffron knows," she whispered to him. "It feels like you've made it real. You've given me a friend. A real friend."

They carried the animals outside, where Lilly's mum had laid out a huge tartan blanket laden with sandwiches, samosas, crudités and dips, bowls of crisps and cans of pop. Admiring it, they went to sit down, when a banging knock came at the front door.

"You girls sit, I'll get it," said Lilly's mum, stepping back into the house.

A moment later they heard the door open before a voice shrieked, "WHERE IS SHE? WHERE IS MY DAUGHTER?"

"You must be Saffron's mum," came Lilly's mum's voice. She sounded taken aback but calm. "She's just out in the garden with Lilly. We're about to have lunch, would you care to join us?"

Tearing into sight, a tall, slim woman with fierce green eyes and tightly pulled red hair, shouted, "SAFFRON! GET HERE, RIGHT NOW!"

Saffron stayed standing by Lilly, her bottom lip starting to quiver. In her arms Priscilla's tail started to flick.

"I'm having lunch with Lilly." She said defiantly, much to Lilly's surprise.

"You are not eating off the ground in the company of animals like a gypsy," growled her mother. "Come here, right now."

"Excuse me, Mrs Jones, but it's just a normal picnic. It's perfectly hygienic. Please take a seat and we can talk about it." Lilly's mum said in a reassuring but firm voice.

"Don't be stupid," spat Saffron's mum.

"Mum, please!" begged Saffron, holding tightly onto Priscilla like a comfort blanket.

Saffron's mum stormed over the grass, grabbed Saffron by the arm and yanked at her. Priscilla was thrown to the ground by the force of it and Saffron cried out in pain.

"Mum! Please!" Saffron wailed, tears starting to run down her cheeks.

"Stop it!" protested Lilly's mum looking horrified. "She's just spending time with her friend!"

"She already has friends," snarled Saffron's mum, her grip on Saffron's arm tightening as Saffron wept silently at her side. "Friends I selected for her before your daughter came along and started interfering."

.Lilly was terrified and clung silently to Jeffrey too scared to move or speak. She watched aghast as Saffron's mum dragged Saffron behind her as she swept from the house, Saffron whimpering as they went.

"Please! Let go of her!" begged Lilly's mum following, her voice straining. "Saffron! Please call if you ever need anything at all! We are here for you!"

The door slammed. Lilly, Priscilla and Jeffrey came into the house and found Lilly's mum sat on the floor crying.

"Mummy?"

Lilly's mum pulled her close for a hug. "That girl needs you," she said into Lilly's neck. "Look after her. She is going to depend on you. She can't live like that."

Jeffrey approached and put a paw tenderly on Lilly's hand. She held it tightly.

Chapter Six

"What are you doing?" came Jeffrey's voice from behind Lilly as she worked at her desk. "You're not even thinking about it now."

"What?" she asked him as a butterfly drifted out of the window.

"Look what you're doing!" he said in an exasperated voice. "You're making butterflies!"

Lilly watched as another she had absentmindedly drawn flew away. "So? It's just a butterfly."

"Am I just a cat?" asked Priscilla from the bed, where she was curled up in Jeffrey's favourite patch of sun.

"Well, no, of course not." She thought for a moment. "But you're different."

"Because I can tell you to treat me with respect, whereas the butterflies can't?" asked Priscilla, narrowing her eyes.

"Erm…" Lilly mumbled, feeling her cheeks redden.

"They may be small and weak," said Jeffrey, his voice calm and gentle, "but they're still lives. Lives that didn't ask to be made. It's dangerous to use your magic without thinking. Without understanding the consequences."

"Sorry," she said, embarrassed. Jeffrey had a way of making her think about things in a way that hadn't previously occurred to her, a way of making her realise she was at fault without telling her off. "I need to go find mum now. I've got to finish this weird History homework."

She picked up the page she had been working on with the details she had been able to fill in by herself. She had her own details, branches coming out with her parents, and then from there aunts, uncles and grandparents. As far as she was aware none of the people she knew of had any powers, but Alex saying magic ran in families gave her cause to question it, and she reckoned her mum might know more than she was letting on.

Before she turned to go, she hesitantly asked, "Jeffrey, do you know Mr Stubbs?"

For a moment the rabbit didn't react. "Who?"

"My history teacher. Mr Stubbs."

"Nope."

Beside him, Priscilla's tail flicked.

Lilly raised a suspicious eyebrow, but without pushing it she left the room and took her homework down to her mother. It was Saturday but her mum was still at her laptop working, a harassed look on her face and a mug of coffee at her side. Her father was in the garden weeding and listening to The Beatles.

"Ready?" she asked, looking up as Lilly approached and folding down the screen on the computer.

They set the page out on the table and Lilly's mum filled in the dates and details that Lilly had missed. "Right, where do you want to go next, up my family or your dads?"

"Well," Lilly said, subtly eyeing her mum and keeping her voice light, "I was hoping to make this super interesting, make a good impression and stuff... so is there anything interesting in our family? Anything different?"

"Well, not really," she replied thoughtfully. "It depends how far you want to go back. We're pretty average for the most part."

"For the most part?"

"Well unless you want to go back further than we have records for, but I don't think that's what your teacher's interested in."

"I'm interested." Lilly insisted, her eyes wide.

"Well, there are actually some rumours. Legends, in both our families. Magic." Lilly felt her breath catch. "My family originally came from Poland and legend has it my great, great, great, well lots of greats, Grandmother was a Healer. She lived in the woods with her daughter, and would heal anyone who came to her. One day the Church came, they dragged her away and burned her for witchcraft. Her daughter survived by hiding out, and then fleeing the country." She shook her head sadly. "If it's true, it's very tragic."

Lilly nodded, trembling, "And on dad's side?"

"Well that's a more tragic tale in many ways, I'm afraid. His lots of greats Grandfather was a powerful man. Vengeful. He was a Condottiero in the time of the Plague in Italy. Everyone was segregated to their towns, trapped, to keep the Plague from spreading. He found out that his wife had been having an affair with one of the men." Her mother looked sad, and Lilly felt her stomach squirming in nervous excitement. "If legend is true he cursed the town. All their crops failed; all their animals died. As the food disappeared all the people started to die too. All the children died. He'd hoarded enough food for himself and his family, and once his wife had watched all the people she was responsible for die, the man she loved die, because of her actions, he then killed her too."

"Oh my God," whispered Lilly in horror. "That's awful."

"It is," she said, sighing heavily. "Your father hates that legend. So, interesting as those stories are we don't know that they're true and they can't really go on your family tree either."

Lilly nodded, barely listening. She let her mum help with her homework, going back through her family as much as they could, but she wasn't paying much attention. She wanted to talk to Jeffrey.

"Thanks mum!" said Lilly as they finished up, grabbing everything and running away from her mum before she could say anything else. She crashed into the bedroom and slammed the bedroom door shut, her heart pounding.

"Are you okay?" asked Jeffrey, a worried look on his face.

"No, not really," she said tensely, sitting down on her desk chair and picking at her thumb nail. "There's magic in my family. A long way back, but it is there."

"Oh?" Jeffrey asked, inspecting a paw nonchalantly.

"There was a Healer on my mum's side, but on my dad's side was this evil man, who killed all the crops and animals so all his people died."

"Wow," said Jeffrey, though Lilly wasn't certain he sounded surprised. "Well I suppose that makes sense."

"No it doesn't," she said, feeling confused and getting fed up of feeling that way. "Why can't mum and dad do magic?"

"Well, it sounds like magic had pretty tragic ends in both cases," said Jeffrey. "Their children may well have had magic, but when it goes unused it dies. Over the generations, what little magic was left will have just died out. But it does explain their acceptance of *your* magic because, somewhere deep in their DNA, magic is normal so they don't notice it as shocking. Their mind automatically transforms what they've witnessed into something they can consciously process, even if their subconscious just accepts it as it is."

"Right… So why do I have magic? What if I'm evil like the magic on my dad's side?"

"You're not evil, nobody is born evil."

"But people *are* evil."

"Perhaps, but they were made that way."

"How?"

"People are often corrupted," said Jeffrey carefully. "Sometimes good people allow their desire for personal gain to become more important than the needs of others. Sometimes, the easy path can be a… well, an all-consuming rabbit hole, where the good are lost to an addiction to power. Sometimes you start seeing what you want as worth fighting for, even if it hurts the people around you."

"I don't want to be evil. I want to be good."

"Well, that's a pretty good sign you will be."

~ƐӁ3~

Emma Bahman sat at her desk, the mirror in her hand showing Jeffrey's face. She tucked her grey hair behind her ear and adjusted her glasses thoughtfully.

"How much are you telling her?"

"Not a lot," he said. "But when she finds things out I can't lie to her."

"No, I realise that, but we can slow down her rate of development," she said thoughtfully, frowning a little. "And you say she's starting to do it without thinking about it?"

"Only once that I'm aware of," said Jeffrey, a note of defensiveness creeping into his voice.

"Yes, but it is still a worrying sign," she said. "We can't have her losing sight of the value of life. You know how dangerous that is. You need to pull her back."

"I do realise that, but it is who she is, we can't deny it. When you brought me on, my job description wasn't to *stop* magic, just *guide* it. Gaining her trust is already made harder by keeping things from her. I can't add lying about what she does discover by herself on top of it."

"I understand that, Jeffrey," said Emma sternly. "But this isn't like your previous jobs and shouldn't be treated as such."

Jeffrey sighed. "I know. She's not like anybody else."

~ƐӁ3~

Saffron was already in form when Lilly got there on Monday morning. Her long hair was pulled back into a ponytail at the base of her neck, hanging limply behind her. Her face looked gaunt and Lilly realised she wasn't wearing make up for the first time since they'd met. Her green eyes looked dull, grey smudges of tiredness underneath them.

"Are you alright?" Lilly asked, sitting down.

"Embarrassed," she whispered shyly, not looking her in the eye.

"Oh! Please don't be!" insisted Lilly. "Your mum should be embarrassed. She's crazy!"

"She really is," whispered Saffron, her voice full of pain. "Are we still friends?"

"Of course! Jeffrey and Priscilla want to see you again soon, if your mum would let you."

"They do?" Saffron asked, looking up with a genuine smile before her eyes dropped sadly. "That's amazing. You're so lucky Lilly."

"It is pretty awesome," Lilly agreed.

That day was the start of a new world for Lilly. Together she and Saffron walked between classes, during which they chatted, laughed and smiled. Even maths was survivable thanks to Saffron's animated conversation. In a heartbeat Lilly's life had changed, and it was this burgeoning friendship with Saffron that impacted her most profoundly. All the other developments in her life, the dramatic changes from what she had thought reality was, carried a weight of expectation and pressure and confusion. Saffron's friendship was pure and free, and in it she was able to rest.

Maisie, Charlotte and Georgina were less happy, muttering and glaring in their direction, but the two girls ignored them.

When they handed in their history homework, Mr Stubbs asked Lilly if she had found it at all enlightening, but she just shrugged and avoided his gaze for the rest of class.

At lunch time, as they stood in the queue for the lunchroom, Alex walked by and said with a smile, "Hey there, ladies."

"Hi," breathed Saffron, pulling her hair out of the ponytail and trying to fluff it up. He smiled at her, winked at Lilly and walked away. Her gaze followed him until he was out of sight then she turned to Lilly and asked with trepidation, "Is he your boyfriend?"

"No! Not at all!" Insisted Lilly. "No, honestly, I wasn't lying. We're just friends."

"Cool," said Saffron, sounding unconvincingly casual. "So... maybe you could, like, find out, maybe, if he might, you know, like me? Maybe?"

"Yeah! Of course! I'll ask him!" She said enthusiastically, but then, remembering how he had spoken about people without powers, referring to them as, 'pathetic mortal types,' she hesitated. "He, erm, might not be into girls younger than him though."

"He likes hanging out with you thought," said Saffron keenly. "So it can't matter that much to him!"

"Okay, I'll talk to him," she said nervously.

"Hey, Saffron," came a voice behind them. They turned to see Maisie. "Are you coming?"

Lilly felt her heart drop, doubt suddenly rushing through her as she met Saffron's eyes.

"No," said Saffron, not looking at Maisie. "I'm staying with Lilly."

"Bitch," spat Maisie, and walked away.

~ƐЖЗ~

"Well, ladies and gentlemen, we have our three semi-finalists!" announced Mr Hogg in his booming voice, as Lilly and Saffron sat at their desks in the art room that afternoon. Saffron grabbed Lilly's hand excitedly. "In third place... LILLY ELIZABETH PROSPERO!"

Lilly's eyes opened wide and she let out a gasp. Her heart banged. Next to her Saffron squealed and gave her a hug.

"In second place… RICHARD ALISTAIR BAKER!"

Across the room Richard's friends grunted and punched him in the shoulder.

Next to Lilly, Saffron was trembling. Her knuckles were white. Lilly held tightly to her hand.

"It'll be you, it'll be you," Lilly whispered, truly believing it.

"And in first place…" The two girls huddled together, pulses racing. "SAFFRON YVONNE TALLULAH MARGARET JONES!"

"Oh my God oh my God," Saffron squealed, dropping Lilly's hand and jumping to her feet.

"Come on then," said Mr Hogg, clapping his enormous hands together with a huge smile on his face. "Let's have our semi-finalists up here, and everyone give them a round of applause!"

Standing at the front, listening to the claps and cheers, Lilly could almost believe they were for her. It was exhilarating. Lilly and Saffron held hands and basked in the glory.

"Right, your next piece is to be handed in this Friday and is an abstract piece." Said Mr Hogg, turning a business voice on and looking at them seriously. "From there, two of you will go through to the finals. Adamantine Power, corporate logo, marvellous opportunity et cetera, et cetera." Formalities over, he gave them all a huge smile. "Well done guys."

They spent the rest of the class learning about techniques for drawing objects in motion, whilst excitedly chattering away about concepts for their abstract piece and what winning would mean to them. Lilly couldn't believe how amazing her life had suddenly become. She had a friend, she had magic, and she was finally being recognised for something she was good at. Everything she had ever wanted was finally happening to her and she felt dizzy with joy.

"Lilly, those people are staring at you," said Saffron as they walked away from the art building at the end of the day.

Lilly turned and saw Ashya Patel, Amy Chan Li, and the freckled boy they were friends with watching them, their eyes fiercely intense.

"What's going on?" Saffron asked. "They look really pissed off."

"I don't know," said Lilly with a degree of honesty. "They don't like me I guess."

"They're coming over here."

"Can we speak with you alone?" asked the boy as they approached,

"Why?" asked Lilly taking a step back, really not keen on being alone with them.

"It's important." He said darkly and looked at Saffron. "It's private"

"We don't keep secrets from each other," said Saffron, sniffily and crossing her arms.

"Please," said Amy in a quiet voice, her eyes carrying a haunted look that gave Lilly chills.

"Oh fine," grumbled Saffron with a grumpy look. "See you tomorrow."

Following the three around the corner, Lilly felt her hands getting sweaty and rubbed them on her top. She didn't know what they wanted and wondered if she was in danger. Alex had said that Ashya had attacked Una and set fire to the school, was she next? She started to look around nervously to see if anyone was around who could help her.

"You need to drop out of the competition," said Ashya, her eyes burning as they stopped behind one of the mobile classrooms.

"No! And why?"

"It's dangerous," said Amy in a quiet voice. She sounded genuinely terrified.

"A competition? How is it dangerous?"

Amy clawed at her face suddenly, violently, and Lilly jumped back in fright. "I don't know yet!" she cried loudly. "I can't see it!"

"What? Can't see what?" Lilly asked, her heart racing.

Ashya put a protective arm around her friend. "Don't push her, she's weak."

Amy knocked her arm away and stared up at Lilly. "I can't see why yet, I can just see it's dangerous. I can see death and pain and danger, if you win this competition bad things are coming. The magic, it has consequences. You are a bringer of death!"

"What?" asked Lilly, bewildered by everything that was happening. "How would you even know that?"

"She's a Seer," explained the boy. Seeing Lilly's confused expression, he explained in a patronising voice, "A Psychic, a Prescient, an Oracle?"

"Oh. Wow," said Lilly, surprised. She had no idea how many different powers there were and, despite not liking what they were telling her, she was impressed by them.

"You need to stay away from Alex too," said the boy.

"Alex? Why?"

"He's dangerous," said Ashya.

"*He's* dangerous. The competition's dangerous," exclaimed Lilly. "Seriously? Didn't you set fire to the school? Didn't you attack Una? I think you're the dangerous one!"

"What? You're so stupid!" Ashya snarled at her in disgust. "She just doesn't think, Billy!"

"Billy?" A memory stirred in Lilly. "Alex mentioned you. Are you Billy who changes the colours of things?"

He looked at her scornfully. "I'm a Chameleon."

"Alex warned me about people like you," said Lilly, angrily. "You are the ones who want to get rid of powers. You want to stop us using our magic!"

"You don't know anything!" cried Ashya, exasperated as her eyes glowed red with heat.

"Leave me alone," Lilly said. She backed off nervously, turned and hurried away. Looking over her shoulder she saw that Amy had tears rolling down her cheeks, but none of them tried to follow her.

As Lilly slowed down, breathing hard, she heard a voice in her ear say, "Well done."

"Alex?" she looked around in surprise.

He appeared in front of her making her jump. "I had your back, but you handled it."

"You were watching?" asked Lilly with an involuntary shudder.

"Of course."

"Why?"

"I've got your back."

"Oh right… thanks." She said hesitantly, creeped out by having an invisible audience. They started walking. "So, Alex, you know my friend Saffron?"

"Yeah."

"She likes you a lot." She said, watching his face for a reaction. He nodded, unsurprised. "And, well, she was wondering if you liked her."

"Mortal kids, eh?" he said, laughing. He elbowed her in an assumed shared joke. "See you soon, Lil. Keep practicing. I'm counting on you."

Chapter Seven

Lilly didn't practice magic that night and she didn't practice on Tuesday night either. She knew Jeffrey and Priscilla were watching her, and suspected they talked about her when she wasn't there, but she didn't want to admit how rattled she was by Amy's warning combined with the evil magic of her father's family legend.

"I can't control it" she said sadly to Jeffrey on Wednesday night, when she could deny her desire to use her power no more. "I can't stop it happening, and I want to use it but what if something bad happens and there's nothing I can do?"

"Have you tried to stop it?" asked Jeffrey, looking up from his newspaper.

"Well, sort of," said Lilly, thinking. "I didn't want those seagulls to come alive and they did."

"True, but you weren't expecting them to so you didn't do anything to actively stop it before it had started," he reasoned. "Draw something now and try thinking about it, making it not happen."

"Yeah, okay," agreed Lilly nervously.

She fetched pad of paper and a pen from the desk, then began to sketch the now very familiar butterfly shape. As she drew she put all her thoughts into instructing the drawing to not come alive over and over again. As she took her pen away from the finished sketch, the butterfly quivered, peeled away and began drifting lazily around the room.

"It didn't work," she said glumly, watching the butterfly as it slowly flitted towards the window and flew off into the world.

"I see that," said Jeffrey.

"What am I going to do?" Lilly wailed, putting her head in her hands. "I can't not practice or I'll never get it under control! I don't want my magic to die, I want to be able to do good things, and I really want to use my power. But what if something bad happens? What if Amy's right?"

"We need make sure you're extra careful," said Jeffrey gently, hopping over to her and resting his head against her arm. "You're not going to do anything to deliberately hurt anyone, and you understand that you're using great power. You respect it. So we just work on it slowly, and carefully, until you have complete control. I believe you can do it, you just have to be patient."

"Thanks Jeffrey," whispered Lilly and stroked his soft, warm, fur for comfort. "Okay, I'll try. But stay with me."

"Always," Jeffrey assured her.

Lilly sat and drew butterfly after butterfly whilst they tried to work out how to stop it happening, but one by one they peeled away and flew off as Lilly got more and more frustrated.

"Okay," he said firmly, after Lilly gave a particularly hopeless wail of despair at another failed attempt. "We'll try again tomorrow night. Don't worry, you won't have to do anything else with your power until you've got this. It'll be fine." He gently nudged her arm with his nose, "Cheer up. I'm here for you."

"At least this round of the art contest is abstract," said Lilly with a sad smile. "Nothing can come alive from that!"

Fetching her paints and a canvas, she set up her easel and started painting shapes and swirls, a sad feeling emanating from the work as blues and greys took form. Jeffrey jumped onto the desk chair and watched her working.

"I just wish I knew what I was doing," she said to the rabbit as she painted, her mind free to explore everything whilst her hands were occupied doing something she found so relaxing. "I hate feeling out of control, you know? I wish my mum could help me, I wish I knew where it all came from. Alex expects so much of me, he's so certain that I'm going to do so much good to help everyone and I'm so scared I'll let him down! And then Amy and Ashya think I'm going to do hurt people, and what if they're right?"

"It's a lot of pressure," Jeffrey agreed quietly.

"And Saffron, she thinks we have no secrets!" Lilly went on. "She thinks that that we're best friends but I'm hiding all this from her! I hate lying to her, I hate not telling her. I mean, I know I can't, but I really want to."

"I understand, but you're right, you can't tell her," said Jeffrey. "It's not fair to her. She will never have access to the parts of the world you have, she will never be able to be part of that community. Keeping her away from it keeps her safe. However much you trust her, you know how some magical people see mortals. She wouldn't be accepted and she'd feel isolated and alone; cut off from something not meant for her in the first place. Not knowing stops her feeling that, it keeps her where she belongs."

"I just hate feeling like I'm letting people down," said Lilly, her face starting to crumple as tears began running down her cheeks.

"Hey, listen," he said, his voice firm but full of kindness. "You will never let me down. Never. I can see you, I know you. You are good and you are kind, you are gentle and loving, and you would never do anything to hurt anyone. I know that, and that is all I could ever ask of you."

Putting her brush down, Lilly picked the rabbit up and sat on the bed, burying her face in the soft, downy fur on the back of his neck. She left her tears gently slide onto him.

"Please never leave me," she begged.

"Never," he promised. "Not 'til the day I die."

~ƐӜЗ~

"I'm getting to know her now, really know her," said Jeffrey into the mirror over Lilly's bedside table where Emma sat watching him.

"And?"

"And I don't believe she's dangerous," he said. "The Seer could be wrong."

"Few have the clarity of the Oracles," she accepted. "Mistakes happen."

"Amy studies the writings of The Oracle of Los Pacos, if we could contact her…"

"The Oracles are private people. Do you know how many approach them for help?" she said and shook her head. "No, she needs guidance from a friend, not a warning from an old woman she has no reason to respect. She doesn't know this world, remember?"

"I don't like hiding things from her!" protested Jeffrey, feeling stressed and wishing he was the one in charge. "We could bring her in, protect her? We could keep her away from their influence easily!"

"Fifteen years ago it was different," said Emma wistfully. "It was easy then. She knew nothing of either world. But now? Now it would do more harm than good. No, keep guiding her, keep nudging her in the right direction. She needs to see it on her own terms. We just need to hope you're right."

"I am right," said Jeffrey confidently. "She would never hurt anyone."

"I do truly hope that you're right."

~ƐӜЗ~

"Right class, we have a particularly excellent lesson today," announced Mr Hogg with excitement from the front of the room. Behind him, on his desk, were three large, round shapes with clothes draped over them.

"Following your studies on objects in motion, today you will be painting *these* objects in motion!" He lifted the cloth with a flourish revealing three large goldfish who were swimming casually around three large glass fishbowls.

Lilly felt her stomach drop. How she was going to get away with this she had no idea. She watched as Mr Hogg placed the three bowls on the three large tables they were grouped around, and her mind raced.

"Do they have names?" asked Saffron, peering at the fish in front of herself and Lilly.

"Of course," he said, pointing them out individually. "That is Horatio, that is Socrates, and this one here is Joe."

"Hello Joe," said Saffron, looking at the fish who ignored her.

"Do we have to actually draw the fish?" asked Lilly nervously.

"Of course you do!" said Mr Hogg in his bellowing voice. "Call it practice. If you get through the semi-finals you'll need to paint something much more impressive than a goldfish to win this contest!"

The colour drained from Lilly's face. She started trying to think of ways to stop the fish coming alive, trying to ignore Saffron who was chattering away about the abstract piece she was working on, how her mum and dad had been fighting a lot and how excited she was for the end of term.

"The fish, Lilly, paint the fish," came Mr Hogg's voice behind her as he leaned over and saw Lilly's painting of the fish bowl and water that was as of yet without contents.

"Erm, okay," she said, looking up at him anxiously.

Gritting her teeth, she dipped her brush into the orange and filled her head with thoughts of the fish not moving. She carefully painted its shape, its scales, its eyes. Joe the fish swam around idly, oblivious to his audience and the chaos that risked being unleashed in his image.

Breathing hard, Lilly pulled her brush away and then felt her stomach tighten.

"That looks good!" said Saffron as she leaned across to examine Lilly's work. "Woah... what's happening?"

"Oh crap," hissed Lilly, panic in her eyes as she turned to her friend. "Oh Saffron, please make people look away! Quick! Please help me! Please!"

Saffron looked at the fish that was beginning to drag itself away from the page and then she looked at Lilly. Their eyes met for a moment and she gave a nod. Lilly watched in surprise as Saffron flung herself to the ground and started writhing around on the tiled floor.

"OH MY GOD," Saffron howled as everyone started staring over at her to see what had happened. "I'M HAVING A HEART ATTACK!"

As everyone started hurrying over to Saffron, Lilly turned to the fish who was now fully free of the page and starting to drown in oxygen, flapping in panic. Quickly, Lilly scooped it up and dropped it into the water beside Joe with a splash.

"Oh, I think I'm okay now actually," said Saffron from the floor beside her, catching Lilly's eye.

"Don't you think you ought to go to the medical room?" asked Mr Hogg as he sat back on his heels and helped her stand.

"No, no I'm fine," Saffron insisted, before taking her seat next to Lilly again and giving her a pointed look. Without taking her eyes from Lilly's, she pointed at the fish bowl and said, "Oh, what's that?"

"That's a... wait! What the hell?" asked Mr Hogg, looking around the room at the other fish bowls but saw they were still inhabited. He turned back and stared at the two fish in front of Lilly with a bewildered look on his face. "Where did that second one come from?"

"I'll take it home if you like, my mum won't mind," said Lilly, dragging her eyes from Saffron's and fixing an innocent look to her face.

"I'll get a jar!" cried Saffron, leaping to her feet and running over to the sink to retrieve one from the drying rack. Mr Hogg watched in mute confusion as Lilly took the jar from Saffron and scooped the new fish from the bowl.

"I'll just run to the office with it," said Lilly trying to force herself to sound calm as her hands shook. "My mum will come and collect it. No problem!"

"Right," said Mr Hogg sounding overwhelmed by the sudden frenetic action around him. "Okay!"

"I'll go with her!" said Saffron, speeding after Lilly as she walked away with the fish swishing around in the jar of water.

"I... what?" asked Mr Hogg, but they were already at the door.

Lilly hurried out of the classroom and into the courtyard. She was aware of Saffron at her side staring at her, but didn't know what to say so decided to be silent. After a moment Saffron let out an exasperated sigh and pulled at her arm.

"Tell me, right now," said Saffron, as Lilly turned to face her friend with a guilty look on her face.

"I don't know if I can," said Lilly, shuffling her feet and looking at the floor.

"Fine. Don't." Said Saffron, turning from Lilly and starting to walk away. "Then you're on your own."

"Wait!" cried Lilly, going to follow her so suddenly that some of the fish water sloshed over the edge of the jar. "I'll tell you!"

"Go on then," said Saffron coldly, turning back to Lilly and putting her hands on her hips.

"Okay," said Lilly, breathing hard, not certain this was the right thing to do but not seeing any alternative. "So, you know how Jeffrey and Priscilla can talk, well, Priscilla can talk because I drew her. Because I draw things and they come alive."

"Like the fish?"

"Yeah," said Lilly, looking up at Saffron and trying to read her reaction, scared she'd be rejected as a freak and a liar. "Like, well, anything really. Any animals I draw come alive."

"I see," said Saffron, a frown on her face momentarily before she broke into a grin. "That is so awesome."

"It is!" said Lilly with a sigh of relief. "But, like, I have to be careful with it. They're lives, they're not just objects, you know? And like some people think I'm dangerous, and other people think I could do loads of good. It's all bit confusing and new."

"What do you think?" asked Saffron.

"I want to do good."

"Good," said Saffron. "So will your mum actually come and get this fish? Does she have magic too?"

"It's a long story," said Lilly, not sure how to explain it all. "My parents don't have any magic that I know of but there's magic in their DNA so they don't react to it like it's weird. They don't even realise it's happening. Even when it's really obvious. They just seem to not see it."

"That's cool." Saffron breathed with excitement. "You could get away with so much stuff."

"I don't think I want to get away with any stuff," said Lilly, realising the thought hadn't occurred to her and wondering if it should have.

"I would," said Saffron darkly.

They started walking, the fish watching them with fascination as it sloshed around in the jar in Lilly's hands. When Lilly knocked on the office door, the same lady as last time opened it and looked at Lilly with a bemused face.

"Hello!" said Lilly brightly, trying to act as if nothing peculiar was going on.

"What now?" asked the woman, looking at the fish and raising her eyebrows.

"Erm…" Lilly hesitated.

"Did your pet fish follow you to school too?" she asked in a sarcastic tone of voice.

"No! No, no, no!" said Lilly, attempting a natural laugh and failing. "This is just a fish Mr Hogg has sent me here with. For my mum to come and get. Again."

Frowning, the woman stepped back and let Lilly and Saffron in to use the phone. Lilly's mum agreed immediately without any hesitation, and the office lady begrudgingly allowed Lilly to leave the fish on her desk.

"So, no more secrets, okay?" said Saffron as they headed back to class.

"I promise," said Lilly, nodding emphatically in agreement, but not sure whether it was a promise she was able to keep.

"Thanks, Lil," said Saffron, smiling happily.

At break time when Saffron went to the loo and Lilly was waiting for her in the corridor outside, Alex appeared at her side making her jump.

"Lunch time, we need to talk to you," he muttered quietly in her ear.

"Today?" asked Lilly quietly, keeping her eyes on the girl's toilets door.

"Meet me at the usual place," he instructed.

"What about Saffron?"

"Leave her," he said dismissively. "She's not involved."

"But…"

"It's important. We need you, Lilly, please," he said, firmly turning her chin so she was looking him in the eye. He breathed slowly with his voice barely above a whisper, but he was so close to her face that she heard every word. "Please?"

She nodded silently, her heard thudding so hard in her chest that it hurt. The toilet door open and Alex disappeared as Saffron stepped out, smiling at Lilly. Lilly felt herself stumble, her head still spinning from the experience with Alex, and put a hand on the wall to regain her balance.

"Okay?" asked Saffron, concern on her face.

"Yeah," Lilly lied. "I'm fine."

~ƐЖƷ~

When the lunch bell rang at the end of biology, Lilly gulped. She hadn't yet told Saffron that she wouldn't be spending lunch time with her and felt like the worst friend. She told herself firmly she didn't have a choice and that Saffron would definitely have done the same in her position, but she still felt sick about it as Saffron chatted away, blissfully unaware.

"Are you excited to hand in your painting tomorrow?" Saffron asked cheerfully as they pushed their belongings into their bags and got ready to leave. "I am. So much is happening at the minute it's amazing, right? With all your stuff and all the competition stuff, you know?"

"Yeah…" said Lilly quietly, picking at her thumb nail.

"What are you going to have for lunch today?" Saffron asked as they headed down the stairs. "I think they've got spaghetti on the menu. Although I might just have chips."

"Erm…"

"Or we could just get sandwiches and sit outside to eat, it's so sunny we could get a bit of tan on our legs!"

"I erm…"

"I can't wait until we're in sixth form and we can just walk into town at lunch," Saffron continued as they stepped outside. "That's going to be way better. Plus, you know, school uniforms suck."

"Erm… Saffron?" Lilly asked, stopping as they started walking towards the lunch hall and putting a hand on Saffron's arm.

"Yeah?"

"I can't have lunch today," said Lilly, looking at her feet.

"Oh okay, no problem," said Saffron, tossing her hair over her shoulder and smiling. "Is everything okay? What do you want to do instead?"

"No I mean, I have stuff I've got to do."

"That's okay, I don't mind skipping lunch. I've got a bag of Wotsits in my bag if I get hungry later, is it something to do with magic? I can totally help out." The eagerness in Saffron's eyes made Lilly hate herself.

"No erm," Lilly said, hesitating and shuffling her feet awkwardly. "It's private."

Saffron's smile broke and she frowned. "Secret?"

"No! No I'm not keeping a secret, it's just that…" She paused and tried to think of something to say that would stop Saffron from being angry. "I'm not supposed to have told you about this. Some people are really funny about it, you know? They don't trust people without magic. So I need to talk to them about you and how awesome you are, and stuff. Tell them that they can trust you. You understand, right?"

"Who?" asked Saffron curiously. "Anyone I know?"

"No, nobody," Lilly lied, trying to force herself to sound innocent. "It's just a little group of people with magic."

"And they don't trust me?" Saffron asked sadly.

"Not yet, but they will!" Lilly insisted. "Look, I'm really sorry but I've got to go. I'll see you this afternoon, okay?"

"Oh, yeah," said Saffron. "I'll see you later."

Hurrying round the back of the building, Lilly saw Alex waiting like normal and hurried over, embarrassed at being late.

"Sorry, I had to ditch Saffron," she said.

"Whatever. Let's go. They're waiting." He led her down the alley behind the kitchens again and they found Una, Max, Tereska and Sophia waiting again.

"Hey," said Lilly waving shyly, wondering if she would ever feel completely confident around those more capable and powerful than herself.

"So, we wanted to talk to you about this party," said Alex. "It's really important. It's at Arrowsend House on the river, Friday next week, and starting at half past six. Can you remember that?"

"Arrowsend House, six thirty, Friday," said Lilly, nodding.

"People will be there," said Una, looking at her sternly. "Important people. We're all working our asses off ready for this, do you understand?"

"Not really," Lilly admitted, feeling confused about why people would be working hard just to go to a party. "Why?"

"Because we have a lot to prove," said Sophia. "We want to impress."

"You think that just because you're the Life Giver that you get a free pass?" scoffed Una. "Well you don't. We're all more experienced than you, we all have better control of our power than you, and you'll be expected to perform to the same standard. Just having a fancy power won't get you far in life, you need to earn your place."

"Don't scare her," said Sophia quietly, putting a hand on Una's shoulder.

"What she means is," said Alex, glaring at Una then turning to Lilly with a reassuring look on his face, "this is a chance to make a good impression on some people who really matter in our world. They're established, they're powerful, and they can make things happen for people who are worthy."

"Oh, I see," lied Lilly. She didn't see at all, but she didn't want to look stupid and thought agreeing was probably a safer option.

"How's the practice going?" asked Sophia. "Made anything else cool?"

"Well, I sort of made a fish," said Lilly, looking a bit embarrassed.

"A fish?" said Max with a snigger.

"Well it was by accident," Lilly admitted. "I was trying not to make anything at the time."

"Trying not to use your power?" asked Sophia, a look of confusion on her face.

"Well, not exactly," said Lilly, shuffling her feet and feeling like a total idiot in the eyes of Alex's friends. "I mean I'm trying to get control of it. I don't want it to happen unexpectedly, you know? I want to be able to stop it happening when I want to."

"Of course," said Alex, a frown on his face as he looked in her eyes. "But a big part of being able to stop it happening is to understand how it happens in the first place. If I never turned invisible then I'd never have learned how to make it happen or not happen. Understand your power and you'll understand how to control it."

"Actually, that makes a lot of sense," said Lilly. "You're right."

"So, Friday. Last day of school. Six thirty. Arrowsend House. Got it?" Alex asked her.

"Got it," said Lilly, feeling determined.

Chapter Eight

When Lilly left Alex, there was still a little bit of time before the end of lunch but she didn't bother going to get anything to eat and headed straight back to form room, thinking hard about how she would impress whomsoever needed impressing at this confusing party she was required to attend. As she pushed open the form room door, she spotted Saffron sitting alone at her desk with her face in her hands, her body heaving as she wept huge and miserable sobs.

"Hey, Saffron! What happened?" Lilly cried, rushing over and sitting down by her friend. She put a gentle hand on her arm. "Are you okay?"

"No," Saffron sniffed, looking up at Lilly with huge, wet, green eyes. "It was awful."

"What was?" asked Lilly.

"I was having lunch, on my own, and Maisie and Georgina came over with some friends and sat with me," she said as tears slid down her cheeks. "I was lonely so I was pleased to have company, you know?"

"I'm sorry," said Lilly sadly. "I'm so sorry."

"Thanks," said Saffron miserably. "So they started chatting and stuff like normal, but when got up to go Maisie grabbed my bag and tipped everything out all over the table. All my stuff fell in my spaghetti and across the floor, and there was tampons and pens and stuff going everywhere!" She started sobbing again, her face bright red with humiliation at the memory. "And they just laughed at me! Everyone just walked off and left me there and everyone was laughing. I don't even think I managed to get all my stuff back because I just grabbed what I could and ran."

"Oh god, Saffron," breathed Lilly, feeling completely awful about herself. "I'm so sorry!"

"It's okay. I know you wouldn't have left me if you didn't have to," said Saffron. She sniffed and smiled a smile that was so trusting and earnest it made Lilly's heart hurt. "I just wish Maisie wasn't so evil to me, we used to be friends. It's okay though, I'd rather be friends with you anyway."

"I'm glad we're friends too," said Lilly as the end of lunch bell rang out.

As everyone started funnelling into the room, Lilly watched as Maisie cackled and elbowed Georgina when she saw Saffron's blotchy face. Lilly glared at her in fury, hating her for making Saffron feel so embarrassed and unhappy. Remembering Saffron's humiliation before and determined to make it even, she pulled out a pad of paper and pencil, and hastily drew a spider. Keeping a protective arm around the pad, she watched as the little spider quivered and dragged its way out of the page.

The spider looked up at Lilly, keen to make a good impression as it began the new life with which it had been gifted. Lilly leaned down and, very quietly, whispered instructions. The spider, eager to please, nodded in understanding and quickly skittered off the table and down the leg. Lilly saw it shimmy its way across the floor, darting around bags and table legs, until it reached Maisie. It waved a leg at Lilly and she flapped her hand at it to hurry it up.

The spider started to climb. Maisie felt the tickle on her calf of the spider's legs and reached down to scratch it, but the spider jumped out of the way just in time. Lilly watched as it reappeared round the back of Maisie's kneecap and waved to her again. Watching, with her heart pounding in her chest, Lilly eagerly awaited the reaction when the spider appeared in front of her.

"OH MY GOD!" shrieked Maisie as the spider crawled up onto her arm and began running towards her hand. She leapt into the air knocking the spider to the floor, and, before Lilly could stop her, slammed her foot straight down on it.

"NO!" screamed Lilly, launching herself across the room at Maisie in horror and rage. "What did you do that for?"

"What are you screaming at me for?" shouted Maisie, shoving Lilly away from her. "It's just a spider!"

"You didn't have to kill it!" Lilly cried, tears streaming down her face, "It didn't do anything!"

Mrs Robinson appeared at Lilly's side and put a hand on her shoulder. "Come on Lilly, why don't you step outside and calm down for a minute," she said gently.

"I'll scrape it off my shoe so you can bury it if you like," said Maisie, laughing coldly.

"SHUT UP!" screamed Lilly, turning on Maisie with hatred boiling inside her, wanting to reach out and smack her in the smug face.

"Come on. Now." Mrs Robinson said firmly and led her out into the corridor, where Lilly fell to the floor sobbing. The teacher crouched down beside her and put a gentle hand on her arm. "What's going on, Lilly? Are you okay?"

"She killed it!" Lilly wailed, her head in her hands and her shoulders heaving as agonised sobs of guilt wracked her body.

"I know," said Mrs Robinson sadly. "I never kill spiders either. I'm not a fan of any animal killing, actually. I've been a vegetarian for years. But this is too strong a reaction, honey. You need to calm down. Are you going to be ready to come back in?"

Lilly shook her head and kept crying so Mrs Robinson gently patted her shoulder and stepped back into the classroom, leaving her alone. Lilly felt sick and dizzy. The spider had been made by her, and died because of her. All it had wanted to do was make her happy and it had been killed because of it. She had caused death and she felt like her insides were dying because of it.

A moment later Saffron stepped out of the form room and closed the door. She sat herself down on the floor next to Lilly and put her arm round her shoulders. "Mrs Robinson told me to come and sit with you."

"Thanks," said Lilly, sniffing miserably.

"Did you make that spider?" asked Saffron quietly.

"Yeah," Lilly whispered.

"To punish Maisie for being mean to me?"

"Yeah."

"Thanks," she said. "I'm so sorry it died."

"Me too," said Lilly, wiping her eyes on her sleeve and nodding sadly.

"I guess being responsible for lives is a big deal, huh?" asked Saffron, leaning back and putting her head on the wall, a contemplative look on her face.

"Yeah," said Lilly, copying her and leaning back against the wall, her tears starting to dry.

"I get it," said Saffron quietly.

They sat together in silence. Lilly couldn't stop thinking about the spider but after a few minutes she sighed, wiped her eyes and stood. As they stepped back into the classroom Lilly saw confused faces around the room staring at her but she didn't care, she felt too wretched to be bothered about people who didn't understand reality.

After the bell rang, Saffron and Lilly walked side by side, talking quietly about magic and the importance of respecting life, when Maisie tapped Saffron on the shoulder.

"Sorry about lunch time," she said with a smile that didn't reach her eyes. "It's such a shame Lilly couldn't take you with her, isn't it? You know, when she was hanging out with Alex."

Lilly's mouth fell open as Maisie looked at her with a sanctimonious smile, then stalked away with her head in the air.

"Alex?" Saffron asked, turning to Lilly with a face slapped by betrayal. "You were hanging out with Alex?"

"I…" Lilly stuttered in panic. "Just a bit!"

"Seriously? After everything?"

"Saffron, I… I couldn't tell you… it's…" Lilly's mind went blank. She couldn't think of an excuse.

"It's what? Because I don't have magic you don't have to include me? Don't have to tell me the truth?" demanded Saffron. "Does Alex have magic too or are you just seeing him without telling me?"

"I can't tell you," whispered Lilly, her eyes on the floor.

"Whatever, Lilly," said Saffron turning away from her. "I thought we were friends."

~ЄЖЗ~

Sobbing on the bed, Lilly felt Jeffrey gently stroking her hair with a soft, warm paw. Priscilla sat by her feet, washing a paw and observing.

"It's all gone wrong, how has it all gone wrong? First I couldn't stop Molly coming alive," she moaned, gestured at the fish in its newly acquired bowl on her desk. "Then I had to tell Saffron about magic when I promised I wouldn't, and then a spider I made got killed, and then Saffron fell out with me. This day sucks, it's plotting against me."

"The day?" asked Jeffrey.

"It's made everything go wrong," she wept.

"It wasn't the day, Lilly, it was you," said Priscilla, flicking her tail. Jeffrey frowned at her and batted at her with a paw.

"I didn't mean to," said Lilly, sitting up and looking miserably at the two animals.

"No, but you had a choice," said Jeffrey carefully. "You always have a choice. You chose to draw Molly, you chose to tell Saffron about magic, you chose to draw the spider and send it after Maisie, and you chose to lie to Saffron about who you were seeing."

"I *had* to draw Molly, I *had* to tell Saffron and I *had* to lie to her!" said Lilly crossly, glaring at Jeffrey.

"I'm sorry, but you didn't have to," he said sadly. "You chose to. It might have been the right choice and you might have seen no other option, but everything you do has a consequence. You chose, and now you're paying for that choice."

"But it's not fair," cried Lilly.

"Unfortunately life isn't built around fairness," said Jeffrey. He sounded genuinely heartbroken.

Lilly went to bed early that night and cried herself to sleep.

~ƐЖҘ~

Saffron wasn't in form the next morning, and she didn't come to maths either. Lilly was carrying her abstract painting ready to hand in, and part of her hoped Saffron didn't show up so she would get an automatic pass to the finals, but that made her feel guilty so she scolded herself for the thoughts. At break time she wandered around alone for a while, finding an odd comfort in the familiarity of solitude, when she suddenly spotted a shock of red hair in a doorway.

"Saffron?" she called out.

"Hey!" said Saffron, stepping out of the doorway alcove and waving to Lilly, a look of delirious glee on her face. Lilly went to speak to her when Alex stepped out for the doorway and grinned at her, looking pleased with himself. Lilly watched in dumbfounded silence as Alex took Saffron's hand and lead her towards Lilly.

"Erm, hi," she said awkwardly. "Where have you been?"

"We… had things to do," said Saffron giggling, brushing her hair behind her ear as her cheeks went pink. Lilly watched her and felt herself judging her. She thought she looked childish and stupid and it annoyed her.

"She's smart," said Alex, holding Lilly's gaze with an unapologetic smile on his face. "She can cope with missing a couple of classes."

"Oh, right, yeah," Lilly muttered. Her chest hurt. Her head hurt. She felt anger at Saffron boiling in her chest and wanted to scream in Alex's face, but she hated herself for it. It wasn't fair to either of them. "Are you coming to art, Saffron? We have to hand in the paintings today."

"She sure is," Alex answered for her whilst Saffron gazed at him adoringly. "She's got a stellar one, haven't you?"

"Yeah," Saffron said dreamily, her head bobbing up and down and her eyes never leaving him.

"See you soon, ladies," he said with a cocky wink. He smiled at Saffron then turned and looked at Lilly, holding her gaze for a moment longer than necessary, then walked away.

"I'm so sorry I was mad at you," Saffron said once Alex was out of sight, and through her arms around Lilly in a tight hug. "Alex told me everything!"

"He did?" Lilly asked in surprise, breaking away from the hug.

"Of course!" Saffron enthused, bouncing on the spot, joy smeared across her face in a way that made Lilly want to throw up. "And thanks so much, if I'd known you were getting people to accept me so that he could ask me out then I'd never have gotten so mad! And Maisie wouldn't have got that smug smile on her stupid face!"

"Oh, yeah, of course," Lilly said. She had no idea what Saffron was talking about but was not going to deny anything.

"He was so nice about you, Lil," she went on with a goofy smile. "I can definitely tell you guys are good friends."

"He was?"

"Yeah, but, he said you waste your potential." She said, suddenly serious. "That you could do so much more if you put your mind to it. He said that you could be really powerful if you weren't so scared all the time."

"He did?" asked Lilly, scowling.

"I told him about your spider and how you're scared," she continued, apparently oblivious to Lilly's growing irritation. "But he said that because those lives only exist because of you, they're artificial so it's not like a real person dying or anything. Plus spiders are just spiders right? So it's no reason not to use your power."

"But, yesterday you agreed with me," Lilly argued. "A life is a life!"

"He's totally right, you know," Saffron went on, ignoring Lilly. "Think about how much you could do! You could be a legend. You could be the absolute bomb!"

Lilly stayed silent as Saffron babbled away about how wonderful Alex was on their way to the art room. She tried to listen, made vague efforts at smiling and nodding, but her mind was too busy. She was thinking about her power. She was thinking about life. She was silently fuming about Alex. As they sat down, they got their paintings out and set them down on the desk side by side. Saffron's was a spikey, fierce work with hot pinks, oranges and reds. Lilly's was a drifting sea of grey tears and blue thoughts.

"You pair are very different beings!" observed Mr Hogg with a chuckle as he took the paintings from them.

"We aren't that different," said Saffron to Lilly after he'd moved away. "Well, other than the whole magic thing."

"Attention please!" Announced Mr Hogg from the front of the class as he positioned Lilly and Saffron's paintings upright on the desk behind him for everyone to see alongside Richard's. "We have an exciting development for whichever two make it to the finals! Keren Archer, herself, will be judging the final round live in front of the year group on the last day of school."

"Wow," Lilly said as her eyes widened.

"Awesome," Saffron whispered, gripping Lilly's hand. "I need this."

~ƐЖ3~

"I'm a bit worried about the last round," Lilly admitted to Saffron as they headed to Geography. "I don't know how to draw an animal without it coming to life. How am I going to enter if I can't paint anything?"

"Dunno, but I guess I'll win then!" Saffron said with a broad smile across her face. Lilly opened her mouth then closed it again, not sure if she was joking or not. "Or you could learn how to control it, I guess."

"I'll have to," she said with a frustrated sigh as they reached the classroom. "I just don't know how!"

"Welcome, welcome," announced Dr Murray as they walked in. Lilly and Saffron exchanged worried looks as they took in the tables that were arranged in large groups around the room, with assigned seating. Dr Murray laughed at everyone's horror and confirmed with delight, "Yes, its group work time."

"Here's us," said Lilly to Saffron, finding their names side by side and breathing with relief.

"And Maisie," muttered Saffron checking out the other names on the table and letting out a groan of despair.

"Our end of year project on Peru will be presented to the year group on Wednesday," announced Dr Murray. "Each group is to create a display board and each person in the group is to perform part of a talk. Right, go."

"Right," Maisie announced to the group, standing up and smacking a palm on the table to command their attention. "Jake and Anthony, you can do about the plants and stuff. Saffron, you can help me do a piece about fashion. Lilly, erm, you can do animals. I dunno, draw a llama."

"What?" Lilly asked in a panic. "No! I, erm, no! Saffron should do it! Saffron's much better at that stuff than me!"

"Saffron is much better suited to fashion than animals, so you'll just have to do it on your own. You should be used to doing things on your own." Maisie said with a cruel smirk. "Call it a chance to get your drawing seen by someone, it's not like you're going to win this competition, is it?"

"You have to work this out anyway, right?" Saffron whispered quietly to her. "And if it goes wrong maybe we'll get bonus marks for bringing a real Peruvian llama!"

"Go on, then," said Maisie, glaring at her with her hands on her hips. "Get drawing!"

Chapter Nine

"Right, this has to work," Lilly cried in frustration. "I COMMAND YOU, BUTTERFLY, TO NOT COME TO LIFE!"

Four pairs of eyes watched as another butterfly drifted lazily into the air. Jeffrey scratched his ear with a long back foot, Priscilla flicked her tail, and Molly drifted around in her bowl. Lilly stamped her foot and tossed her pen on the carpet in a strop.

"Maybe try drawing it with your eyes closed?" Priscilla suggested.

"Erm, okay," Lilly agreed with a shrug and retrieved her pen. Closing her eyes tightly, she repeated the extremely familiar shape. Despite that slightly wonky appearance, the butterfly peeled away and began flying lopsidedly towards the window. "Dammit!"

"How do you feel when it happens?" asked Jeffrey, "Are you happy? Sad?"

"I don't know really," Lilly said trying to think. "I guess excited? Anxious? I think when I want it to happen I'm excited but then when I don't want it to I'm scared."

"So, perhaps you need to feel something different?" suggested the rabbit. "Have a less emotional response?"

"How do I do that?"

"Be calm. Watch the fish. Fishes are soothing." Suggested Priscilla.

Lilly sat still and watched Molly in her bowl. Molly, on seeing she was being watched, began an elaborate series of loop-the-loops whilst waving and blowing bubbles.

"Okay, maybe not," sighed Jeffrey.

"This has to work!" Lilly wailed, slamming her hand on the floor in rage. "I literally got someone killed with this power. That spider is dead because of me! I can't do it. I can't let this happen. I don't want to be *that*."

"I know," Jeffrey said gently, jumping off the desk chair and sitting down beside her. "You're not going to be anything you don't want to be, Lilly, and you've got us right here. We are going to help in any way we can."

"Thank you," Lilly said miserably. "I'll try some more."

Butterfly after butterfly flew out of the window. The animals tried making her calm and they tried making her angry. They tried making her happy and they tried making her scared. She drew in the dark and she drew whilst thinking about other things. But still butterfly after butterfly peeled from the page and experienced a life it was never supposed to have. By the time Monday rolled around Lilly was exhausted, fed up, and determined never to draw another animal again.

"I probably won't end up in the finals anyway," she reassured Jeffrey as she got dressed for school. "Richard's brilliant and we all know Saffron always gets everything she wants. She got Alex after all."

"Alex is dating Saffron?" Jeffrey asked in a surprised voice.

"Yeah, I found out on Friday," Lilly said as she brushed her hair.

"He doesn't seem the type to have time for someone without power," mused Jeffrey thoughtfully.

"Well, he isn't generally, but… well Saffron's different. Saffron's special."

"If you say so," he said, sounding unconvinced.

~ƐӜƷ~

"I am so nervous," whispered Saffron as she and Lilly sat side by side in art. "If we don't both go through I think I'll cry!"

"Me too," agreed Lilly. She felt torn between her desperate ambition to get through and her terror at having to enter an animal painting in the finals. She suspected she would cry either way.

"Can we have our semi-finalists to the front, please?" asked Mr Hogg. Lilly, Richard and Saffron stood and made their way up nervously as Mr Hogg initiated loud a round of applause. "Congratulations to the three of you for getting this far. However, only two of you can go through. Please put your hands together for our finalists… SAFFRON AND LILLY!"

He began hammering his hands together, a huge beam across his enormous head as the claps echoed around the room. Lilly stood in frozen surprise for a second before Saffron's squeals of delight shook her back into reality.

"OH MY GOD!" cried Saffron, launching herself at Lilly so hard Lilly lost her balance and nearly fell to the floor. "It's us! It's us!"

After class they headed for break time, Saffron chattering away excitedly, eager to recount her victory to Alex. Lilly nodded along until she felt a soft, strong hand take hold of her arm and the hot, damp of breath on her neck. She spun round but saw nothing.

"Well done," came Alex's voice, though he remained invisible. "I knew you could do it. You're finally proving how special you really are."

His grip released and she stopped feeling his closeness. Saffron, so busy chatting about her impending victory, hadn't noticed Lilly stop, but as they stepped into the courtyard she spotted Alex leaning on a tree and waved excitedly to him. He approached and leaned over, giving Saffron a slow kiss whilst he winked at Lilly over her shoulder.

"We're through to the finals," Saffron said excitedly. "We find out on Friday."

"Big day," he grinned, looking at Lilly again. "Are you ready?"

"Definitely," said Saffron confidently.

"I hope so," said Lilly nervously.

"See you later, ladies!" he said, laughing as he walked away from them.

"I wish I had powers," Saffron said with a sigh, watching him go.

"Why?"

"He pays more attention to you than me," she said, looking down at her feet and twisting her hair in her fingers. "If I had power he might see me. You know, really see me."

"I see you," said Lilly, gently.

"At least someone does," she said miserably.

~ƐЖӠ~

That afternoon, Lilly sat through History day dreaming. Mr Stubbs reeled off information with less enthusiasm than normal, apparently distracted from his usual vigilance by the approaching end of term, and nobody paying as much as attention as normal anyway. Outside the summer sky beckoned, promising weeks of freedom ahead, weeks away from the mundanity of school. Just one llama drawing, one art contest, and one mysterious and troublesome party to get through, thought Lilly, then she could escape.

"Lilly, would you stay behind a moment?" Mrs Stubbs said as the end of school bell rang out. Saffron raised her eyebrows and said goodbye in a worried tone, then Lilly was left alone with the peculiar teacher.

"Did I do something wrong, sir?" she asked, racking her brain, fairly sure she hadn't.

"No, no, no," he reassured her, and perched on the edge of his desk in a failing effort to look casual. "I heard about you going through to the finals of the art contest. A very well done to you, obviously."

"Erm, thanks," Lilly said, confused. She shuffled on the spot awkwardly, eyeing the door.

"The thing is, I was thinking that perhaps you would be better suited to something different," he said, a serious look on his face. "Perhaps we could start a history club together!"

"What? There's four days left of school…"

"Oh, well, yes there is that," he admitted and rubbed at his eyes for a moment. "It's just, perhaps it would be better to let your friend Saffron take this prize."

"Why?"

"I think she's better suited to it."

"What?"

"It's just…" he hesitated for a moment then sighed. "You have certain gifts… talents… that are potentially troublesome and I fear that this competition could lead you down a path that there is no turning back from."

"Wait," Lilly said, frowning and taking a step back. "Do you know Amy Chan Li, sir?"

"Yes actually, quite well," he admitted, looking guilty.

"And you think I should stop using my 'gifts', do you?" she asked, putting her hands on her hips.

"Well not stop altogether, exactly," he said quietly, his eyes flicking as he searched for the right words. "Perhaps just hold off for the time being."

"I deserve it," Lilly said angrily. "I'm good enough, I'm talented enough."

"That's not in question. It's not whether you *can* win it's whether you *should* win," he said, stepping towards her with a pleading look on his face. "Whether you *should* be using these talents for your own gain."

"I'm not what you people think I am," Lilly said, her fists clenching and blood pounding through her head. "I'm not giving this up. I'm not going to just pretend to be something I'm not because you don't trust me, because you don't think I'm capable of handling myself." He stood and went to say something more but Lilly stopped him, tears starting to fill her eyes with angry frustration. "No! No. Nobody has ever believed in me, believed I could achieve anything. Nobody has ever thought I had value! And I finally do! I finally have something about me that's special, I'm finally being respected. I finally have friends and success. I am getting everything I have ever wanted and you think I should just stop? Just pretend I'm somebody... some *thing*... else? No!"

"Lilly... wait..." he said, stepping forward with a hand out, but she ran and slammed the door shut behind her, breathing hard as tears flooded down her cheeks.

She hurried away from the history room and down the stairs, stopping to lean back against the wall when she was out of sight of the classroom, leaning against the wall and breathing hard.

"Good for you," came a voice at her side. She turned in surprise and Alex flashed into appearance, smiling at her.

"I'm not giving up," she said, angrily. "I am going to get control of this and I am going to be able to use it properly."

"Yes, you are," he said encouragingly.

"And I'm going to win this competition!"

"Yes, you are," he agreed again. "You're the best one, Lilly. You're the most talented."

Lilly looked him in the eye and paused. "What about Saffron?"

"What about her?"

"She's my best friend," she said, a horrible knot of worry squirming in her tummy. "She's your girlfriend."

"I know, she's great," he said dismissively. "But come on, Lilly, she's not you."

"I've got to go home and practice," she said, backing away and feeling like she needed a shower.

"See you soon," he said with a grin, then disappeared.

Lilly held her breath and looked around, trying to sense where the invisible boy was but she couldn't. She hurried away down the corridors with a tingling sensation in the back of her neck with the distinct sensation she was being watched.

~ƐЖӠ~

"How about on Friday night we invite Saffron over?" suggested Lilly's mum on hearing that Lilly was through to the finals. "One of you is going to be celebrating so we might as well make a bit of a party of it!"

"Oh, I…" Lilly hesitated. At her feet she saw Jeffrey and Priscilla exchange looks with one another. "Saffron's mum probably wouldn't agree to it."

"True," Lilly's mum said with a sad sigh. "We can check at least. It would be so lovely for you to start the holidays together. Especially if one of you is going to be spending so much of your summer time at this Adamantine Power place!"

"I was actually invited to a party already," Lilly confessed.

"With Saffron?"

"Erm, no."

"Alex?" she asked suspiciously. Lilly nodded nervously, picking at her thumb nail. "What sort of party is this? You're only fifteen, I'm not sure I want you going to a party with an older boy on a Friday night, Lilly."

"It's important mum!" Lilly whined.

"Why can't Saffron go too?"

"She just can't…"

"I'm sorry Lilly, but I'm going to have to say no. We'll have a nice celebration at home as a family, and if Saffron can join us then that's great, but I'm not comfortable with you going off with some older boy on your own."

"Mum!"

"Lilly, no."

Lilly shoved her chair back and stormed upstairs, slamming her bedroom door. A few minutes later she heard a scuffling on the landing, then the door swung open and Jeffrey and Priscilla stepped into the room together.

"Do you want to talk about it?" Jeffrey asked.

"I just want people to stop telling me what to do," said Lilly crossly.

"Who's telling you what to do?" asked Priscilla, leaping gracefully onto the desk chair.

"Everyone!" Lilly cried, lying back on her bed with a thud. "I just need to figure out what I want to do for myself, not because other people are telling me to do it!"

"What do you want to do?" asked Jeffrey.

"I don't know!" she moaned, then buried her face in her pillow. "I just don't know."

Chapter Ten

"What do you want to do?" asked Alex, a tone in his voice Lilly hadn't heard before, angry at Lilly's revelation that she wasn't going to the party after all. "Are you going to use your power, grow, win this competition and let me get you to this party, or are you going to just give up now and let this part of yourself die? Time to decide Lilly. Are you in or out?"

"But my mum! It's not my fault!"

"In or out, Lilly?" he demanded, a note in his voice she hadn't heard before. His reaction when she said she couldn't go to the party had seemed almost fearful. He sounded angry but also worried. She picked at her thumb nail and stared at her feet. "I can fix this for you, but you have to decide right now. I don't want to waste any more of my time if you're not the girl I thought you were. The girl I've been convincing everyone else that you are."

"I'm in," she insisted, her eyes wide and her hands shaking. "I want this. I want to do this. I don't want it to die."

"Then it will happen," he said in a dark voice with a fierce look in his eyes, then stepped out of her way and vanished.

Lilly headed into school with a new focus in her mind. He was right. She was going to do it and she was going to do it properly. She was going to embrace her truth and live up to her potential. She was going to live for herself and not just for other people. She would master her magic and, somehow, she would go to this party.

~ЄӜӠ~

Keren Archer's phone rang and she picked it up.

"Alex?"

"I've got her," came the earnest voice of the young man, so desperate to prove his worth. "She's coming. She's in."

"Are you certain?" she asked.

"Yes," he said confidently. "She needs help getting to the party, but we can sort it. She's ready."

"Good work, Alex," said Keren Archer with a smile, leaning back in her chair in relief. "Thank you."

~ƐӜƷ~

"Are you alright, Lilly?" asked Saffron, sitting next to her at lunchtime. "You're distant."

"Yeah, just a lot on my mind," said Lilly, pushing spaghetti round her plate and not looking up.

"Me too," said Saffron quietly.

"There's a lot of pressure at the minute, you know?"

"I do," Saffron agreed with a sad nod. "A lot of pressure."

"I shouldn't even be here today," Lilly moaned, not really paying attention to Saffron. Nothing she said could be as serious as what Lilly was dealing with after all. "I need to go home and work on my magic. I need to get back to reality. This crap doesn't matter."

"I'm glad you're here," said Saffron quietly.

"I've got to draw this stupid llama, I've got to get to grips with my power," Lilly went on, dropping her fork on the plate with a clang. "And I've got to win this bloody competition!"

"Yeah... Right..." Saffron said glumly. "Your power."

The rest of the day Saffron remained quiet, not trying to get Lilly's attention anymore. Lilly's face sat in a permanent frown whilst she ignored what was going on around her. As they walked silently together out of school at the end of the day, Lilly spotted her mum waiting by the gates.

"Mum?"

"Hi girls," Lilly's mum said with a big smile on her face. "Hello Saffron, dear."

"Why are you here?" Lilly asked, irritated by the surprise and not bothering to hide it.

"I wanted to talk to Saffron," said Lilly's mum looking a little taken aback by Lilly's tone. Lilly's mouth dropped, knowing what was coming and could do nothing to stop it. "We're hoping you'd come to ours on Friday night. We could order in, have a bit of a party to celebrate the art competition and the end of term. What do you think?"

"I'd love to!" enthused Saffron, her eyes shining. "I'll ask my dad, he'll agree. Definitely!"

"See? Sorted!" said Lilly's mum proudly, patting Lilly's shoulder.

Lilly didn't say anything but glared silently at the floor. This was not okay. She was fuming and she couldn't even tell her mother why without revealing that she was still planning to go to the party. In that moment she hated her mother.

"See you tomorrow, Lilly," said Saffron cheerfully, the first real smile she'd managed all day spreading across her face. "Hope the llama goes well!"

"Yeah, bye Saffron," Lilly said with a half wave.

As they walked home, Lilly's mum asked about Saffron's llama reference, but Lilly just grunted. As they got to their street she asked where Lilly thought they should order the pizza from on Friday, but Lilly just shrugged. When they got home she offered Lilly a cup of tea and a muffin, but Lilly ignored her and went straight upstairs. Jeffrey and

Priscilla were sitting together on the bed, but on seeing Lilly's thunderous face they had the sense to remain silent.

"Right," Lilly said as she banged her school bag onto the floor and angrily kicked her shoes into the corner of the room. "I am going to control this power right now. It is mine, it only exists because of me, therefore it has to do what I want."

"I don't think it works like that," said Jeffrey, tentatively.

Lilly ignored him and pulled out her sketchpad, sat down, and furiously drew a butterfly. It immediately peeled away and flew into the air. She swore loudly. Jeffrey put his head on his front paws and Priscilla flicked her tail. Lilly tried again, and again, her vocabulary descending further and further into the profane with each failure.

"NO!" she finally roared, and slammed the pencil down.

"Okay, draw something for me," suggested Jeffrey. "Draw me a worm."

"A worm?" she repeated, making a face. "That's gross."

"Just try," said Jeffrey. "Do it for me."

Lilly frowned and picked up a muddy coloured pencil, glared at the rabbit suspiciously, then drew a long, thin earthworm on the page. Nothing happened.

"What the hell?" whispered Lilly, staring at the squiggled shaped on the page as it stayed flat and still, no life at all.

"Well, I think we've cracked it," said Jeffrey, sitting up and looking pleased. "Very interesting!"

"Is it?" asked Lilly, thoroughly confused. "I mean it is, but, I don't understand!"

"Well, you didn't want to draw a worm, did you? So it didn't come to life."

"So I can only draw things I don't want to draw?" Lilly sighed, exasperated. "That doesn't help me! I want to win this contest on Friday!"

"Well, you don't have to win it, do you?" observed Priscilla.

"I guess not," she agreed, unwilling to give up the chance just yet. "At least I can draw a llama tomorrow without problems. I didn't want to do it from the start, so it's not like that can come alive anyway."

"As long as you're careful," Jeffrey reminded her.

"Always," said Lilly with a dramatic eye roll.

Lilly fell into a troubled sleep that night, Priscilla purring by her feet and Jeffrey snoring in his box.

She was finishing her llama drawing. Saffron and Alex were watching her at the table, Ashya and Billy were in the corner whispering, and Amy Chan Li was pointing at her from by the door with a haunting look in her eyes. By her feet Jeffrey lay on the floor and he was crying, his brown fur matted and wet with tears. He was weak. Broken. As she finished the drawing, it began to twitch and move, and suddenly, as a leg poked out, she felt a stinging tug on her heart. As the llama pulled away from the page the pain intensified, ripping at her, until she fell from the chair. In front of her the llama grew bigger and bigger, stronger and more powerful, while on the floor Lilly felt everything in her being ripped away from her as she grew weaker and weaker.

At her side Saffron fell to the floor and held onto Lilly's hand. "Help me, Lilly, help me," Saffron wept. "Save me!"

"I can't," cried Lilly, trying to grip Saffron's hand but finding her fingers too weak. "I've got no power left!"

"Help me," wept Saffron. "Only you can save me!"

"I need more power!" Lilly screamed, as above her the llama laughed, its enormous body rippling with strength.

She felt Saffron's fingers slip from her grasp as the classroom began to swim away, spiralling around her, until it was just Lilly on her own in the middle of a swirling sea of mist and chaos, crying, hopeless and alone.

She sat up suddenly awake and looked around room, grounding herself in the familiar. The sky was still dark and a slither of moonlight was licking at the edge of her curtains. Lying back down she turned over and went back to sleep, forgetting quickly the nightmare she had just jolted awake from.

~ƐЖЗ~

"Ready?" asked Saffron, as they sat together in geography the next day.

"No," said Lilly with a sigh, looking at the nearly finished llama sketch in front of her.

"What is that?" demanded Maisie, slamming a fist on the table. "You had one job, Lilly! One! We are presenting to the year in ten minutes!"

"I, erm, yes, right," Lilly stuttered. "I'll just pop out and finish this then."

"Out?" screeched Maisie. "Out where?"

"She just works better when there is less noise around," Saffron interjected quickly. "For her artistic... stuff..."

"Impress me," Maisie instructed, glaring at Lilly as if she was a naughty child that needed discipline.

"Okay," Lilly nodded and quickly stood, hurrying into the corridor with Saffron tailing her.

"Ready?" Saffron asked, excitement on her face as she eagerly bobbed on the spot.

"No," said Lilly, pulling out a pencil. "But we might as well do it anyway!"

As she started to draw, Lilly repeatedly reminded herself that she did not want to do this. She finished his face, giving him big eyes and long lashes, a dopey smile and big teeth. She told herself she wasn't happy about doing this. That she didn't want to draw the llama. This was not an experience for herself. She sketched his shaggy coat, his spindly legs and knobbly knees.

Saffron gazed over Lilly's shoulder, holding her breath in anticipation, watching Lilly's every movement. Nothing happened. Lilly sighed in relief and Saffron sighed in disappointment. Then it started. The quiver.

"No!" Lilly wailed.

The quiver intensified as the llama stuck a leg out of the page.

"Awesome," whispered Saffron, stepping back with eyes wide.

The back legs kicked out, dragging the tail and body with it. The llama grew larger and larger as more pulled away from the page, until, with a pop like a balloon bursting, the head sprung free and a full sized llama stood in the geography corridor looking nervous.

"Hello," he said shyly, peering at them beneath long eyelashes through dark brown eyes, his voice deep like liquid chocolate and heavily accented. "I am Pablo."

"Oh god oh god oh god," muttered Lilly, her face in her hands. "How am I going to explain this?"

"Hi Pablo, I'm Saffron," Saffron said, holding out a hand to the llama, then suddenly retracting it with an embarrassed look on her face. "And that's Lilly. She drew you."

"Many thanks to you, Miss Lilly," the llama said respectfully, and dropped to a deep bow. "I am most grateful."

"Pablo, can you do me a favour?" asked Lilly nervously, feeling extremely guilty about putting pressure on someone who had only just come to exist. "I need to take you on stage in front of my school and you need to promise me you won't talk. Please?"

"Well of course, Miss Lilly," Pablo agreed immediately. "For you, anything."

"Thank you," said Lilly feeling relieved, and guided the llama into the classroom where it was met with gasps and the clattering of chairs being knocked down as around the room people jumped to their feet.

"I, erm, thought maybe a real llama would have more impact than a drawing," she said awkwardly.

"What?" demanded Dr Murray, standing up and staring with his mouth open. "What's going on? What's going to happen with that?"

"My mums going to come and pick him up! Right after the presentation! I swear."

"If he makes any messes on the floor you have to clean it up, Lilly," said Dr Murray sternly, eyeing the llama suspiciously.

Next to her Pablo huffed in indignation and looked like he was about to argue. Lilly elbowed him and quickly said, "He's toilet trained."

"So, are we all ready to go?" Dr Murray asked the rest of the class.

Everyone followed the teacher out, Lilly leading Pablo as around her everyone whispered and stared. They gathered around the hall door where the rest of the year was sitting inside waiting, bored looks on their faces.

"I'll just run to the office so they can tell my mum we're going on now," said Lilly quickly. "Stay here, Pablo."

"I'll watch him," said Saffron with a reassuring smile, patting the llama gently on his long woolly neck.

"Hello? Oh, it's you again," said the office lady looking around suspiciously when Lilly knocked on the door. "What have you got for me this time?"

"A llama."

"A what now?" she asked in surprise, looking around again. "Where is it?"

"He's just going to come and do our geography speech in the hall, then my mum needs to come and pick him up, please," Lilly said with a sweet smile, trying to act as if there was nothing completely bizarre about this situation.

"Let me get this straight, I'm phoning your mother and asking her to come and pick up a llama."

"He's *our* llama," Lilly emphasised.

"*Your* llama," repeated the lady with a look of sheer disbelief on her face. "Of course. Of course! I don't know why I'm surprised. Right, I'll get her on the phone."

"Thanks," Lilly said and hurried back.

"First up, on our Peru presentation, is Lilly Prospero's group with their able assistant, Pablo the llama!" announced Dr Murray as he ushered Lilly's group into the hall.

Maisie bristled furiously and put the poster up on the display. Lilly stood nervously beside Pablo, watching as Maisie started her rehearsed speech with Saffron, but seemed to get more and more angry as everyone around the room ignored her, instead staring at Pablo in excitement. When Jake and Anthony started their speech nobody paid any attention to them either. Then Lilly stepped forward, everyone in the room sat up, fascination on their faces. She stood in silence for a moment, basking in the glory of having an entire room of people focussed in her direction because of something she had done. She felt powerful. She felt proud.

"This is Pablo," Lilly said and Pablo stepped forward with a goofy smile on his face. "He's a llama which is an animal native to Peru. They are farmed for their fur, to make clothes, and for their meat."

Pablo spun and stared at Lilly with a look of horror in his eyes, then stamped his foot, snorting in horrified protest. The room erupted in laughter.

"Don't worry, we're not going to eat you!" Lilly reassured him quickly. He cocked his head at her and stamped again, unconvinced. She held her hands in the air. "I swear!"

Laughter filled the room again as the llama batted his eyelashes gratefully at Lilly. She continued her speech as Pablo paraded up and down, his head high as he smiled happily at the adoring crowds. Every so often he would stop and allow someone in the audience to stroke his nose, lowering his face to them, then he would stand again and continue his display, tossing his hair back proudly. As she finished, Pablo bent a knee and dropped into a deep bow. The room erupted in applause, children stood from their chairs to clap and cheer, teachers flooded forward to stroke Pablo, who gave each one a turn and proudly posed for a selfie with several.

"You were wonderful, Pablo, thank you," Lilly whispered as she lead him away from the room.

"You're most welcome, Miss Lilly," he said, resting his warm, hairy cheek against the side of her face adoringly. "Thank you for drawing me, to be alive in the most wonderful gift."

Outside the office her mum was leaning on the wall, chatting to the office lady. "Hello there!" she greeted.

"Thanks for picking up Pablo, mum," said Lilly, hoping the magic DNA was doing its job as promised.

"Come on then, handsome, let's walk home," said Lilly's mum with a vague smile. She held up a collar and lead and clipped them round his neck. "I'll see you later, Lilly!"

"Well, you proved your point," came Alex's voice close against her ear as her mother walked away with the llama in tow. "You're definitely using your power."

"Yeah" she breathed, the hairs on the back of her neck standing on end, her fingers twitching as she wanted to reach out and touch him.

"That's my girl," he whispered.

Chapter Eleven

Jeffrey and Priscilla were less impressed with Lilly's efforts, despite everyone in the house seeming remarkably attached to the llama. Pablo now had his own shed in the garden and was happily trotting around eating Lilly's dad's begonias whilst her mum cooed over him and took photographs of him posing in the sun.

"I tried!" protested Lilly in response to their judgmental looks as they sat in the garden that afternoon whilst Lilly's mum cooked dinner. "I did everything we said. I didn't want to draw him, I was actively thinking I didn't want to draw him, but he's here!"

"I want to be here," insisted Pablo. "I like it here."

"We have to get this under control, Lilly," said Jeffrey.

"I know!" exclaimed Lilly. "I've only got one more day until the competition!"

"Not just for the competition, Lilly," said Jeffrey seriously. "For your whole life."

"Oh, yeah," she said. "But you know. I still need to win this contest."

"You don't *need* to," said Priscilla. "You *want* to."

"Same difference," said Lilly, flapping her hand dismissively.

~ЄЖЗ~

Saffron wasn't in registration again on Thursday morning. When Lilly spotted Alex talking to Una and Sophia in the corridor she hurried over to them.

"Oh good, it's you," muttered Una sarcastically, plastering an extremely fake smile across her face with contempt. Lilly gave her a withering look and turned away.

"Where's Saffron?" she asked Alex.

"How should I know?" Alex asked, leaning on the wall and folding his arms, a smirk on his lips.

"You're not still seeing that silly little red headed mortal are you?" Una asked with a cackle, elbowing Sophia who rolled her eyes.

"She's not silly," argued Lilly, glaring at them.

"We're hardly seeing each other," scoffed Alex. "We just have a bit of fun sometimes."

"But I thought…" said Lilly, her head pounding as she thought of how Saffron so obviously adored him, her heart available with no questions or boundaries. She was completely vulnerable to him, and he didn't even care.

"Don't be daft," he said with a laugh. "She's alright and stuff but it's not like someone like *me* would be really into someone like *her.*"

"But Alex…" she stuttered, feeling completely heartbroken for her friend and desperately wishing he would tell her he was joking, that somehow she was misunderstanding him. Una and Sophia whispered together, giggling.

"Don't look so worried, Lilly," he insisted, putting a hand on her shoulder. "Saffron's cool. She gets it."

"Are you sure?"

"Of course!"

"There she is," said Sophia pointing as Saffron approached down the corridor.

Spotting them, she paused for a moment, then started forward again. Her face was blotchy and her red hair was tied limply into a pony tail.

She looked quite different without it framing her face in a mane of brilliant auburn. She looked younger, thought Lilly, more fragile.

"Ready for class?" she asked Lilly, not looking at the others.

"Yeah," Lilly said quietly. "Let's go."

"Good luck for tomorrow," called out Alex behind them as they walked away. "Hope you've got a killer painting ready."

~ƐӁƷ~

With two days left of school, none of the teachers were motivated to make them work, much to Lilly's delight. Most handed out quizzes, some just let them chat. Saffron didn't chat.

"What's happening?" asked Lilly at lunch. "Are you nervous about tomorrow?"

"No," said Saffron, her voice flat. "I'm not going to win anyway."

"Why not?"

"Because you get everything. Why would I win?"

"Me?" Lilly asked in surprise. "I always say that about you! So, I guess your mum said you can't come to mine tomorrow, did she?"

"I've not asked her. I want to ask my dad but…" she stopped mid-sentence.

"Well, don't worry about it," said Lilly, trying to sound reassuring but secretly relieved. "We'll have loads of chances to celebrate over the summer! So long as I can stop my painting coming to life an attacking Keren Archer on stage. I'm sure that's not what Alex meant by killer painting!"

"You know what, Lilly," Saffron suddenly spat, slamming her knife and fork down and picking her bag up. "I don't care. You go off with my boyfriend and talk about all your amazing powers, sort out your fabulous painting to win this competition, let your mum and dad celebrate with you about how wonderful you are and go off and live your amazing life. You don't need me weighing you down, *obviously.*"

"Wait, Saffron!" Lilly cried out in shock, as Saffron stormed away from her.

But she was gone. She didn't come into registration that afternoon and Lilly didn't see her anywhere around school. Lilly sat alone in classes, missing her friend more than she knew she would.

~ƸӜƷ~

"Has she seemed down recently?" asked Jeffrey.

"Dunno, sort of I guess," said Lilly with a shrug after recounting the peculiar outburst to Jeffrey and Priscilla.

"Have you asked her why?" asked Priscilla.

"Not exactly, I've kind of been caught up in my own stuff," Lilly admitted. Jeffrey gave her a pointed look. "I've got a lot going on!"

"Sounds like she has too," said the cat, her lamp like eyes gazing into Lilly's intently. "And sounds like she's been there for you with your stuff as well as carrying her own."

"Well when you put it like that," grunted Lilly, feeling annoyed. She didn't like it when they didn't side with her. "What can I do?"

"Well, what do you think is going wrong in her life?" Jeffrey asked.

"She kind of lost all her friends," Lilly said, thinking hard about the reality of Saffron's life rather than the glossy image Lilly always gave it. "And I think she's having a bad time with her family. And I don't think things are going well with Alex. And she thinks she's not going to win the competition." Lilly hesitated. "And she's jealous that I have magic."

"I see," said Jeffrey, raising his fluffy eyebrows and nodding slowly.

"But I can't change any of that!" Lilly insisted, exasperated. She felt like she was being blamed for Saffron's unhappiness and it felt wholly unfair.

"Are you sure?" asked Priscilla.

"I guess, maybe, if…" Lilly hesitated and rubbed at her temples with her fingers. "If she won the competition then she'd have something special of her own. But I want to win! I can't throw it!"

"You *can,*" said Priscilla. "If you *want* to."

Lilly looked from Jeffrey to Priscilla, then up to the desk at Molly. She found all three sets of eyes giving her a meaningful look that she didn't need magic to interpret.

"Oh fine!" she grumbled. "I'll do something rubbish and I'll let her win. But I still have to figure out how to stop it coming alive!"

"You put no life into that worm," mused Jeffrey.

"I know."

"No, I mean, when you draw things normally you give them life in their eyes. You put life in with your dedication to doing something beautiful and worthy."

"Just look at me!" agreed Priscilla enthusiastically, standing up and looking down her glistening grey body with admiration. "Beautiful. Worthy. Full of life."

"So I paint something dead behind the eyes?" Lilly asked, pulling a face. "That's weird."

"Paint like you hate it," said Jeffrey. "Paint like it's not your life to paint."

"Okay. I think I get it. Sit still." She told the rabbit as she gathered her painting equipment together and set her canvas up in front of her. Soon it was filled with a sad, flat painting of Jeffrey. It didn't sparkle with passion, it didn't quiver with life. The image she created was flat and meaningless. And it didn't move. She gasped. "I did it! I actually did it!"

"It's pretty dreadful," agreed Priscilla. "Saffron will definitely win."

Lilly scowled at the insult then took the painting downstairs to show her parents. They're reaction confirmed that Priscilla was correct.

"Wow, that's erm... great!" enthused her Mum with an artificial smile and over exaggerated nod.

"Sure is," agreed her dad with far less commitment to the performance. "It's really... great."

~ƐӜƷ~

When Lilly got to school the following morning she went straight to her form room, seeing no point in sitting around outside alone, but she found Saffron there already. She hesitated in the doorway then stepped inside, closing the door behind her and shuffling her feet.

"Hey," said Saffron.

"Saffron, I'm so sorry" rushed out Lilly, as though Saffron's greeting had given her permission to speak. She dropped her bags by her desk and dropped to her knees by Saffron's chair.

"No, I am," said Saffron quietly, looking embarrassed. "You didn't deserve that. I'm just having a really hard time. My mum and dad had this massive fight, my dad's moved out, my mum's being a total cow and I just... I took it out on you and I'm sorry, Lilly. I'm so sorry."

"I'm sorry too," Lilly said sniffing and wiping her eyes, relieved that Saffron had apologised because it vindicated her, but still feeling a troubling sense of guilt. "I'm sorry about your parents."

"Me too," said Saffron sadly.

"I'm here for you, okay?" promised Lilly, putting her arms around her friend who fell gratefully into her hug. "I promise."

"Thank you," Saffron said into Lilly's shoulder before sitting back up and wiping her eyes on the sleeve of her jumper. "Can I see your painting?"

"Oh, erm…" Lilly said nervously. With an embarrassed smile, fully aware that she was entering a total dud of a painting, she held up the image of Jeffrey. "Here."

"Oh, it's great!" Saffron lied enthusiastically, her eyes moving quickly from confused to joyous. She held up her own with a look of pride on her face. She was right to be proud, her canvas held a stunning painting of a horse running on the beach; its golden hair blending then disappearing into the luminous sunlight that shone down on its glowing body.

"Wow," said Lilly, in awe of her friend's ability. "That's amazing."

"Yeah. I mean, thanks!"

~ƐЖƷ~

Mr Hogg stood on the stage in front of the school. His usual leather waistcoat was now accompanied by a rather fetching leather bowtie, and the paint that normally stained his hands and forearms had been mostly scrubbed off. Lilly and Saffron looked at each other nervously, the realisation that it would all be over imminently suddenly taking hold.

"Ladies and gentlemen, the day has finally come!" Mr Hogg announced grandly, the usual cynicism about corporate jargon apparently washed away with the paint. "The winner of the art competition is going to be decided right now. To do the honours, I would like to welcome Keren Archer, CEO of Adamantine Power, to the stage!"

A round of applause welcomed the woman from the wings of the stage, where she strutted forward confidently, seemingly unconcerned by the audience. Lilly watched her in awe. She was slim and tall, with stormy grey eyes and neat brown hair in a bun. Her suit was unwrinkled and elegant. Her heels were high with scarlet red soles.

"It's great to be back," she said clearly as she smiled around the room. "When we decided to have a company rejuvenation we wanted to get the most out of the power we have, and getting the most made us want to give the most. What we want to give to one lucky winner is the chance of a lifetime. A chance to join us at Adamantine Power over the Summer, train with us, work with us, and design the new company logo with professional level payment. Hopefully, by the end of these six weeks, we will have a relationship with the winning entrant that will lead to as lifetime of success in the Power industry."

Lilly sighed and began to regret her decision to throw the competition. Next to her Saffron was twitching with excitement as Keren Archer listed the opportunities she was about to be given in exchange for her horse painting. Lilly reminded herself of all the reasons she was doing this, but hated herself for it every step of the way.

"I would like to welcome to the stage our two finalists, Saffron Jones and Lilly Prospero!" Keren Archer announced. She began clapping and stepped away from the centre to allow the two girls to take their positions. At the side of the stage two display easels were set up with red sheets over the girl's paintings. "Would you like to reveal your paintings now, ladies?"

Lilly and Saffron smiled nervously at one another then pulled the sheets back away from the paintings. Quiet gasps and hushed whispers circulated the room as everyone took in the entries. Lilly caught Mr Hogg staring in bemusement at her painting from the side of the stage with folded arms.

"Crap," she whispered under her breath. Reminding herself of all the honourable and good reasons why she had done this was providing no comfort at all now. She felt humiliated, ashamed, and angry. It was a stupid decision and she was certain she would regret it for the rest of her life. Just feet away she saw Saffron proudly standing beside her work of art, a confident look on her face that Lilly realised she hadn't seen since they first met.

"It's very nice to meet you two girls," Keren Archer said as she approached them with a smile, her eyes lingering on Lilly's for a moment longer than Lilly was comfortable with, then she inspected their work. She looked at them closely, then at a distance, each in turn then back again. Lilly and Saffron exchanged nervous looks. Lilly felt utterly miserable. There was no way she could win and she wished Keren Archer would stop dragging it out in such a humiliating way. "Well, I am certainly pleased that these two exceptional young ladies made the finals. They're a true credit to your school. However, I have to choose just one winner, so I would like everyone to give a round of applause to our new colleague at Adamantine Power... LILLY PROSPERO!"

Lilly didn't move then, hearing the claps coming from the audience, looked up and realised it was for her. Next to her Saffron looked like she might break down, her face hung and her eyes brimmed, but she had a generous smile stretched out and her hands clapped together louder than anyone else's.

"Thank you!" Lilly said, her voice muted with disbelief as she stepped forward and allowed Keren Archer to shake her hand

"Well done, Miss Prospero, I look forward to working with you."

"Thank you," Lilly said again, wishing she could be more articulate but finding even those simple words were getting stuck on the way out.

"And now I must be getting back," Keren Archer said speaking to the watching audience again. "Businesses don't run themselves and we have an important event to prepare for this evening, otherwise I would love to stay and celebrate with you!"

Mr Hogg stepped forward and shook her hand and Mrs Krank fawned around her on her way out of the room. Lilly watched in stunned silence for a moment, then she and Saffron stepped off the stage and took their seats. Saffron's smile was still glued to her face though her eyes held an intense and real pain that made Lilly hurt inside. After the assembly, they headed back to form rooms to finish for the summer, chatter all around them, but Saffron and Lilly remained silent.

"I am so sorry, Saffron," Lilly whispered as they sat together. "You should have won. I don't understand."

"Well, it's fine. It is what it is," Saffron said hollowly. "You can go home and have fun with your family and friends and celebrate. I'll go home to my mum who hates me, and my au pair who hates me, and see if I can get hold of my dad who can't be bothered with me."

"Oh Saffron," Lilly cried, feeling like the worst person in the world as she put her arms around her friend. "I am so sorry!"

"It's not your fault," Saffron said, shrugging Lilly's arms away miserably.

The bell rang for the final time that term and everyone headed out of the school in a sea of excitement. Lilly saw Ashya, Billy and Amy but they ignored her. She saw Alex but he ignored Saffron. The party later suddenly seemed like the worst idea in the world, an ominous dark cloud looming ahead of her.

"Well, maybe I'll see you around," Saffron said as she spotted Marika's car parked at the side of the road. "You're going to have a pretty busy summer by the sound of it."

"We'll definitely see each other," Lilly insisted. "Definitely."

Saffron waved sadly as she got into the car next to Marika, and Lilly watched the car pull away before she headed up the path. Ahead of her she was surprised to spot her mother waiting, talking intently to someone Lilly didn't know. As she got closer she saw a strange expression on her mums face, oddly vacant and unfocussed. The girl, long dark hair to her waist, was nodding slowly as her Lilly's mums head following her movements exactly.

"Mum?" Lilly called out. She felt an odd sense of trepidation and fear as she approached. The girl stayed just a moment longer, then crossed the road and walked away without looking back. Lilly hurried up to her mum who seemed not to see her, her eyes focussing on something in the distance. "Mum?"

"Oh, Lilly," she said, suddenly spotting her daughter. She smiled and kissed her cheek. "Hello darling. I was thinking, I was very unfair to say you couldn't go to the party tonight. It sounds like a lovely opportunity for you."

"It does?"

"Definitely," she said in an almost robotic tone. "You will have a lovely time."

Lilly looked over the road where the girl had walked and saw Alex and Tereska watching her, Tereska's long dark hair down past her waist. Alex looked at her and winked, then together they walked away. Lilly felt herself shiver, but knew Alex had made it so she could go to the party. She wouldn't let him down.

"Thanks mum. I will."

Chapter Twelve

Lilly frantically rummaged through her wardrobe, desperate to find something to wear that didn't make her look like a child. However much the party filled her with anxiety, if she was going to go she was going to look good.

"You're stressed," observed Priscilla.

"It's an important party," said Lilly, pulling a pale grey dress out of her wardrobe and holding it up against herself in the mirror.

"It's hardly life or death," said the cat snarkily, her tail swishing.

Lilly ignored her as she pushed the grey dress back in and pulled out a green skirt.

"I thought you weren't allowed to go to the party?" asked Jeffrey, sitting up on his haunches and keeping his tone light.

"I wasn't. But I am now," said Lilly, chucking the skirt on the floor and rooting in a draw for a pair of jeans, wondering if it was more of a casual party than a glamorous one.

"With Alex?" asked Priscilla, her tone not even slightly light.

"I'm meeting him and some other friends there," said Lilly as she decided it definitely wasn't a jeans occasion and went back to her wardrobe.

"What about Saffron?" asked Jeffrey.

"She's not allowed to go," said Lilly, holding up a black dress with beading round the neckline. "Do you like this dress?"

"Was she upset about losing?" asked Priscilla, ignoring the question.

"Yeah, kind of," Lilly nodded, examining herself in the mirror with the black dress, then shaking her head and throwing it on the floor angrily. "I look stupid in everything! This sucks!"

"What was her painting like?" asked Jeffrey.

"Awesome," Lilly admitted. The two animals exchanged looks, something Lilly was both getting used to and finding increasingly frustrating. "Look, I know you thought mine wasn't that good, but I guess I'm better than I realised because Keren Archer loved it."

"I'm sure she did," muttered Jeffrey, his voice low.

She pulled out a purple dress and put it on, brushed her hair and started putting mascara on. She ignored the stares from both the animals on the bed and the fish in the bowl, all eyes seemingly filled with judgment she just didn't want to deal with. The party felt like enough pressure for that night, everything else they had to say could wait.

"Maybe you should just stay home tonight," suggested Jeffrey. "I think you should call Saffron and celebrate with your family."

"No, I want to go to the party."

"Why?"

"It's a party!" Lilly said in exasperation as she rolled her eyes at the rabbit. "Back off, okay? I won the competition fairly, I was allowed to go to the party because mum trusts me, and you just have to learn to trust me too. I'm not a walking time bomb of death, okay?"

"Lilly..." Jeffrey started to say, but Lilly ignored him and stalked out of the room, slamming the door behind her.

"You look beautiful!" said her mum enthusiastically as Lilly came into the kitchen. "Have a wonderful time celebrating with your friends. You deserve it."

"Thanks mum" she said, looking into her mother's eyes and feeling perturbed by the cloudy look of them. Hesitating for a moment she asked, "Are you okay?"

"Of course," her mother said dreamily.

Lilly wanted to stay, check on her mother, ask Jeffrey what had happened. She felt sick with nerves and frightened about what was going on. So much of her wanted to kick off her heels, put on her slippers, and order a pizza with her mum. But instead, she waved goodbye and stepped out of the house into the soft, warm July sun.

~ƐЖЗ~

"She's gone, I don't know how but they've got her," Jeffrey said miserably into the mirror. "I was so sure."

"Archer?" Emma asked, her voice full of disappointment.

"Yes," said Jeffrey, feeling wretched. "We were right about the competition, it was a set up. The boy, Alex, he's meeting her there. I think the time has come to step in again. We can't let them get her."

"Are you still sure she's not dangerous?"

"Left to direct herself? I'm certain," he said confidently, then hesitated. "But if they get her, if they turn her, if she gets taken in by them… I'm not sure what could stop her."

"We should have been more aggressive with our tactics," said Emma, rubbing at her temples.

"No, you were right. It just makes her more defiant," said Jeffrey sadly. "I don't know what are choices are."

"Get hold of Errol." Emma instructed. "He might be able to get to them before she does."

"I'll do what I can to bring her back," Jeffrey promised, then put a paw on the mirror so Emma's image dissolved.

~ƐЖЗ~

Lilly headed through town to the river, then walked down the river
path to wear the houses started to get larger and set further back from the
woodlands that surrounded her. Her heels crunched on the rough ground
and the trees got thicker, obscuring her shadow from the evening sun.
The river that rushed past her was deep and full, the sound of the water
incredibly loud in the quiet of her surroundings but Lilly barely registered
it, her brain too flooded by thoughts.

"Calm down," she muttered to herself, shaking her hands. She felt like
she was drowning in emotions and it was clouding her ability to focus.
She was excited to see what happened at the party, but nervous about
what she was expected to do. She was both delighted and terrified about
the prospect of seeing Alex. He seemed to have changed and become
almost cruel, but still represented a world she longed to be part of and
wasn't willing to let go, and it left her feeling overwhelmed and confused.
Then she thought of Saffron. Poor, lonely Saffron whom she had lied to
and betrayed, who would be devastated if she found out where Lilly was
going and who she was meeting without her. It made her feel sick. She
hated herself for what she was doing but couldn't bring herself to stop.

She reached a narrow wooden bridge over the river with a large sign
reading "ARROWSEND HOUSE" against one of the wooden pillars. She
paused to collect her confidence and heard a crunching sound rushing up
behind her. She spun around in surprise and saw Saffron running down
the river path towards her.

"Lilly!" Saffron cried out, her arm waving.

"Oh no," she hissed to herself, panicking. She quickly stepped onto the
bridge to get away from her.

"Lilly! Please!" Saffron called out again and she skidded to a halt, her
trainers sending grit flying.

"Why are you here?" Lilly asked, guilt surging through her as she turned slowly to see Saffron stepping up onto the bridge with her, her eyes wide, her cheeks pink and her hair wild.

"I went to your mums," Saffron said, panting. "She said you were at the party. Jeffrey caught up to me as I was leaving and told me you'd be here."

"How did he even know?" Lilly asked, bewildered, but shook her head because it was irrelevant. "You can't come anyway, Saffron, it's not for people like you."

"People like me?" Saffron looked like she'd been slapped. "People like your best friend?"

"Please, Saffron, you know what I mean," Lilly said, turning away to cross the bridge and leave her.

"Lilly!" Saffron cried out, reaching out and grabbing Lilly's hand, forcing her to turn back. "You lied to me! Do I mean nothing to you? Why are you doing this? We're friends!"

"Go home! I'll talk to you later!" Lilly insisted, her voice full of anger and frustration, whilst her head felt heavy with guilt and shame.

"I can't!" Saffron wept, her face starting to crumble. "I ran! My mum hit me and I ran! I can't go back, Lilly, I can't! Please, please stay with me, please Lilly I need you. I need my friend. I'm scared. Please, Lilly, please."

"I can't, not now, I have to do this," Lilly said quietly as she tried to pull away, her own eyes filling with tears. She wanted to go with Saffron, take her home with her and be the friend she deserved. But she couldn't. The lure of power, the desire to be accepted into that world, was too strong. She felt drunk on it. Addicted. "Please go away!"

"I thought we were friends," Saffron sobbed, letting go of Lilly's hand and dropping to her knees, her face in her hands as huge choking cries racked her body.

"We are!" insisted Lilly, wanting to run whilst she had the chance but not able to leave.

"No!" Saffron spat, forcing herself to her feet and turning on Lilly with rage. "No we are not! You're obsessed! You're obsessed with power and magic. Nothing else matters to you anymore! I don't matter to you anymore!"

"Saffron I'm sor…" Lilly began but suddenly froze. A hideous noise of ripping, cracking, creaking tore words from her mouth. Beneath them they felt the bridge jolt violently and lurch forward, flinging them heavily into the bannister.

"Lilly!" Saffron cried out, going to grab for her friend as Lilly reached out for her, but before they could touch hands the bridge went, collapsing underneath them and tossing both them and the wooden structure they perched so precariously on into the water below.

Lilly struggled in the swirling water, wooden fragments smacking into her face and body in agonising jabs. She couldn't tell which way was up as she thrashed around in the green grey water that buffeted her and dragged her down. Suddenly she broke the surface and gasped as oxygen flooded her lungs. She forced herself to open her eyes properly, the sunlight suddenly painful, and saw Saffron just feet away.

"Lilly," Saffron choked out, struggling in the water. Lilly went to swim towards her when suddenly a huge wooden beam rocketed over a break in the water and crashed straight into Saffron's face. Blood shot from her pale skin and she sunk below the water.

"Help!" Lilly cried out, swimming as fast as she could through the current to the spot where Saffron had been. She felt beneath the surface of the water, trying to feel for a hand or a tangle of red hair but there was nothing. Looking around frantically she reached out more, desperate to feel something of into her friend. "Help!"

The water was fast and deep, the broken bridge battering her as pieces slammed at her cold skin. She swam as fast as she could, screaming for help every chance she got. A large lump of wood smacked her in the chest and she got dragged down by the current again but she forced herself to swim, grabbing the branches of a thorny bush at the edge of the river and pulling herself up and out of the water as she cried out from pain and horror.

"Saffron! Saffron!" she cried out, her voice weak and her head dizzy. On the muddy verge she crawled on her knees, coughing up dirty water onto the ground. "Help me! Help! Somebody help us! Saffron! Help us! Please help us!"

All of a sudden, over the sound of the river and her own tears, she became aware of a buzzing in the air and hooves pounding on the path. She looked up, staring around wildly as Pablo came into view, Priscilla on his back, and the air filled with swarms of butterflies, seagulls and bees that began to whizz frantically around the river's surface.

Lilly watched, stunned, as the insects gathered together in one huge spinning ball over a spot on the river and Pablo immediately began wading into the water. The currents tore at him, threatening to wash Priscilla from his back. She clung on by her claws, which Pablo was stoically ignoring, as seagulls chattered in the air around them. The llama was visible struggling, the water strong, but he kept fighting. He dunked his head below the surface time and time again until he slowly pulled it up, Saffron's t-shirt gripped in his teeth. As her head broke the surface, her pale face hanging limply, the seagulls swooped down and in a cloud of feathers and squawks, all began to pull at her t-shirt and jeans until together they managed to work her hanging form onto the llama's back. Pablo began to force his way forward again to the bank where Lilly was waiting in shock, his teeth gritted with determination whilst on his back,

Priscilla, kept her body weight on Saffron as she clung onto Pablo with her back claws.

Exhausted from swimming and dragging the weight, Pablo dropped to his knees, allowing Saffron's body to fall with a wet splat onto the mud below. Priscilla jumped down and daintily poked at her face with her paw before leaning down and licking at her cheek tenderly.

"Saffron?" wept Lilly, crawling forward through the slippery mud and pulling her friend's head into her lap. Her skin was deathly pale; translucent with blue veins showing through. Her lips were grey and she was completely limp, a dead weight as Lilly tried to pull her further into her arms. Lilly wept as she stroked Saffron's face, feeling her skin and neck but she showed no sign of breathing or movement, with blood smeared across her head and caked into her hair. "Saffron?"

"Is she...?" asked Priscilla, too terrified to finish the question.

"No!" Lilly sobbed, pulling Saffron close to her and pressing her cheek against the stone cold, clammy wetness of Saffron's face. "No, no, no! Saffron don't be dead, you can't be dead, you have to live. Saffron! Saffron please. You have to live. You can't die. Live, Saffron, live!"

In her lap Saffron suddenly coughed, rolled over, and vomited copious amounts of river water onto the mud at Pablo's feet. The insects in the air whizzed around in excitement, as the flock of seagulls began to spin and flap. Priscilla cried out in joy, and Pablo leapt to his feet and stamped frantically at the ground.

"Lilly?" Saffron's voice came out weak and cracking as she looked up at Lilly through eyes that looked too pale.

"Saffron!" Lilly cried. "Oh Saffron I am so sorry, I am so sorry!"

"What happened?" Saffron asked, her eyes unfocussed and her voice faint.

Behind them they heard a cough. Turning, Lilly was stunned to see Keren Archer standing at the top of the bank looking down at them, with

Alex by her side and a crowd of people behind her. She didn't know how long they had been there, she didn't know what they had seen. She stared open mouthed, her arms wrapped protectively around Saffron. Without a word, Priscilla climbed onto Pablo's back and he trotted away down the riverbank as fast as he could. The swarms of insects in the sky dissipated and vanished, and the seagulls launched themselves away, disappearing through the trees.

"The Life Giver," said Keren Archer calmly, looking at the soaking, bleeding girls. "Well done, Alex. Why don't you go and help them up."

Alex nodded and climbed down the bank. Too exhausted and confused to resist or demand answers, Lilly allowed him to help her to her feet then pulled Saffron up after her.

"Come on," said Alex, holding his hand out to Lilly. She didn't want to take it, she felt too freaked out by his presence, but the combination of overwhelming dizziness and physical exhaustion, and the slippery unsteady ground below, gave her little choice. She took his hand in her right, and a firm hold of Saffron's in her left, and allowed them to be lead carefully up the bank towards the watching party above.

"Impressive work, Lilly," said Keren Archer as the two girls arrived, filthy and broken, in front of her.

"What?" Lilly asked, confused. Frightened.

"Let's get you dried off, shall we?" Suggested Keren Archer casually, gesturing away. Lilly followed her hand and saw a large house set back behind the trees. "Then Alex can walk you both home."

In shock and confusion Lilly followed her through the grounds and over a large drive way then inside, Saffron trembling at her side. The watching crowds parted as they moved through, staring at them as they passed. Lilly wanted to grab Saffron's hand and run, it all felt too wrong, but she didn't have the strength and she was certain Saffron had even less.

The inside of the house was what Lilly's mother describe as opulent. It dripped with wealth from the chandeliers to the large gilt framed mirrors. The marble floor gleamed through the entrance hall with a thick cream rug spread across it. Lilly looked around in amazement and, despite the agony and fear that was filling her, felt horror at the trail of grim they left in their wake as blood and mud dripped from their bodies as Keren Archer led them straight across the rug without looking back.

They walked down a long, clean corridor and were lead into a large, gleaming bathroom. Keren Archer gestured for them to sit on an elegant loveseat with gold fleur de lis woven into the cream fabric, then leaned back against the white tiled wall. Lilly wondered if she was supposed to say or do anything, but before she had a chance to a small, elderly woman shuffled into the room.

"Multumesc ca ati venit," said Keren, from where she leaned.

"Orice pentru tine," croaked the woman, not looking at her.

She examined the girls and wiped their faces clean with wet cotton wool, then held their hands and began to hum. Lilly thought she looked exactly like gypsies from old drawings. Her shawls were heavy and her hands laden with rings. Her skin was leathery and tan, and her eyes were dark with hooded lids. The tune she hummed was beautiful. Lilly, already exhausted both physically and mentally, found herself beginning to drift off. Her eyes were heavy and her head swam with swirling clouds of confusion.

Sometime later, it could have been seconds or hours and Lilly would have believed it either way, the old woman stopped humming and dropped their hands gently to their laps. She nodded respectfully to Keren Archer then shuffled from the room again.

"How do you feel Lilly?" asked Keren, stepping in front of her and looking at her intently.

"What happened?" Lilly asked, looking up groggily and suddenly realising she no longer felt any pain. She looked at her hands which had been shredded by the thorn bush, but no trace of the cuts showed. She felt her chest, savaged by the beam that had knocked her down, and it felt fine. Looking at Saffron she saw the bloody wound on her head was replaced by the fair skin that was supposed to be there, and her face looked as confused as Lilly felt.

"Alina is a Healer," said Keren in a calm, matter of fact voice. Oddly business like, Lilly thought, as if she expected Lilly to understand fully without explanation. "A powerful one. Her work takes time but, we find, it is more successful than those who work with more speed."

"Why are you here?" Lilly asked after a moment, glancing to the side at Saffron, who remained silent, her large green eyes just watching in disorientated awe.

"This is my house, I live here," said Keren.

"But…" Lilly started, shaking her head, trying to focus. It didn't make sense. Keren Archer was the boss at Adamantine. She was just judge of their paintings. Why would she be there? Why would the party be at her house? None of it made sense and she couldn't make her brain work well enough to articulate her confusion. "But the party?"

"Yes, I threw the party," said Keren, speaking slowly and clearly. She seemed almost amused. "Alex and his friends are ambitious. Keen to impress. They have been working with me for some time now and there are opportunities I can offer talented young people, such as yourself. Opportunities that people fight to get. Parties are a wonderful chance to make connections that can lead one to greater things."

"So, you're magic?" Lilly asked, realising the question was stupid, but needing to think aloud to ensure she fully understood everything.

"Yes, Lilly," she said, another amused smile. Lilly was getting fed up for people finding her bewilderment funny. "I am of power."

"And Adamantine? Is that real?" Lilly asked.

"Let's leave this until another time, shall we?" suggested Keren with a smile. "I think you need to be returning Saffron to her world, she doesn't belong here. It's hardly fair to her to expose her to things too great for her mortal mind to fully comprehend."

"Oh, okay," Lilly said hesitantly, casting a guilty look at Saffron who seemed to not have heard any of the conversation, her face blank and her eyes staring at nothingness.

"Alex?" Keren called out as she went to the door, her heels clacking on the tiled floor.

"Yes?" Alex stepped in from where he had apparently been waiting, and flashed a grin at Lilly.

"Make sure you get them home safely," instructed Keren, then stepped aside.

"Of course," he agreed, and stepped forward holding a hand out to Lilly. She took it and he pulled her to her feet and went to walk out of the door.

"Saffron too," said Keren Archer, a note in her voice that Lilly couldn't place.

"Oh yeah," said Alex, and held out his other hand to Saffron, who didn't move or react.

Lilly dropped Alex's hand and took Saffron's instead. Alex winked at Lilly then turned and walked out of the room. Lilly carefully pulled Saffron to her feet, and she stood up with a hollow look on her face, but silently agreed to go with her.

Following Alex, they walked together back through the house, where people now mingled with drinks in hands, and all turned to watch them pass. Lilly spotted Una and Max talking in one corner, Sophia with someone else in another. Tereska stood alone by the stairs, silent, watching. As they stepped outside into the now empty garden, Lilly saw the bridge was back in place and gasped.

"Things in reality are different than what you're used to," explained Alex, catching her surprise.

"Is it safe?" asked Lilly as he stepped on it, too scared to follow.

"Of course it is," he said with a laugh as he walked across and stepped onto the other side, arms out in proof. "See?"

"But... but it collapsed..." said Lilly, rubbing at her temples and feeling so confused.

"Well, sometimes things happen for a reason," chuckled Alex. "It's fine now, come on."

The two girls stood at the steps to the bridge, looking at the rushing water below. In her hand, Lilly felt Saffron tense, her fingers tightening their hold. Lilly tried to catch her eye, tried to give her a look of reassurance and strength, but Saffron's gaze were lost.

"If you're too scared, we can just go the long way," he said with a shrug. "If you're scared."

Lilly looked at Saffron again, this time catching a look of pleading fear on her face, but she stepped onto the bridge anyway, pulling Saffron with her. Next to her Saffron started to cry as they walked over. Lilly held her breath, concentrating hard on each foot placement and the sound of the water below, only breathing again when they stepped onto the ground on the other side. Alex laughed again and then started walking confidently down the path that Lilly and Saffron had walked up before.

"So, that was pretty cool," Alex said after a while, looking back over his shoulder and flashing a cocky grin at Lilly.

"Cool?" asked Lilly.

"Yeah, you kicked ass," he said, turning back to smile at her. "Totally impressed everyone, I'm definitely in the good books."

"I wasn't trying to impress anyone," Lilly said coldly. She stopped walking and put a protective arm in front of Saffron to stop her. "I didn't even do anything."

"Well, you did!" he said, stopping and turning to face them, his eyes sparkling with excitement. "Seriously, you're going to be in for a great summer. Everyone's going to want you. I bet old Archer herself is going to try and get you on her team."

"Team? What team?" Lilly asked, confused.

"At Adamantine," he said. "There's so many projects going on, everyone knew you were strong but, you know, now you've proved it and taken away any doubt."

"I have?" Lilly asked. At her side, Saffron sniffed and let her long red hair fall over her face in a veil of tangled curls.

"Totally. You're going to need to rest up over the weekend, you know," Alex went on, ignoring Saffron and looking only at Lilly. "They're expecting you in first thing on Monday."

"Expecting me where?" Lilly asked. "Who? What?"

"Oh don't worry, someone will be sent," he said, and turning away casually and starting to way down the path again. "You'll be looked after. Especially since you've not been raised in reality."

Lilly slipped an arm through Saffron's as they started to follow him again. Saffron tried to sniff back further tears but they began to crawl miserably down her cheeks.

"Are you okay?" Lilly asked her quietly.

"No," Saffron whispered, still looking at the floor as her feet scuffed over the pebbled ground.

"Alex? Can we stop a second?" asked Lilly, turning and putting her hands on Saffron's cheeks, tilting her head up so she could look into her eyes. Her whole face looked broken, pale and lost. She had none of the sparkle that she'd once carried with ease, none of the life that had been effervescent in her eyes. "Saffron, are you alright?"

"Oh she'll be fine. Don't stress it." Said Alex dismissively, not turning back.

"No, seriously, Alex she's not okay," Lilly insisted, gently brushing the hair from Saffron's face.

"Come on, she's just a mortal, she'll recover," he said, turning back to look at them again. "They're designed to bounce back."

"Why are you being such an ass?" Lilly demanded, turning on him with fury. "She's meant to be your girlfriend and you're talking about her like she's not even human!"

"It's not like she's one of us, is it?" he said, sounding exasperated. "Come on, Lil. Stop over reacting!"

"She's right there!" Lilly cried, gesticulating wildly, disgusted with him in a way she never thought possible. "Jeez, Alex!"

"Let's just go alone," Saffron whispered quietly, tugging on Lilly's arm. "We know the way."

"Nah, can't let you," Alex said and shook his head. "If I lost Lilly now there'd be hell to pay. You can go alone though, if you like. That won't bother anyone."

"Shut up!" Lilly shouted at him, feeling completely intoxicated by rage now. It bubbled in her. It made her face, her brain and her skin ache with the venom of it all. "What the hell is wrong with you?"

"What?" Alex asked, looking confused. "What's the big deal? It's just a mortal."

"It? *It?*"

"Sorry… *She,*" he said sarcastically, rolling his eyes.

"You know what, Alex?" Lilly shouted, the anger almost too much to bare now. "Just drop dead."

Alex's face seized, his eyes rolled back in his head, and he fell to the floor with a smack.

Chapter Thirteen

The two girls didn't move for several seconds, then Lilly ran forward to where the lifeless boy lay in the dirt.

"What do I do?" Lilly cried. "What happened?"

"I... I... I..." Saffron stuttered, looking absolutely terrified.

"LILLY!" Came a man's voice from down the path. "SAFFRON! STAY RIGHT THERE!"

"Oh my god!" Lilly cried out, watching someone racing down the path towards them. "Oh my god we're going to prison."

"Mr Stubbs?" asked Saffron, her mouth dropping open as the history teacher came into focus as he raced towards them.

Lilly watched in absolute bewilderment as Mr Stubbs crouched down and put his fingers to Alex's throat and shook his head sadly. "Right girls, we need to get you out of here."

"What's happening?" Lilly asked, the shock of seeing the teacher appear beside the body of the apparently dead Alex felt like too much to process.

"Jeffrey called me, I had hoped I'd get here in time." He said sadly, shaking his head again and standing up. "Come on, we really need to go."

"Jeffrey called you?" Lilly asked, feeling dizzy. She stumbled, her balance lost in the confusion. Beside her, Saffron gripped her arm tightly. "Jeffrey? My rabbit Jeffrey?"

"Please, just come," Mr Stubbs insisted. "You can't be here now."

Side by side the girls followed their history teacher down the path and out of the woodlands into a carpark by the park. They climbed into the back of his car and he started the engine as they buckled their seatbelts.

"Jeffrey called you?" Lilly asked again as they pulled away.

"Yes," said Mr Stubbs, looking at her in the rear view mirror. "I'll leave it to him to explain."

"But... you mean Jeffrey?" Lilly asked, leaning forward and putting a hand on his seat so she could be sure she was hearing him correctly. "My Jeffrey?"

"Did anyone hurt you?" he asked, ignoring the question. "Has anyone said anything or done anything?"

"Jeffrey the rabbit?"

"Lilly! Focus!" he instructed sharply, looking angrily at her in the mirror again before turning onto a roundabout. "Did anything happen at your party?"

"I died," said Saffron quietly, gazing out the window at the people in their party clothes gathering outside pubs and bars, relaxing in the early evening sun.

"I see," he said, not looking back this time, a rigid look coming over his features.

Lilly sat back in her seat. She felt frustrated and confused, frightened and upset. Nothing made sense anymore. Nobody spoke again until they pulled up outside Lilly's house.

"My mum's here," said Saffron miserably. "That's her car."

"Do you want me to come in with you?" offered Mr Stubbs gently, turning round in his seat and looking at Saffron with great sympathy in his eyes. "It might raise more questions than we need, but we can work around it."

"No, we'll be fine," said Lilly, not sure how they could explain it in a way that wouldn't make the night any harder to handle than it already was. "What's going to happen to Alex?"

"I'm not sure," he said sadly, turning back in his chair to look out of the front window. "Go in now, and stay safe."

"Jeffrey?" Lilly asked again as she opened the car door.

"Goodnight, Lilly," he said, not looking at her.

With Saffron behind her, Lilly pushed open her front door and was met by Saffron's mother screaming into her phone. "IF I FIND OUT YOU'VE GOT HER!" Then she turned and saw her daughter standing beside Lilly, looking terrified. "SAFFRON! SAFFRON. OH MY GOD!" she screamed. She slammed the phone onto the table and grabbed Saffron to her.

"Oh, Lilly, darling!" Lilly's mum ran over and took her in her arms. "I'm so sorry about all that. I had no idea Saffron had run away! I didn't even know where your party was! How could I have not asked that? I'm so stupid!"

"Car! Now!" Demanded Saffron's mum, taking Saffron roughly by the arm and pointing at the door.

"Lilly…" Saffron started to say, but her mum pulled her away shoved her out of the door.

"Bye Saffron!" called Lilly, but Saffron's mum slammed the door shut in her face.

Lilly ran to the window and watched as Saffron was manhandled into her mum's car, and the door shut on her with a loud bang. As her mother got into the car and started the engine, Saffron's pale, haunted face gazed out. Her eyes stayed on Lilly's for as long as they could, before the car disappeared around the corner and out of sight.

"Your pretty dress is all ripped!" exclaimed Lilly's mum, coming up behind her and plucking at the damaged and stained purple fabric. "What happened? Are you okay?"

"Nothing mum, I'm fine," Lilly lied. "I'm really tired. I'm going to go up to bed."

"Oh right. Okay, sweetheart, if you're sure," Lilly's mum said anxiously, not sounding at all happy about it but seeming to sense now wasn't the time to push for information.

"Thanks mum," said Lilly with a tired nod.

Suddenly Lilly's mum reached out her arms and pulled Lilly into her for a hug, breathing hard and holding onto her daughter tightly. Lilly held onto her for a moment, smelling the familiar floral scents of the Anais Anais perfume and clean, fresh Simple moisturiser her mother always wore, and finding such comfort in the warmth of her arms. She wanted to stay, wanted to be cuddled and loved and to let her mum make everything better. But she broke away. Life wasn't that easy anymore. Her mother couldn't fix everything. Some things just couldn't be fixed.

"I'm sorry your lovely day ended on such a bad note," said Lilly's mum, tenderly stroking Lilly's short brown hair off her face. "We can start your holiday properly tomorrow."

"Thank you, mummy," Lilly said quietly, before heading upstairs. "Goodnight."

Lilly opened her bedroom door and found Jeffrey and Priscilla sitting on her bed looking innocent. She kicked off her shoes, dropped her bag on the floor and kicked the bedroom door shut. Neither animal moved or spoke.

"You," she pointed at Priscilla. "How did you and Pablo know we needed you? And you," she pointed at Jeffrey, "You called Mr Stubbs? You know Mr Stubbs? You can *call* people?"

"Pablo and I felt you," said Priscilla. "Like a tug. It hurt. It pulled us to you."

"Really? That's amazing. Thank you," Lilly said, collapsing down on the floor by the bed and putting her chin on her knees, too tired to do anything else. "Thank you so much. I'll go and give Pablo a cuddle too. I really don't know what I'd have done without you. I thought it was over."

"What happened after we left?" she asked, hopping down from the bed and winding gently about Lilly's legs.

Lilly hesitated then looked up at Jeffrey, hating what she was about to tell him. "Alex died."

"Died? How?" Jeffrey asked, jumping down from the bed and sitting in front of her. Priscilla sat down firmly at Lilly's side and gazed up at her in concern.

"I don't know, but I think I did it!" Lilly sad, then felt her face crumple and she began to sob, finally allowing herself to feel it. Her heart broke and her body shook as she remembered the way his eyes had clouded over and how heavily he had landed on the ground, his head cracking violently off a stone. "He was being awful and I told him to drop dead and… he just died."

"Oh my god," whispered Priscilla.

"Are you sure?" asked Jeffrey, putting a paw gently on her foot.

"Yes," she said, nodding in despair as tears splashed heavily onto her hands. "I said 'drop dead' and he did. He just died right there. Dead."

"It was an accident, right?" Jeffrey said gently. He hopped over and sat in front of her on his hind legs, ears back, and gently touched her hand with a paw. "You didn't want him to die?"

"I meant it though," Lilly sobbed, the honesty of her desire for him to die making her whole chest splinter in agony as tears cascaded down her face. Jeffrey climbed into her lap and lay his body against hers. She buried her hands into his soft, warm fur, holding on so tightly she knew it must be hurting him, but he didn't once complain. "I meant it, Jeffrey. I really meant it."

"I know," the rabbit said darkly.

"I'm going to bed," she said after a moment, sniffing heavily and wiping the tears off her face with the back of her hand. She kissed Jeffrey's head and set him gently on the floor. "I am so tired."

She took a long time to fall asleep, lying in the dark staring at the ceiling, remembering the way Alex's eyes had rolled and how his body had crashed to the ground as the life was ripped from him. She had done that. She didn't know how she had done it, she didn't even know for sure it was possible that she did it, but it felt like she did. It felt like she was a murderer. She *was* a murderer.

~ƐӁろ~

"What are we going to do about the boy's parents?" Fawn asked her boss as Keren Archer returned to the party and picked up a glass of champagne from a silver tray.

"I'll phone them," she said, before taking a sip of the drink. "They'll understand. He gave his life in the development of the ultimate Power."

"I shall make arrangements for the body," said Fawn, nodding respectfully. "And the Life Giver?"

"One of them must have got to her and taken her before we could get there," she said, feeling frustrated. It wasn't often she felt like her team had failed her, so when it did she wanted to lash out violently. She sucked breath through her teeth and forced herself to calm down, taking great care to not lose control, to not unleash her rage. "If they're going to make a move to obtain her we're going to have to be fast. We need her trust, especially now she's going to be feeling so vulnerable."

"I'll go in the morning," promised Fawn, before walking away and disappearing through a door at the side of the room into Keren's home office space.

Keren Archer pulled out her phone and stepped away from the crowds. "Hello, it's Keren. Alex was killed," she said in a matter of fact voice, not feeling the need to offer any sympathy or cushioning with the news. She listened for a moment to the voice of Alex's mother reacting. "Yes, it was honourable and it has accomplished great things, you should be proud. Your place at the Final Gathering is assured by his sacrifice."

~ЄӁӠ~

The next morning, Loriana Archer sat at her desk, enchanting a key to work only with her own touch, when Emma Bahman's face appeared in the hand mirror by her side.

"Update?" she asked brusquely, her usually calm face appearing strained and tense.

"And hello to you too, Emma," Lori said with a sigh as she put the key down.

"Sorry, yes, hello."

"I am getting word of a Final Gathering," Lori said, picking up the mirror. "My sister is being very secretive and only letting certain people in. Apparently I don't qualify as trustworthy. Either that or I am not subservient enough."

"I don't like the sound of that," said Emma seriously, her face looked even more strained than normal and her voice was filled with stress. "You don't have any more? Any idea what the gathering could be in aid of?"

"No, and I've only got that from bits I've overheard," said Lori, feeling frustrated. When she'd approached Emma all those years ago she had not imagined she'd be gradually sucked into the inner workings of the opposition. She wasn't cut out for a life as mole, especially for an ideology she didn't believe in. All she really wanted was to teach, help develop powerful young minds, and live a comfortable life. Yet, despite this, here she was having more and more demands made on her and being too scared of the consequences to not step up and help. "I'm trying, alright?"

"You're sure that's it?" Emma asked again, sounding irritated.

"Do you still not trust me?"

Emma hesitated. "Of course I do, I'm sorry," she, running a hand through her short grey hair. "Things are getting stressful and I fear I am not handling it well."

"Fifteen years ago I put my ass on the line for you enchanting that bracelet, Emma, and I haven't regretted it a day since," Lori reminded her. "I might disagree with your political stance a lot of the time, but I don't want the Ultimate Power being held in the hands of someone as extreme as my sister. You know that."

"Yes, of course. I'm sorry Lori, I know." Emma said, nodding in gratitude. "Speaking of, any word?"

"She's coming in this morning. Fawn has been sent to get her."

"They're moving fast," Emma observed nervously. "Jeffrey was convinced she's not dangerous. I fear the Tomson boy's death could have a serious impact on him."

"Tell him to shake it off," Lori said, not feeling particularly sympathetic to the rabbit's plight. "She needs her Guardian now more than ever."

"Well, good luck," Emma said. "You might need it. Keep me updated."

"I always do," Lori said with a sigh, before pressing her finger to the middle of the mirror, Emma's image dissolving into her own.

~ƐӁƷ~

When Lilly woke up Jeffrey wasn't there. She looked out of her window but couldn't see him in the garden either, just Pablo chewing idly on her father's favourite rose bush. Memories of the nightmares she had endured through the night came rushing back to her and she wished the rabbit was there for comfort and reassurance. She swung her legs out of bed and tried to force the images out of her mind. She felt exhausted; drained of energy and enthusiasm and joy. Despite the bright sunshine that illuminated the room, everything seemed tainted by shades of grey.

Heading downstairs, she saw her mum talking to a blonde woman she didn't recognise at the kitchen table.

"Lilly," said the woman in a dainty voice. Her eyes were so shockingly pale blue that they looked almost white. "My name's Fawn. I'm Keren Archer's personal assistant."

"Hello," said Lilly nervously, embarrassed by her Minnie Mouse pyjamas and scruffy hair.

"We were just talking about the possibility of you going into Adamantine today," explained Lilly's mum, a tense look on her face, her fingers gripping her coffee mug tightly. "But, as I told Fawn, it's your first day of the holidays and I had hoped we could spend some time together."

"And I suggested that getting acquainted with the environment before the normal work week starts might ensure you feel more comfortable," said Fawn, her pretty voice carrying an edge that betrayed the strength that was hidden within her fine frame.

"But of course, you're fifteen and won't be doing a normal work week," said Lilly's mum, sternly, glaring at Fawn.

"Ms Archer feels that giving Lilly the opportunity to be treated as a woman, not a little girl, will give her the best opportunity," Fawn said, fixing Lilly's mum with a steely gaze.

"But she *is* a little girl!" insisted Lilly's mum, exasperated.

"I'm not a little girl," said Lilly crossly. Her mother had no idea how much she could do, how strong she was. She didn't need to be wrapped in cotton wool. She had seen and done things her mother couldn't comprehend. The only people who could comprehend it were those at Adamantine. Those with power. "And I am quite capable of deciding what I want to do for myself!"

"Excellent," said Fawn, a knowing smile creeping over her lips. "You'll come in just for a few hours, then I can bring you home to your mother."

"I'll get dressed," said Lilly without looking at her mum, though she could feel the waves of disappointment rolling off her. She almost expected her mum to step in, to insist that she stay at home, but she didn't. Before she got a chance to try, Lilly ran upstairs. Quickly, she pulled on a pair of jeans, purple sandals and a Batman t-shirt, snatched her bag from her bedroom floor, then trotted back down and went to the door with Fawn on her heels. "See you later mum."

Before her mum had a chance to say goodbye, Lilly stepped outside and Fawn closed the door behind them. A small red Yaris sat on the driveway. Fawn bleeped the locks open and Lilly climbed in, dropping her bag on the floor by her feet and resting back on the headrest. Fawn climbed in, buckled up, and started the engine. They drove in silence as Lilly gazed out of the window.

Lilly eyed Fawn out of the corner of her eye, and wondered whether they knew yet about Alex.

"We do," said Fawn.

"What?"

"Know about Alex," said Fawn, not taking her eyes from the road.

"Oh, right," stuttered Lilly. "How did you…"

"I'm a Listener," she said, as if that explained it. "And we do know about Alex, well… some of us do. Ms Archer felt it best that it was kept as private as possible. For your sake. Alex was popular."

"I'm so sorry," Lilly whispered, looking at her hands and picking at her thumb nail. The now familiar sickness and guilt began to surge in her guts.

"Many of us feel it was the best possible outcome," said Fawn lightly, indicating the car and turning right.

Lilly tried to think, tried to understand. Nothing about the situation seemed like a good outcome however she looked at it. How could her killing Alex ever be seen as a positive? She didn't understand.

"You will," said Fawn.

"Do you hear everything I'm thinking?" Lilly asked, nervously.

"Only the conscious thoughts," she said, turning onto a large industrial estate. "And only if I'm listening."

Lilly felt sick and her hands started to sweat. She wouldn't be able to hide anything.

"What do you want to hide?"

"Nothing!" Lilly insisted, panic in her voice as she furiously tried to force her mind to go blank while Alex's death, his collapsing body, the greying of his eyes, flashed repeatedly in front of her.

Fawn shot her a sympathetic look as they pulled up to an enormous factory surrounded by a large, metal fence. An armed guard examined Fawn's ID badge, then the gate opened allowing them in. Lilly noticed with surprise that the carpark was remarkably full for a Saturday.

"Working here is more of a calling than a job. Weekends are often spent in the office by people's own desire," explained Fawn as they pulled into a marked parking space close to the front of the building. "Many colleagues choose to sleep here at times, too devoted to their work to leave."

Lilly's skin crawled, responses to questions she hadn't yet asked making her feel distinctly uncomfortable. Like her brain was being entered without her permission. She felt violated.

They got out of the car and Fawn led across the carpark, up a ramp, and in through double doors. Inside was a tangle of corridors and staircases, different coloured doors scattered everywhere, many blank, others with names etched on them in gold. Fawn led her through the maze with experienced ease, talking as they went.

"The blue doors as for invisibility powers, yellow are healing," she explained as they passed different areas. "Green are flight, purple are mind powers and white are communal. Powers are not permitted through one another's doors, but communal areas are open to all."

Lilly listened, trying to take it all in, overwhelmed and feeling insignificant. Everything seemed so big and organised, the people that moved between rooms and busily through the corridors around them looked efficient and grown up. Even though everyone was dressed in casual attire, Lilly still felt like a child on a field trip rather than a potential colleague. As they went, Fawn greeted several of the passers-by who greeted her back with cheerful hellos and wary smiles. Lilly became aware that everyone was casting curious looks over her before looking quickly away.

"You will find communal rooms in all power areas," Fawn continued as they climbed stairs and moved down further labyrinth like corridors. "And many groups gather there to study and practice, as well as enjoy recreational activities. We are well stocked with technology both for business and pleasure."

Fawn gestured up another staircase and Lilly followed mutely, having long given up trying to memorise where she was going, but still trying to take in everything Fawn said. Soon they came to a long corridor with a plush cream carpet and shiny black doors.

"What's black?" Lilly asked, looking at the names in swirling script.

"Senior level staff," said Fawn, her voice now hushed respectfully as they walked to the end of the corridor. "The restrictions do not apply. Senior staff can enter any room they choose, but you may only enter through their doors with express and advance permission."

"What do I do?" Lilly asked as they reached a door labelled 'Keren Archer CEO'.

"Be honest," said Fawn, with a wry smile as she pushed open the door and gestured Lilly inside.

Chapter Fourteen

"I'm a failure," said Jeffrey miserably as he sprawled dejectedly on one of Mr Stubbs's lawn chairs and sipping a mug of coffee. "I've lost her."

"You're giving up?" asked Mr Stubbs, eying the rabbit over his morning paper. "That's not like you, Jeffrey."

"I told Emma she's not dangerous. I swore to it," he said, shaking his head miserably. "And under my watch she killed someone." He sat up and carefully placed the specially adapted mug on the wrought iron garden table. "Seriously, Errol, what am I doing? How have I let her down so badly? I should just quit. I've failed her. I'll ask Emma to replace me."

"You're up against people without your morals," Mr Stubbs said slowly, putting his paper down on the table and folding his arms thoughtfully. "People who are not above manipulation and mind control. I'm not saying it was a losing battle at the start, but I am saying that if she's in their world now she's going to need you more than ever."

"I've been a Guardian for thirty years now, and I have never let anyone down like this before," said Jeffrey, feeling hopeless and ashamed. "I'm losing my touch. Lilly deserves the best and I am not good enough for her."

"Now listen up, Jeffrey," said Mr Stubbs, turning on his stern teacher voice that made Jeffrey jump a little and instantly feel small, even for a rabbit. "That little girl needs *you*. Not someone else, not a stranger. She needs *you*. She loves *you* and she trusts *you*. If you walk away from her now you are handing her to them on a plate. She's a smart girl, you know that, and she has a balanced heart, but she's only a child. She can't be expected to carry adult responsibilities without support. She won't be convinced easily but, without you there to guide her, it will happen. You only fail when you stop trying."

"Thank you, my friend," said Jeffrey, picking his coffee cup up again, trying to push the self-doubt and self-hatred away from his mind, but finding it holding on tight.

~ƐЖƷ~

"Have a seat," advised Fawn, as she and Lilly entered a waiting room with plush furnishings, soft lighting, and walls lined with abstract art.

Lilly sat down nervously on the edge of an emerald green sofa as Fawn disappeared through another door. She looked round at the paintings on the wall and was surprised to see they looked like originals. Matisse, Picasso, Kandinsky. She did a double take when she got to the back wall where, sandwiched between a Matisse and a Rothko was her own painting, the abstract she had entered into the art contest.

"Come through," Fawn said, coming back into the room and holding the door open. Lilly frantically wiped the sweaty palms of her hands on the legs of her jeans and stood up, following Fawn through into the pristine white office on the other side.

"Lilly," smiled Keren Archer, standing up behind the sparkling white desk that sat on the thick white carpet in front of an enormous glass window which took up the entire wall. She looked impeccably turned out, as always, and had a warm smile on her face. "It's lovely to see you again."

"Erm, you too," said Lilly, though she wasn't sure she meant it. Events of the previous night were clawing at her mind, and how Keren Archer fit into everything left her with an uneasy feeling she couldn't shake.

"Do sit," said Keren formally, gesturing to the chair as Fawn backed out and closed the door behind her. Lilly watched her leave and felt herself wishing the door had been left open. She felt caged. Nervously, she crossed the white carpet, hoping desperately she wasn't leaving dirty marks, and sat on the edge of the chair. "I understand you're anxious about the Alex situation, and that's why I brought you in earlier than initially planned. The rate your powers are developing is impressive and exciting, but dangerous. You need us, Lilly."

"I do?"

"Do you want to kill again?" she asked, fixing her piercing grey eyes on Lilly's own.

"No! No, of course not!" Lilly insisted, shaking her head in panic and feeling sick at the idea.

"Well, here you will learn how to stop that happening," said Keren, confidence and calm emanating from her as she rested her elbows on the desk and leaned forward. "We can train you, teach you, and harness your power in a way that will benefit the most number of people possible."

"But isn't this just a Power company?" Lilly asked. She already knew the answer, the doors and the powers she had seen on the way up at proven that to her quickly enough, but she needed to ask. She needed clarity.

"Well, in a manner of speaking, yes," said Keren with a chuckle, leaning back in her chair and smiling mischievously. "It's a facility for people with power. We find ways to enhance existing powers, utilise them, and develop them for uses in the outside world. There are any number of projects running at all times, and I am hoping you will become involved in mine."

"But... what about the art competition?" Lilly asked, remembering how hard they had worked for this opportunity and how far they wanted to push Saffron away from their world. "What if Saffron had won?"

"Oh Lilly," she exclaimed with a laugh, before delicately wiping her eyes, avoiding smudging the mascara that perfectly decorated them. "That wouldn't have happened."

"But Saffron worked so hard," she said quietly, a hard knot forming in her gut.

"I know, I know," said Keren, giving what Lilly suspected was supposed to be a sympathetic nod. "But we needed you here, and we needed a valid reason to get you here. But obviously we are very sorry about your friend." Keren paused, giving regretful face. Then looked back up and smiled broadly. "I'll get Fawn to show you to your room, and introduce you to some of the communal activities, and I look forward to seeing you on Monday to start work!"

"What exactly will I be working on with you?" Lilly asked as she stood.

"Do you know what happens to powers that go unused, Lilly?"

"They die," she said. "Alex told me." Mentioning his name tightened the knot in her gut so hard she thought she might throw up.

"They do, indeed," she said sternly, folding her arms and looking seriously at Lilly. "When those powers could be used to benefit people, do you think that's fair? Do you think that's good?"

"No," Lilly said hesitantly, knowing it was the correct answer but not sure she agreed fully with it.

"And the people who seek to use their own powers against us… to destroy power with power. Do you think that's fair?"

"No," Lilly said again, more confidently.

Keren Archer lowered her voice and said quietly, "We are finding a way to make it right."

At the back of the room, Fawn opened the door and gestured for Lilly to follow her. Lilly felt Keren's eyes following her out of the room as she stepped back into the waiting area.

"Wait here a moment" Fawn advised Lilly then stepped into Keren's office and shut the door.

Lilly sat on the emerald sofa. She felt small, vulnerable and unprepared. She wondered what they were talking about behind the door.

~ƐЖ3~

"Well?" Keren asked as Fawn walked towards her and sat in the chair Lilly had occupied.

"She's hesitant," said Fawn. "Definitely uncertain."

"What about?" Keren asked, sitting and leaning forward, her elbows on her desk and an intense look on her face.

"Her loyalty to her friend, the whole premise of your project," said Fawn. "She definitely wants to use her power and likes the prospect of helping people, but she has doubts about your motives. She doesn't like the fact she was lied to, and Alex's death is causing her a great deal of stress and anxiety."

"I see," said Keren thoughtfully. "Owen O'Donnell is in Lori's group, isn't he?"

"Yes," said Fawn, nodding to the unspoken words her boss was thinking. "No problem. I'll see to it."

~ƐЖ3~

The car ride home with Fawn was stressful, she tried not to think too loudly but found the more she tried the worse she managed. Fawn drove silently, a smirk on her face, as Lilly thought of the amazing building she had been round and how terrified she was about screwing up and looking incompetent. Everything had amazed her and she was now longing to get back, the conversation with Keren now barely entering her mind.

"Hello darling, how was it?" Lilly's mum asked when Lilly pushed open the front door. Jeffrey was sat on a chair beside Lilly's mum, a serious look in his eye as he chewed idly on a carrot.

"Oh my god it was AMAZING!" Lilly said, landing heavily in a chair beside Jeffrey, excitement bubbling inside her. "I'm so excited for Monday."

Her initial hesitation and nerves had soon been shoved aside from the moment Fawn had shown her to her room. Behind a grey door with "Lilly Prospero" on was a world designed with Lilly in mind. It was bright colours with music playing, a huge table covered in art supplies and fabrics, and several easels with blank canvases ready and waiting. To the left was a bathroom complete with Jacuzzi bath, to the right was a kitchen which Fawn informed her was kept fully stocked to her own tastes. Fawn had informed her that it was her room and her room alone, a space she could stay in, visit or leave when she wished. It was her home away from home. Lilly felt incredibly grown up looking around that room. She felt like she belonged.

After she had fully explored everything her room had to offer, she had been led to a communal room. Inside was a huge squashy seating area with a big loaded fridge and coffee machine, a pool table, a ping pong table, and a selection of top of the range computers and accessories. Some teenagers were sat in there chatting, playing with their powers, and generally relaxing. Lilly had gawped in absolute awe at the world she was being invited into. The world she could spend as much or as little time in as she chose. The world where she was wanted, admired even. She was desperate to prove herself worthy, to become as powerful as she could and achieve everything she had the potential to achieve.

"Let's do something fun this afternoon!" suggested Lilly's mum, closing her laptop and smiling at Lilly with a hopeful look on her face. "We could have a girly day? Go shopping?"

"Yeah, yeah," Lilly said, not really listening and picking Jeffrey up in her arms. "I'll just be a minute okay?"

She ran up the stairs, Jeffrey bouncing uncomfortably in her arms, and kicked the door shut behind her. Priscilla was sunbathing by the window on her back, a contented look on her face. Lilly bounced herself down onto the bed so the cat was flung in the air, and dropped Jeffrey down beside her.

"So, it was good?" he asked, ignoring Priscilla protestations.

"It really was," she said happily. "I'm going to learn how to control this power and really use it properly. They're going to help me."

"Why do they want to?" Priscilla asked. "What's in it for them?"

"Because that's what they do," Lilly said, annoyed by the lack of enthusiasm the animals were showing. "They work with people's powers. Make them better and make them safer."

"Then what do they do with them?" Jeffrey asked. "Do they profit from it or are they a charitable organisation?"

"No, they have projects," said Lilly, frowning. Wishing they would stop asking questions, and wishing she knew the answers. Feeling stupid she hadn't thought of these questions herself. "I guess they use the powers somehow. Do something with them to make money. It's got so much stuff it's amazing. They must make a lot of money actually."

"What project are you working on?" Jeffrey asked.

"I don't know, okay?" Lilly said, the interrogational way the animals spoke to her making her angry. They should have been happy for her, shared in her excitement. "But its Keren Archer's own project, and that's a really big deal! She said there's a lot of projects going on but she wants me for her own. It's a real honour."

"That's really great," enthused Jeffrey, smiling a determined smile at her. "Will you keep me in the loop?"

"Of course I will!" said Lilly, relieved that he was finally showing enthusiasm. Happy that he was impressed by her opportunities.

"Why don't you go and have a nice day with your mum," he said, putting a paw on her hand gently. "She's missed you."

"I will," she said, smiling.

"And Lil," said Jeffrey as she opened the bedroom door. "I really am pleased to see you feeling so much better."

"Me too," said Priscilla.

Lilly smiled at them, breathing a sigh of relief to see them both looking happy with her for the first time in ages. "Thanks guys."

She trotted downstairs and greeted her mum, who gave her a big hug.

"Let's go," she said happily.

~ƐӜƷ~

"So?" asked Emma, her face appearing in the mirror as Jeffrey pressed his paw to it.

"She's far less impacted by Alex's death than she was. She's more excited now," he said sadly, hating what he had to report. "She's obviously still upset by it's been pushed aside by whatever they've said to her. No doubt played it as a positive somehow."

"I see," said Emma gravely. "This lack of respect for life has been an issue for her before, has it not?"

"Not exactly," said Jeffrey defensively. "Anyway, I think we've made her start to question things. She didn't know how they make money nor what they actually do and it annoyed her. She didn't like it."

"That's a good start, I suppose," said Emma with a sigh, rubbing at her temples. "Of course, not trusting them would be an improvement but a niggling worry will do for now."

"It was only her first day," said Jeffrey, irritated. He was doing the best he could and hated feeling like it wasn't enough. "Bearing in mind how excited she was by her experience and how they've obviously brought out the big guns to lure her in, I'm pretty happy with that result."

"Fair enough," acknowledged Emma. "I'll take what I can get at this point."

"Indeed," he said darkly. "Lastly, she has met with Keren and is being brought into her project. Whatever she's doing, she is planning to use Lilly."

"Oh yes? That is excellent news," said Emma brightening up, much to Jeffrey's surprise. Of all the updates he had for her, he had been certain that this was the worst. "Lori can't get any information anymore and we need someone on the inside. I had hoped she'd be brought in on that quickly. I was worried they would wait until she was settled, until they'd built up her loyalty and trust, but they must have a need to move fast. Instead of trying to pull her out we will leave her there whilst maintaining her trust in you. She is in the prime position to feed back to us the inner working of Keren's project in a way we've never had access to before."

"I'm not sure I like this, Emma," said Jeffrey anxiously. "She's a little girl. We can't use her as a spy."

"If Lori helps Lilly keep her head, we could find out exactly what Keren is trying to pull off," said Emma, staring at him intensely. "I don't believe this is run of the mill Power-play. She's being too secretive, there are too many whispers. The Seers are convinced something huge is coming, something catastrophic. We can't do anything to save people if we don't know what it is. With Lori out of the picture, Lilly is our only hope to stop them."

"I understand that," said the rabbit, nervously. "But our goal was to protect Lilly, not bring down Keren Archer."

"Goals change, Jeffrey," said Emma. "Keeping her away from this world failed. Now we work with the new reality we're faced with."

"But this isn't a method I'm keen on utilising at the best of times, let alone with a child," protested Jeffrey. "She's too young! It isn't fair!"

"She's not just a child though, she's the Ultimate Power," said Emma, speaking calmly, persuasion in her tone. "She's one of a kind and she could do some serious good. Or, if we make a terrible mistake, something devastating. What do you think she would want?"

"All she's talked about is how she wants to be good, how she wants to do good," said Jeffrey, shaking his head slowly, too conflicted inside to know what the right choice was. "But I don't like lying to her. I don't like using her like this. It feels like tactics they use themselves. She might be the Ultimate Power but she's still just Lilly. She's just a little girl. Can we tell her? If she knew the good she could do, she'd definitely want to help."

"Not yet," said Emma sternly. "She's too overwhelmed by their world. She won't leave this life she's discovered on a whim. We still need her to understand on her own terms, choose on her own terms. Nothing about that has changed but whilst she does we could get information more invaluable than we've ever had before, even with the Seers."

"I understand," said Jeffrey, his heart heavy. He felt like he was betraying Lilly, but he knew where his loyalty lay and he was true to it. Above all else, he was a professional. "I'm on board."

"Very good," said Emma in a business like tone. Jeffrey suspected she had known from the start that he would agree. "I'll talk to Lori. If she seems to be moving away from them then don't push her back in, we'll respond to her in the same way as planned, but until then get what information you can. Keep the Balance."

They offered goodbyes, then Emma's finger pressed the middle of the mirror and Jeffrey saw his own face again, but looking older than it had before their conversation.

~ΣҜჳ~

Amy Chan Li sat on the bench on the back wall of a little artisan coffee shop on the edge of town. She held a rapidly cooling mochaccino and gazed into space. To anyone else it would look like she was people watching, taking in the surroundings of people talking and moving around. But she wasn't. Everything was surrounded by a constant grey mist, flashes of futures both good and bad sprang into her eyes every so often like dazzling, blinding lights that were gone as fast as they had appeared, usually before she could decipher what she had seen. It happened more and more now; the times where future events uncontrollably blurred out current ones.

On the table in front of her was a copy of the diary of The Oracle of Los Pacos that she had been studying before the vision mess began. The Oracle, Patricia Gutierrez, had written about learning to comprehend her gift, harness it. Focussing on one of the things she saw and picking it apart like a finely woven shawl until the strands became clear. Amy was finding the book of great comfort. Whilst she was never destined to be an Oracle, the woman's words were giving her comfort in the knowledge that clarity and control could be achieved. That one day she would command her visions, rather than they commanding her.

"Amy?" Saffron said, coming into the coffee shop and watching Amy's unfocussed eyes as they roamed through the fog of the future.

The sound of Saffron's voice seemed to part the mist, and the world around her slowly trickled back into focus. Relieved, Amy looked up and smiled at Saffron, forgetting momentarily they had not shared kind words. "Hello."

"May I sit?" Saffron asked nervously, shuffling on the spot and looking anxious about being there; her face was pale and blotchy, her eyes seemed to radiate pain.

"Yes," said Amy, folding a long red fabric marker down through the book before closing it.

"You're a Seer. Right?" she asked in a hushed voice, her eyes flitting around nervously as she checked nobody could overhear them.

"Yes," she said again, looking at Saffron in curiosity. She had never seen her look so vulnerable, nor so young.

"Can you tell me my future?" Saffron asked.

"No," she said, looking down and feeling embarrassed. She fingered at the book and longed to the control The Oracle spoke of. "I have not yet mastered visions on command. I See what I See."

"Can you try?" Saffron asked, her voice pleading and strained, her lip quivering. "Please?"

Amy hesitated. Everything about the girl in front of her screamed out for help, and refusing it felt like the cruellest thing she could do. "Okay," she said, quietly. "I can't promise anything. But I can try."

Saffron nodded in gratitude and sat with her palms out in front of her like they do in movies when visiting fortune tellers. Amy ignored the hands and looked into Saffron's eyes.

A flash hit her, blinding her with the violence of the light. Amy seized it as quickly as she could and tried to untangle the threads. Her head throbbed in pain, the intensity agonising, like a sharp stabbing to the brain through the forehead.

Saffron. Flash. Lilly. Flash. Something was tying them together but she couldn't make it out. No, it wasn't tying them, it was a connection, a stream of light holding the two together. Binding them.

"I can't make it out," she muttered, screwing her face tight as she fought through the pain and tried to make the vision clearer. "There's light, there's something there."

Suddenly a full, clear vision blasted into her and shot her back against the wall behind her with the force of it. She saw Lilly and Saffron standing in front of a woman with the light connecting them, and lightning emanating from the woman with scorching violence. She saw the two girls cower before her, their faces contorted in horror. The woman seemed to be sucking light and energy from Lilly, growing bigger and stronger and more powerful the more she took. The woman's arms raised as she howled in victorious triumph. She saw Lilly falling to the ground, her body broken in death. The light that connected them pulled Saffron down to die at her side. Then she was hit by a flash was so bright that her head burned in searing agony.

The vision faded and Amy slumped down, exhausted. Her whole body ached, her head spun, she felt sick. The vision left her with an overwhelming sense of horror in a way she had never felt before, something wrong, twisted and evil seemed to sit in her heart. Something she felt she could never be rid of. A grime or filth that clung to her insides, festering in her, invading her.

"Why did you ask me to do that?" Amy whispered, her eyes flicking open and tears running down her cheeks.

"I died on Friday," said Saffron quietly, looking first at her hands then nervously up at Amy.

"You're dead?" Amy asked. Her grandmother had been a Necromancer and had spoken many times of the gift, but it wasn't a power Amy had thought she shared.

"No, not now," said Saffron, shaking her head. "But I was, and now I feel… different. What did you see?"

"You *are* different," said Amy, remembering her vision, examining it, picking it apart until she could make sense of it. "It seems your life energy has changed and you are now connected to Lilly on the most fundamental level. You're bound to her. Your life is tied to her life. When Lilly dies, you will die too."

"What do I do?" asked Saffron, trembling. "Can I stop it?"

"I don't know," said Amy. "But there's more. There's danger coming, it is huge and insurmountable, and Lilly is going to cause it. And she will die," Amy looked into Saffron's eyes, hating herself for what she was saying, wishing she had never seen it. "And so will you."

"I need to find Lilly," said Saffron, pushing her chair back as she stood.

Amy watched her leave, her heart racing. She needed to find Ashya and Billy.

Chapter Fifteen

"Saffron?" Lilly said in surprise when she opened the door. She had only been home from shopping with her mother for a couple of minutes when a knock had sounded at the door.

"My mum doesn't know I'm here," said Saffron, looking around nervously. She looked wild and frantic, speaking rapidly, barely pausing to breathe. "We need to talk. Where's Jeffrey? He knows things, right? He knows stuff about magic. We need him."

"Oh, erm, garden I think," Lilly said, stepping back and allowing Saffron into the kitchen.

"We need him," Saffron repeated, nervous energy seeming to shake her entire body.

Deciding to wait until the rabbit was with them before asking what had happened, Lilly led the way into the garden.

"Jeffrey," she called out to the rabbit who was sunbathing on the swing seat. "Saffron needs you"

"Are you alright?" he asked, sitting up when he saw the state Saffron was in.

"No, I'm not," she said, shaking her head frenetically. "I spoke to Amy."

"Amy Chan Li?" Lilly asked, confused and cross. "Why? She's vindictive, what did you speak to her for?"

Jeffrey held up a paw to silence Lilly, much to her annoyance, and looked at Saffron seriously. "What did she say?"

"Lilly is going to cause a catastrophe," Saffron said hollowly, sitting on the ground in front of Jeffrey and looking up at him with desperation in her eyes. Lilly opened her mouth to protest indignantly but Jeffrey held up a paw again. She sat down beside Saffron and let her continue. "It's going to kill us. We are connected now. When Lilly dies, I die."

"Of course," said Jeffrey, shaking his head sadly. "I should have seen it coming."

"Of course Amy said I'm going to cause something bad!" argued Lilly, unable to stay silent any longer and standing up angrily. "She's one of them! She wants to stop me using my power! She told me to drop out of the art competition or I'd be causing death and… and… Oh god… Alex…"

Saffron looked up at her, her face drawn and pained. "I believe her."

Lilly sat down again next to Saffron, pulled her knees up to her chest and tried to stop her head spinning. "Jeffrey? What's happening?"

"Did she explain why?" Jeffrey asked Saffron.

"No," said Saffron. "Just that my life energy has changed and I'm now bound to Lilly's."

"I don't understand, what does bound to me mean?" Lilly asked. "And *why* is she bound to me?"

"Okay, I think I need to explain some things," said Jeffrey, hopping down from the swing seat and sitting in front of the two girls. "Magic is not a right. It is not free. Everything has a consequence or a price. Your power Lilly, the power of life and death, the Ultimate Power, will come at a very high price."

"Why didn't you tell me any of this before?" Lilly asked in disbelief. "This sounds bad! This sounds like something I needed to know!"

"I'm sorry," he said, looking into her eyes earnestly and with great sadness. "I should have. I really believe I should have."

"What's the price?" asked Saffron, her voice barely above a whisper.

"I don't know for sure," Jeffrey said hesitantly, looking from girl to girl. "To make life you have to give life. You know how when a woman gets pregnant she puts her own energy and well-being into that baby to grow it? How she doesn't *lose* her own life, she just uses it. But if she dies, the baby dies."

"Yeah," said Saffron.

"Well I think this is the same thing," he explained. "Lilly didn't lose her life to save you, but she used it."

"My life is in Saffron?" asked Lilly, feeling bemused.

"It would appear so, yes." Agreed Jeffrey.

"But I didn't do anything!" protested Lilly. "I didn't put anything in her! Have I got less life now?"

"No," said Jeffrey gently. "You don't have less life in you, but Saffron has... Saffron has a different life now. It's not the same energy as if it were her own life. Saffron's life is now... limited."

"If Lilly dies, I die," Saffron said, her voice empty.

"What about the big catastrophe?" asked Lilly. "Was that Amy stirring up trouble or was it real?"

"I'm not a Seer, so I can't know," he said, then looked down. "But I do know Amy. Not well, but I know her. And I trust her. She has never given me reason not to."

"You know Amy Chan Li?" Lilly asked, standing up in exasperation. "You know Amy Chan Li. You know Mr Stubbs. What the hell, Jeffrey? How is this happening? How do you know all these people? You're a rabbit! You're just a rabbit!"

"Please, Lilly," he said. "That doesn't matter right now. What matters is what she said. You need to know that if you see something happening that you think is wrong, or dangerous, or just makes you anxious you can come to me. You need to know I am here for you, no matter what. You must come to me."

"I promise," Lilly said, sitting back down and looking at Saffron nervously. "I don't want to be the cause of anything bad and I don't want to be the reason Saffron dies!"

"I don't want to die…" whispered Saffron, tears sliding down her cheeks. "Not again. Not yet. I died, I watched my boyfriend die… I can't deal with anymore death, I just can't!"

"I'll protect you," Lilly said, taking Saffron's hand in her own and looking into her eyes. "I promise. I will find a way to make it right."

~ƐЖƷ~

"What do you mean, gone?" asked Ashya when Amy appeared at her door, a terrified look on her face. "Gone where?"

"Gone! Just gone!" said Amy, her voice shaking with panic. "I went to his to get him first and he's gone! His mother's an Empath and she can't feel him at all. She can usually tell if he's happy or sad or frightened, but she's got nothing. She's had nothing for two days now."

"How is that even possible?" demanded Ashya angrily.

"I don't know!" wept Amy. "But they're scared. They're so scared. They've even called the police! The actual mortal police!"

"Have you Seen him?" Ashya asked, walking into the living room with Amy at her side and starting to pace like a caged lion.

"No! I tried!" Amy insisted desperately. "I can't see anything at all."

"Try again!" insisted Ashya. "Billy wouldn't just disappear on us! How could he?"

"I can't!" Amy started sobbing. She cursed herself for being so restricted with her power. She longed to learn, to improve, but nothing seemed to be working and nobody could guide her. She felt so desperately alone with just her books to understand her.

Ashya hesitated and stopped pacing, and her voice softened. "He's dead, isn't he?"

"He can't be," Amy said, shaking her head. "His mum would feel that. He's not dead. He's just… gone."

~ƐЖӠ~

Fawn arrived at 8 O'clock on Monday morning and Lilly was ready, and not just for her start at Adamantine Power. Since Saffron's visit she had been deep in thought, consumed by her desire to make things right for Saffron, and the idea that someone at Adamantine might be able to help. There were more powers than she knew, more things people could do, and surely there would be someone who could help. She just had to find them.

Fawn stayed quiet on the journey and Lilly knew she was listening, so she sang "I Went To The Animal Fayre" in her head.

"Are you going to do that all the way?" Fawn asked, rubbing her temple with her left hand whilst steering with her right.

"If it bothers you stop listening," said Lilly, not looking at her, a smug smile on her face as the big baboon by the light of the moon was combing his auburn hair.

"Fine," said Fawn with a sigh, but Lilly didn't trust her so just kept singing, allowing her own thoughts to be completely drowned out by the song.

When they pulled up in the carpark at Adamantine, Fawn breathed a sigh of relief as she stepped out of the car. Lilly grinned at her but Fawn just turned to walk away. Cackling inwardly, proud of sussing out a way around the woman's intrusive power, Lilly hurried across the carpark to catch up.

"You've got a group session this morning with Loriana Archer," said Fawn as they walked through the corridors of the large building and approached Lilly's own grey door. "Someone will come and get you in due course. After that session you'll be taken to meet with Keren and her team."

Lilly watched Fawn leave, rubbing her temples as she went. Once she was out of sight, Lilly quickly stepped inside her room and locked it behind her, feeling a strange need for the security and protection that came with the key. Taking a breath, she inhaled the delicate smells that reminded her so much of her mother, soft florals and a faint scent of incense, then went into the kitchen for a lemonade. Being in command of her own fridge in her own kitchen made her feel incredibly grown up and she indulged that feeling for a moment, leaving the fridge door open for longer than her mother would ever have approved of, always knocking it shut and complaining about wasted electricity.

A few minutes later, a knock came at her door. Setting the lemonade down on the table beside a large box of fabric, Lilly hurried to the door, smoothing her dress as she went, anxious to make a good impression on whomsoever was there.

"Hey there, I'm Owen," came the soft Irish accent of the fair skinned, dark haired boy she opened the door to. "You must be Lilly Prospero?"

"Uh... I... Yes," Lilly nodded, staring into his blue eyes and cursing herself for not being cooler.

"Lori sent me," he said with a lopsided smile on his face.

"Oh," she said dopily, wanting to kick herself repeatedly and ensure him she did speak English and wasn't completely thick. She felt her cheeks redden and cringed. You suck, she told herself. This is truly pathetic.

"Do ye want to come?" he asked, an amused look on his face. "With me?"

"Erm... Oh... I..." she nodded enthusiastically and picked up her bag.

She fixed a smile to her face as inside she swore at herself for being completely hopeless, stepped into the corridor with Owen and locked the door behind her. They started walking whilst Lilly tried to encompass a relaxed and confident stroll, but worried she was actually looking a little constipated.

"So, Lilly Prospero," he said, smiling at her. "Yeh the one everyone's been making such a fuss about?"

"I am?" she asked, gawping at him. "I mean... I am."

"Quite the impressive power you have there," he said, looking straight ahead while Lilly stared at him, nearly bumping into several people as they moved through the corridors.

"Thank you!" she smiled proudly. He was right, she just had to keep reminding herself of that.

"Welcome," he said with a nod, chuckling to himself. "So, how come I've not seen ye around here before?"

"I've only just started having magic," said Lilly, feeling embarrassed. Aware that she was proving herself to be far less impressive that Owen had been lead to believe. "I didn't have any before."

"That's a funny turn of events," said Owen, raising his eyebrows. "How'd that happen then?"

"I don't actually know." Lilly admitted, feeling her face get hot.

He looked at her sideways, curiosity across his face. "You're a mystery, Lilly Prospero." He said, stopping at a white door. "Ready?"

"Erm..." Lilly hesitated, pretty certain she wasn't even a little bit ready but unwilling to admit it. She looked up at him, feeling the fear widening her eyes.

"In here," said Owen with another amused smile, pushing the door open and stepping aside to allow her through.

"Ah, you're here," greeted a plump woman with a warm smile and a mug of coffee in her hand. "I'm Loriana Archer." She looked remarkably like her sister, the same grey eyes and the same brown hair, but with softer edges, colourful loose clothes, and a less tightly wound appearance. She held out a hand and took Lilly's, shaking it enthusiastically.

"Oh, erm, hi. I'm Lilly," Lilly stuttered nervously, then on hearing laughter, turned and saw she had an audience. On the sofas behind her were Una, Tereska, and two people she didn't recognise. Owen was perched on the edge of a sideboard, arms crossed and a smile on his face that crinkled the corners of his blue eyes.

"Oh good. It's you," said Una dryly, rolling her eyes and leaning back with a huff.

"Play nice," Owen scolded her playfully. "Lilly's one of us now."

"Whatever," she said, not looking at him.

"Obviously you know Una and Tereska, and now Owen," said Loriana, gesturing for Lilly to sit on the sofa as she lowered herself down. "This is Caroline, she's a Replicator, and Matty here has invisibility."

"Cool," said Lilly faintly, as her heart slammed in her chest and her hands felt clammy. Invisibility like Alex. She smiled weakly, did they know? She felt sick and tried to concentrate on the room, not on the memories that kept chewing at her gut.

"Owen here is a Wiper, and I am an Enchantress," Loriana went on.

"Wiper?" she asked.

"I could show you," he said, tilting his head and gazing into her eyes. "If ye like."

"Careful now, Owen," advised Loriana sternly.

"I will be," he said, an excited twinkle in his eye. "What do ye say, Lilly Prospero?"

"Erm, okay," Lilly nervously agreed. She didn't want to, she didn't know what was going to happen and something about it made her uncomfortable, but she didn't want to look childish and afraid, and she didn't want to let anyone down and face any consequences. Consenting seemed a safer option than refusing.

Slowly, his eyes fixed to hers so intently she felt grateful she was already sitting down it knocked her so off guard, Owen approached her.

Tenderly he placed his thumb between her eyes. For a moment they stared into one another eyes, whilst the room around them was silent, then he took his thumb away and stepped back, smiling.

"Who's this, here?" Owen asked, gesturing to the girl that Loriana had introduced her to moments earlier.

Lilly stared at the girl. Thick dark curls, Kewpie doll mouth and a smattering of dark freckles. Lilly knew her name. She knew her power. But she had nothing to offer as an answer. She knew she had the information because she remembered Loriana giving it to her, but she could feel just blank space where the information should have resided.

"It's... I..." She stuttered as she clawed at her mind, rummaged through her memories, but nothing came.

"Wiper," said Owen with a wink. "I wiped the memory from you. This is Caroline, she's a Replicator."

"Oh, right," Lilly said quietly, trying not to give away how sick she felt. Her skin crawled and her brain felt unclean. She felt violated. "I didn't know you'd do that to me."

"It'd ruin the surprise if I told you," he said, grinning. "Plus you might have said no and it's always better to demonstrate than describe."

Lilly knew he was right. She'd definitely have said no. She wished she'd said no.

"Don't worry, we won't do that to you again," Loriana reassured her. "Here we are working on using our powers together; using multiple powers at once to achieve something new." She turned to Owen again. "Do you and Tereska have an update?"

"Mortal brains are less substantial," said Owen in a matter of fact voice, turning away from Lilly and looking seriously at Loriana. "The memories Tereska gives them easily take over. We're getting pretty deep with the mortal subjects. It's quite cool actually."

Lilly listened, trying to figure out what was going on with a frown on her face. She didn't really understand, but it sounded like mind control and it made her feel sick.

"And on those with power?" asked Loriana thoughtfully.

"As Lilly so beautifully demonstrated for us there," Owen said. "Taking fresh memories is a doddle. They just lift out. Deeper memories are proving tougher to remove. We are also finding that they're more inclined to reject Tereska's replacements. She can Speak through my Wiping just fine, it's the acceptance on the other side we're struggling with. When they're fighting with the new memories they can end up..." he hesitated for a moment as though searching for the right word, "troubled. I've had to Wipe the new memories more than once to rectify it, but that in itself is problematic as they're left with nothing."

"Well, you're a solid team," Loriana said reassuringly. "I can think of a few project leaders who could use your combined forces, application in surveillance and counter terrorism just as a start! It'll take time, but you'll get there. Keep working and bring me a written report on progress at the end of the week. Something I can present at the senior staff meeting."

"Of course," said Owen.

Lilly was embarrassed by instinctive negative reaction, and wanted to see the positive in what they were doing. Counter terrorism was definitely a good thing. Her lack of familiarity with this reality and how it worked made her feel stupid but she was determined to learn. The rest of the session saw them sharing ideas, thoughts on what powers could be created with blending, what practical applications these new powers could have. Lilly was fascinated, and found herself warming greatly to Loriana who listened and advised, but without the critical tone of teachers. She was genuinely interested, and genuinely respectful. As the session ended, which appeared to come naturally rather than with the clanging of a bell, Loriana asked Lilly to stay and chat as the others started filing out.

"I'll wait for ye out here," said Owen to Lilly, flashing her a smile before stepping out and closing the door.

Loriana smiled at Lilly and suggested they sit on the sofa. "You'll be going to work on my sister's project this afternoon," she started, a slightly nervous look on her face. "Keren is a notoriously private person. She will swear you to secrecy about everything you learn."

"Okay," said Lilly, unsure what the relevance was. "I can keep a secret."

"She's also a difficult person to connect with," Loriana went on. "Many of the people here find her unapproachable. She's dedicated and brilliant, there's no doubt, but not always the easiest to talk to. I would like you to know that if you're worried or unsettled by anything she has you working on or doing then you can talk to me. My sister and I are not always in agreement, but we both value the loyalty we offer one another. You can always talk to me about anything."

"Oh, thank you," said Lilly gratefully. Not being able to share this reality with her mother was leaving a hole in her heart, and Jeffrey was so concerned about what she was going to do with her magic that she didn't feel as able to share as she'd have liked. If Loriana was willing and able to step into that void it would give her a connection she craved. "I do have a question."

"Yes?"

"The Wiping thing that Owen and Tereska do," she asked, nervously. She didn't want to offend but it was the one thing that was making her reluctant. "Can it hurt people?"

"Progress sometimes involves a degree of sacrifice, so yes as you felt, sometimes it can be a little unpleasant," said Loriana, a sad look in her eyes. Lilly looked at her feet and shifted a little. "But, Lilly, I promise you this, if lives are saved and the world is improved, a little bit of unpleasantness to achieve a greater good is worth it. If you don't take risks you can never achieve greatness."

"I guess," said Lilly, thinking hard. It did make sense, though something about it still sat unpleasantly in her gut. She tried to rationalise it, reminded herself that achieving good in the world was what she was there to learn, that all progress came at a price. After a moment of thought she nodded firmly. "You're right. I understand."

Loriana smiled and put a hand gently on Lilly's shoulder. "Go and relax, you'll have a busy afternoon coming."

Chapter Sixteen

When Emma Bahman's face came into view, Amy gulped nervously. It was not in her nature to step forward and be the one to demand attention and it always gave her a sickness in her stomach when she felt too compelled to not step forward. She had never felt a need to involve herself in any political issues, certainly never given herself enough credit to warrant contact with someone so senior in the magical community, no matter what vision she had experienced. Next to her Ashya looked nervous, but fixed her eyes forward, and Amy could tell she was unwilling to betray any weakness or vulnerability that she felt inside.

"I'm told this is important," Emma said, a distracted look on her face. She sounded neither annoyed nor interested, but didn't look concerned by their appearance in her office mirror.

"Billy Dawkins is missing," said Ashya, not bothering with any greetings.

"Dawkins," said Emma, suddenly concentrating on them, a serious look on her face. "The Chameleon? The son of the Empath and the mortal?"

"Yes," said Amy, her voice faint, wishing she had Ashya's confidence.

"And his mother, the Empath," Emma went on, her eyes hard. "What does she say?"

"She can't sense him," said Amy. "Nothing at all. He's not missing he's... he's gone."

Emma's face fell, and she rubbed at her temples. "Another," she said with a sigh.

"Another?" asked Ashya, her voice suddenly turning sharp.

Yes," said Emma looking crestfallen. She looked older than Amy remembered. Her hair was greyer, her face more haggard. She looked tired. "I would appreciate it if you girls did not share this information with anyone who does not need to know," she paused, the weight of what she was about to say seemed too much to bare. "We are losing people."

"But how can we lose people?" protested Ashya with a furious heat, her body starting to tremble. "It's not like we don't have ways of finding people, it's not like there aren't powers out there that can help! Billy's own mother can't feel him! What's happening to people? Where are they going? How can you not know? It's your job to know! It's your duty! You're supposed to keep us safe!"

Amy put a hand gently on her friend's arm and softly squeezed. Ashya's temper made her nervous.

"Ashya, Amy," Emma said, her voice heavy. She paused for a moment, looking down before looking up at them with a face full of pain, her authority seeming to slip. "Unfortunately my efforts have so far revealed nothing. I have feelers out, people on both sides, but things aren't always simple and loyalties can be split."

"What do we do?" asked Amy.

"Find out what you can, See what you can, tell me what you can," said Emma. "I'm so sorry girls. This is more than you should be having to deal with."

"We'll do what we can," Amy promised, putting her hand on Ashya's arm again before her friend could fire out more rage.

"Thank you," said Emma, putting her finger to the mirror and disappearing.

"So what now?" asked Ashya, her eyes burning with anger.

"Stubbs?" suggested Amy.

Ashya sighed dramatically. "Go on then."

~ƐӜЗ~

"So," said Owen as they reached Lilly's door. "Did ye enjoy your first session?"

"Yeah, very much," said Lilly enthusiastically, fumbling with her key and wondering if inviting him in was polite or would give a bad impression.

"You and Una seem to have some issues between ye, eh?" he asked, an amused look on his face.

"She doesn't like me," said Lilly awkwardly.

"I got that impression!" he said with a laugh.

She hesitated then unlocked the door, pushing it open to reveal the music, bright colours, a floral smells from within. He leaned against the door frame and smiled at her.

"Erm, do you… would you…" she hesitated. She had never invited a boy into her own space before. She had seen it in films, heard people talking about it, but it was an alien experience and she found she had no idea how to do it properly She felt every bit the fifteen year old she was and she hated it. "A drink? Lemonade?" She cursed herself. Offering him a lemonade seemed to be the most childish thing she could have done when attempting to do something grown up.

He laughed again and shook his head. "Tell ye what, you keep hold o' that lemonade and I'll have it with ye another time."

"Oh, yes. Okay," she said feeling her face burn red.

"See you around there, Lilly Prospero," he said with a smile, then walked away.

She watched him leave then slipped inside the door, slammed it shut, and slid to the floor with her head in her hands, completely mortified.

~ƐӜЗ~

"You are not going back to your father's house ever again!" screamed Saffron's mother, slamming the door as her daughter stepped inside, dropping her bag in the corner of the kitchen.

"You can't stop me!" spat Saffron, storming past her mother, trying to force herself not to cry.

"Don't you dare speak to me like that you little bitch!" her mother snarled.

Saffron spun and glared at her mother. She wasn't going to tell her that hadn't been at her father's, she had been alone by the river, watching the water and thinking about death. She had been crying and missing her friend, but resenting her even more. Before Lilly had come she hadn't been happy, she had been lonely and sad, but she had been popular. She had been the smartest, the coolest, the prettiest and the most talented. It's amazing, she thought, how much loneliness one can cope with when surrounded by people. This new loneliness, this all-consuming solitude, was eating her alive... and yet even the feeling of being alive was now artificial. She couldn't even feel pain with authenticity. She was alone in a way nobody else in the world could comprehend.

"I will speak to you however I want!" Saffron said with a painful anger boiling inside her. "It's not like you give a crap anyway!"

"This is my house and my rules," said her mother with disgust. She looked at Saffron as if she was dirty. "If you don't like it you can get out!"

"You know what?" Saffron screamed at her mother. "Fine! I'll go!"

"If you walk out of this house you will never be welcome back," her mother spat at her, her usually neat hair flying wildly around her head, her face contorted.

Saffron picked up the bag she had dropped, stuck her middle finger up at her mother, and stormed out of the door slamming it behind her. From behind the shut door she heard her mother's voice scream, "You'll be back! You need me! Nobody else will want you!"

Into the warm evening air Saffron started walking, coldness eating her flesh. She couldn't go to her father's because she didn't know where he was, and she couldn't go to her friends because she had none. Walking away from her entire world the fifteen year old girl with nothing and no one determined to find herself a life that mattered… despite not having one to use.

~ƐӜƷ~

"Right, we have a new member of this team," Keren Archer announced to the room full of people that Lilly had been escorted into. It was a room very different to the comfy, homely style she was familiar with in Adamantine. It was white and stark. The white table was surrounded by people in lab coats, the only one of whom she recognised was Tereska who didn't look at her, remaining characteristically mute. "This is Lilly Prospero."

"Hi," Lilly said awkwardly, waving a hand shyly and wishing she owned clothes that were grown up and didn't give away the fact she was just a child.

"Our work, Lilly," said Keren, pulling a seat out and gesturing for Lilly to sit, "is exceptionally confidential. We are on course to change not only reality, but the world the mortals perceive to be reality. We are on course to stop powers being wasted, and ensure only those with the best intentions keep the powers they have."

"How?" asked Lilly as she lowered herself into a seat, intimidated and overwhelmed by this incredibly formal place she had now been thrust into.

"I can answer that, if I may," said an elderly woman standing. "It's nice to meet you, Lilly. My name is Odessa. I am an Eidetic with a special interest in the history of power," she said, introducing herself with a respectful air that Lilly wasn't accustomed to from adults in her life. "There has been legends of a set of words that can be used, combined with certain enchanted objects and forces of nature that will allow powers to be transferred. Removed from one person, and given to another."

"Wow," said Lilly, leaning forwards, her brain sparking.

"The problems we have faced were two fold," Odessa continued. "Firstly deciphering the exact accuracy of the legends. As with many ancient works, the adaptations, translations and interpretations have changed the fundamentals of the original law itself. Secondly, the need for a catalyst; an Ultimate Power that will allow this spark to happen. A catalyst so intense that it can warp Nature itself."

"As you may have realised by now, Lilly," said Keren Archer, placing a hand on Lilly's shoulder. "It is believed that you are that catalyst."

"Me?" Lilly asked faintly, her eyes wide. She had definitely not realised it. She stared around the room and realised everyone was watching her with fascinated looks on their faces.

"You," confirmed Keren. "With you, we could save those from the burden of powers they don't want. We could give powers to those most deserving who could use them to help people. We could remove dangerous powers from those who seek to do harm."

"There are some amazing powers out there," Odessa said, a hopeful look on her face. "When used in union they could end terrorism, end global warming, prevent war, drought, floods… but they're in the control of the wrong people. If this works, we could fix that."

"In short, Lilly," said Keren. "You could save the world."

"Oh…" Lilly stuttered, staring up at her, then at those around the room who sat silently watching her, their eyes mirroring the hope in Odessa's.

Keren smiled at her proudly then changed the subject, taking on a more business like tone whilst the Lilly let the information she had been given settle. "How are the lists coming Ron?"

"Ours is complete," said a middle aged man with close set dark eyes and a thick, bristly moustache. "We have a thousand names, strong, capable and committed. We're still a couple short on the other side, but we're getting there I can assure you."

"We still have a little time, but push harder," she said to him sternly. The man nodded nervously. "Tereska, I assume your efforts continue?"

The silent girl nodded, her eyes flashing up to Keren's just for a moment before she looked down again. Soon the room was filled with conversation, ideas and progress being discussed, difficulties being analysed. Lilly tried to focus, follow what was going on, but everything was drowned out by the swelling of her own self-importance and thoughts of saving the world.

"We've completed our fifth round," said the large, hairy man sat to Lilly's left, his booming voice snapping Lilly back into reality.

"How have they coped?" Keren asked, looking at Tereska whose eyes flicked up momentarily as she shook her head slowly.

"We are getting closer," a woman with long dreadlocks quickly interjected, shooting an angry look at Tereska. "There is definite progress in power lifting, and some signs of movement. But without the catalyst we can't possibly achieve full transference. Especially on the scale we need."

"Well, we might be able to change that soon," said Keren, looking over at Lilly. "Lilly, we will need you fully in control and confident with your power. This will be hard work, and you need to be at full strength to achieve it. Do you understand?"

"Erm, yes," Lilly said, not sure what full strength with her power entailed, not convinced she would be able to get control of her power anyway, and totally at a loss about what she was supposed to do with her power if she managed.

"Very good," Keren said.

The discussions moved on to language interpretation and Lilly couldn't follow it, so she allowed her gaze to wander around the room, taking in the people around the table, as she listened to the confusing words. As her eyes drifted over Tereska, she realised she was staring straight at her. They held eye contact for several seconds before Tereska looked away. Lilly felt her hands get clammy, the girls stare held something Lilly couldn't place, but she knew it made her uneasy.

The session ended and Lilly copied everyone else as they started to stand and leave. People broke into groups and separated off, chatting and heading in different directions. Keren and Odessa disappeared through a small door at the back of the room, their conversation low and intense. Lilly stepped out of the room into the corridor, trying to remember how to get back to her own room, when Tereska fell into step at her side.

"I know you killed Alex," she said after a few minutes, her voice barely above a whisper.

"Tereska, I, I'm so sorry..." Lilly started to stumble across her words, her heart racing and panic taking over, but Tereska held up a hand to silence her.

"It proved what I already knew," the girl said in her voice that was both barely audible and incredibly carrying. "What we all already knew. The Ultimate Power."

"I don't know if I am what she wants me to be, I don't know if I'm as powerful as everyone thinks." Lilly started to confess, when ahead of them a door opened and Owen stepped out into the corridor, deep in conversation with a middle aged woman. Lilly caught his eye and smiled shyly at him, before noticing with surprise that following behind them in a white hospital style gown was Billy Dawkins. "Billy?"

The freckle faced boy didn't respond, he didn't give any indication he had heard at all. His face hung slack and disturbingly pale, his eyes vacant. He continued to walk forward slowly, his arms hanging limply at his sides and his feet shuffling. Owen opened a purple door to their right, and the woman guided the zombie-like Billy through it and out of sight.

"I'll catch ye later for that lemonade, yeah?" said Owen hurriedly, before stepping out of sight and closing the door behind himself.

"What was that?" Lilly asked turning to Tereska in bewilderment. "Why was Billy here?"

Tereska silently ignored her and slipped inside the purple door after them. Lilly heard a lock click into place and stood alone in the corridor feeling completely confused. She stared momentarily at the purple door, a feeling of nausea creeping up in her gut, then rushed away. She couldn't concentrate on where she was and soon the maze like corridors consumed her. She raced around another corner, completely lost, when she bumped straight into Loriana, who was chatting idly to a woman outside a white door.

"Lilly, are you okay?" she asked in surprise, then looked into Lilly's eyes. "Come on, let's go to your room."

Lilly nodded in relief and allowed herself to be lead away through the labyrinth of Adamantine to her own grey door. She fumbled in her pockets, unlocked it, and stepped inside with Loriana following her.

"Okay, what's happened?" asked Loriana, sitting on the sofa and gesturing for Lilly to do the same.

Lilly sat on the edge of the sofa, and tried to organise the overwhelming thoughts that were blinding her enough to decide where to start. "I saw Billy Dawkins," she said eventually. "Something was wrong."

"In what way?"

"He was just…" she paused, trying to find the right words. "Gone"

"Is Billy your friend?"

"No, not exactly, but that's not the point" Lilly said. "He went to my school but he hated people who used their powers. He was with Ashya and Amy telling me to stop. He'd never be here."

"People can change," said Loriana casually. "Maybe he wanted to study and train, really do something with his power?"

"Maybe," said Lilly, not convinced. "But what was wrong with him?"

"There's always a price to pay with magic, perhaps he did something wrong or pushed too hard," suggested Loriana. "It happens when the inexperienced are over ambitious. That's why it's so important we learn, so important we practice. It's why our work is sometimes so confidential. We need to perfect it before bringing it to the wider world. Our people here are advanced, if he can be brought back he will be. Inexperience breeds danger, unfortunately."

Lilly felt sickness in her gut, "I'm inexperienced."

"You are," Loriana said gently. "But you can learn. Being here is the first step in the right direction."

Lilly started crying, tears running down her face, the weight of expectation suddenly too much to bare. "I can't! I don't have time! Keren says I need to be perfect now or I'll ruin everything! They want me to be a catalyst or Ultimate Power or something, and to save the world..." She put her head in her hands and wept. "I'm just a child. I can't do it! I can't do it! I'm going to ruin everything and it will be all my fault!"

"Oh sweetheart," soothed Loriana, putting her arms around Lilly's shoulders and cuddling her tight. "This is definitely a lot of pressure on you. What are you a catalyst for?"

"Oh, erm," Lilly hesitated, remembering she was supposed to keep the entire thing a secret. "Can I go home now? I want to see my rabbit."

"Of course," said Loriana, taking her arms away and sounding disappointed. "You can go whenever you want."

"Thanks," said Lilly, grabbing her bag and tucking her hair behind her ears. "I, erm... thank you for listening to me."

"Any time, Lilly," Loriana assured her. "I'm always here if you want to tell me anything at all."

Lilly led the way into the corridor, carefully locking the door behind her. Before they parted ways, Loriana stopped her, putting a hand on Lilly's shoulder and looking at her seriously.

"Remember Lilly," she said, her voice low. "To control your power you need to use your power. But, whatever happens, it is *your* power. If you're not willing to pay the price, nobody has the right to force you. Your power is your life, and nobody else's."

Chapter Seventeen

Amy sat awkwardly on the edge of Mr Stubbs's sofa, Ashya at her side. She could feel heat radiating from her friend's skin as Ashya tried to keep her stress levels down.

"We didn't know who else to go to," Amy said, accepting the cup of tea the teacher handed to her.

"You did the right thing," he said, those his voice didn't sound as confident as his words. He sipped at the cup he held, but his hand shook so much that the china rattled. He set it down on the table, slopping a little bit of brown liquid out onto the saucer. He looked frightened, Amy thought, genuinely afraid.

"You know something," Ashya accused him, leaning forward and glaring. "What is it?"

"Ash," Amy whispered, putting a hand on her arm. "Don't."

"No," she said, knocking Amy's hand away. "I know he knows something and this isn't something we can tiptoe around," she turned back to Mr Stubbs. "What's happened to Billy?"

"When a mind is drained, but a life left intact, the human is essentially rendered the living dead," he said, his voice wobbling but the words coming out clearly, words he had clearly a great understanding of. "A mind contains all that makes up a person's soul; their humanity, their conscience, their emotions, without which the body can thrive as an empty vessel. To exist without existing, to live without a life, is surely the cruellest and most unusual punishment. It reduces a human being to an object and nothing more."

"What?" asked Amy, feeling horrified. "That can happen?"

"I'm afraid it can," he said, a look of misery on his face. "And if it has happened to Billy then something truly terrible is going on again."

"Again?" asked Ashya.

"My mother," he said, taking off his glasses and wiping his eyes with a pocket handkerchief. "My mother was a rebel in the 70's. She fought for equality, and fought against the men who dominated our world, using their powers to oppress anyone and everyone."

"What happened to her?" whispered Amy, terrified that she already knew.

"A Wiper took her," he said, looking Amy straight in the eye, his face haunted. "A Wiper took her and erased her mind. So many of the rebels were taken in that way. One day she was my mother, fighting and leading women's rights and magical equality meetings. The next day she was a zombie. She didn't know me and I barely knew her."

"Oh my god," whispered Ashya.

"A Guardian was sent," he said, his face softening. "Our Community were aware of it, and though there was nothing they had been able to do to stop it, the children of those whom had been Wiped were cared for. Our people are invested in protection of the most vulnerable and because of that I'm able to be the man I am today. Without it, who knows? My Guardian and I remain friends to this day and I owe everything to him. But my mother never recovered. Not fully. She was never the woman I'd known and loved again."

"We need to find Billy," Amy said, her hands shaking.

"If you want to find young Mister Dawkins, you need to find someone with the will and power to destroy his mind but leave his body intact," Mr Stubbs said, his voice heavy. "And I would recommend you talk to Lilly Prospero."

"Lilly did this?" asked Ashya, standing up, fury in her voice and heat radiating from her flesh.

"Oh good grief no!" exclaimed Mr Stubbs. Then he sighed deeply, his head dropping low. "But she might know who did."

~ƐӜϨ~

Outside in her garden, Lilly lay on the soft grass and leaned back on Pablo's chest as he lay on his side in the evening sun. Jeffrey and Priscilla sat at her sides, listening as she talked.

"And they need a catalyst," she explained. "And they think it's me. But… But I can't be it. She referred to it as the 'Ultimate Power' and I'm barely in control of what little power I have. I thought I was going to be taught slowly how to use it not expected to be fully in control immediately."

"You don't have to do it if you don't want to," Jeffrey said gently, placing a soft paw on her right hand. "You don't have to do anything you don't want to do."

"I do," she said, sadly. "Without me, without what they think I am, they can't do it. It won't work. It would be all my fault."

"When do they want this to happen?" Jeffrey asked, his voice almost unnaturally calm.

"I don't know exactly," she sighed. "Soon I guess."

Priscilla flicked her tail and said thoughtfully, "So what happens when someone's power is removed?"

"It goes to the person they're putting it into," said Lilly, looking at the cat as if she were stupid.

"No, I mean to the person it has been removed *from,*" explained Priscilla.

"I don't know, nothing I guess," said Lilly, sitting up and thinking. "They just don't have it anymore. She said it would be taken from people who want to let the power die anyway, or people who would use it to hurt people, so it would just mean they can't do that anymore."

"No," said Jeffrey, shaking his head. "There is always a price. Maybe you should find out what that price is, and whether you're willing to pay it, before you agree. Ask some questions, get all the information."

"I don't want to cause a fuss," said Lilly nervously, picking at her thumb. "It won't be that bad because everyone's so excited to do it. They're really nice and really smart. I can't be questioning them, they're all grown-ups who know what they're doing."

"They need you, remember?" said Jeffrey. "They can't do it without you so you can afford ask questions. You need to find out what's going on. The truth."

Lilly was going to reply when she heard her mum call her from in the house. She, Priscilla and Jeffrey said goodbye to Pablo and went inside where they were shocked to find Lilly's mum sitting at the kitchen table with Saffron at her side, hunched over, her shoulders shaking.

"I had nowhere else to go. I'm so sorry," Saffron whispered, then burst into tears.

"Oh darling," said Lilly's mum, leaping to her feet and wrapping her arms around the crying girl. "You always have here. Always."

"What happened?" asked Lilly in surprise, sitting down and putting a hand on Saffron's arm.

"I had a fight with my mum," Saffron said, sniffling wetly and peering up at Lilly. "She told me not to come back."

"Disgusting way to treat your little girl," said Lilly's mum, stroking Saffron's hair tenderly. "You can stay for as long as you like. The spare room is yours."

"Are you sure?" Saffron asked, her eyes brimming with tears as she looked up first at Lilly's mum, then at Lilly, a pleading and desperate look on her face.

"Of course!" insisted Lilly's mum. "We'd love to have you here, wouldn't we Lilly?"

Lilly slipped into the seat on the other side of Saffron. "Definitely," she said, putting a hand on Saffron's back. Despite the complicated relationship they had, their connection was real and true and Lilly felt responsible for Saffron's pain. Maybe with her there Lilly could protect her, stop anymore sadness coming into her life. Maybe in some way make up for everything that had happened.

"Thank you," Saffron said, nodding heavily. "So much."

"Where are your things?" Lilly asked, looking around for bags.

"I didn't get a chance to pack," said Saffron, clearly embarrassed. "I've only got my normal bag with my phone and stuff in."

"Well no mind, you can wear things of Lilly's," said Lilly's mum, turning to Lilly. "Why don't you show Saffron up to her room. Make up the bed, the sheets are in the airing cupboard, and get her some of your pyjamas. I'll phone for a Chinese and we can put our feet up with a movie. Might as well make Saffron's moving in night something fun, right?"

Saffron looked at Lilly's mum with a face full of gratitude, her eyes wide and her skin pale, then let Lilly lead her upstairs. Lilly pulled a set of purple sheets out of the cupboard on the landing, then Priscilla, Jeffrey and Saffron followed her into the spare room. Saffron sat down on the floor and rested her head back against the wall, the animals climbing into her lap and resting against her as she ran her fingers through their fur.

"I just wish I had something, you know?" Saffron said, her voice heavy as she watched Lilly putting sheets on the bed. "I have nothing. Just nothing. I have no friends, no family left, no real life."

"You've got me," said Lilly, frowning as she stuffed a pillow into a purple, flowery pillow case.

"Yeah, and look how well that worked out for me," she said with a tragic laugh, looking up at the ceiling in despair. "You and your magic are why I'm here!"

Lilly went to protest, to argue that she was trying to make for it now when a thought suddenly occurred to her. "Saffron, would you have felt better if you had a power too?"

"If I had a power too none of this would have happened," she said, as if she had already thought about this many times. "I wouldn't have been left out, I wouldn't have been arguing with you on the bridge, I wouldn't have died, and I wouldn't have been treated like crap by Alex. Alex wouldn't have had to take us home and so he wouldn't have died either. If I had power too I'd have my own life not a pathetic half-life that depends on you. If I had a power too I'd matter. Of course I'd have felt better if I had a power too because if I had power too I'd have had nothing to feel so rubbish about in the first place!"

"I know what to do," said Lilly eagerly, dropping the pillow with the case still hanging loose onto the bed.

"Lilly… wait…" said Jeffrey, sitting up suddenly and stepping forwards but Lilly ignored him.

"I think I can get you power," Lilly said, dropping to her knees in front of Saffron, her heart racing with excitement. "I think I can fix everything."

"Seriously?" whispered Saffron, her eyes widening. "I could have magic?"

"Yeah, seriously," said Lilly in a hushed voice, a huge smile on her face. Jeffrey dropped to the floor. "Oh crap."

~ƐӜƷ~

"That must be the Chinese food!" said Lilly's mum as they heard the door knock. She jumped up, pausing the movie. Saffron and Lilly sat side by side on the sofa, Katherine Heigl's frozen face on the screen in front of them. They were about to speak when Lilly's mum voice called out, "Lilly! Your friends are here!"

"Friends?" Lilly asked Saffron who looked as bewildered as Lilly felt. "What friends?"

The two girls walked out of the living room and found Amy and Ashya standing awkwardly together in the kitchen.

"We've got food coming," said Lilly's mum, turning on her hostess smile and clearly thrilled by her daughter's apparent popularity. "But I'm sure we can make it stretch if you girls would like to stay?"

"No!" said Lilly quickly. "No, it's fine. They won't stay long."

"I see," said Lilly's mum, raising her eyebrows and eyeing the girls suspiciously, Lilly and Saffron facing Amy and Ashya with a wall of tension between them. "Well, shall I leave you girls to it then?"

"Yeah," said Lilly, trying to sound calm. "Thanks mum. We'll be through in a minute."

"Okay, honey," she said again, an anxious note to her voice as she turned to leave.

"Where's Billy?" demanded Ashya with her hands on her hips after Lilly's mum had shut the living room door.

"What?" asked Lilly, taken aback.

"Have they got him?" she demanded. "Have those power mad lunatics got him?"

"Nobody's 'got' him," scoffed Lilly. "And they're not lunatics. If he wants to work on his power maybe you should just let him!"

"Something has happened to him," said Amy softly, putting a hand on Ashya to silence her. "And we need to know what."

"You can't See it?" asked Lilly, snarkily.

"No," said Amy, her dark eyes wide and full of angst. "Whatever happened has stopped it. He's gone. I can't See him and his mother can't feel him. His mind has been… taken."

Lilly felt her stomach drop, "Taken?"

"Do you know something?" demanded Ashya, stepping forward, fury on her face.

"I might do," said Lilly, nervously picking at her thumbnail.

Ashya went to speak but Amy silenced her again. "Please, tell us"

"I saw him today. At Adamantine," she said, her eyes flicking to the floor and back up to them.

"And?" asked Amy, looking frightened.

"He was with a Wiper," said Lilly, looking down, guilt and fear starting to surge in her.

"I knew it!" cried Ashya, clutching at her gut as if she needed to vomit, her face contorting in pain. "I knew those bastards were evil!"

"We aren't evil!" protested Lilly. "I'm certain Owen wouldn't have done anything to hurt him, they're probably working on something together and just need to fix something that went wrong!"

"If you're in league with them then you're just as bad as them," spat Ashya, glaring at Lilly. "You're just as evil as them."

"Hey!" Saffron protested, stepping forward and squaring up in front of Ashya. "Lilly's made mistakes, I know, but she's not evil! She'd never want to do anything that could hurt someone!"

Amy looked at Saffron with a ferocity in her eyes that frightened Lilly. "If you're wrong, Saffron, then we will all pay for it."

~ƐӜƷ~

"Tereska?" Lilly called out, spotting her walking towards the purple doors early the following morning. "Wait!"

"What?" she asked, turning round and staring at Lilly through her strange amber eyes.

"I want to help," Lilly said quietly. "I want to practice. I have an idea."

Tereska frowned but allowed Lilly to lead her away to her room. Once inside Lilly said, "If we can figure out how to transfer power, see whether I really am the catalyst, we could fix this problem they're struggling with immediately. Right?"

"Yes," said Tereska, her voice betraying no emotions from within.

"Saffron," whispered Lilly, despite the privacy of the room keeping her voice low.

"What?"

"We practice on Saffron," said Lilly. "I find out if I really am what they say I am, and you find out if you have the right words. If she gets power, the research is proven right, and then together we can save the world."

"Keren would never approve it," Tereska said, a hint of conspiratorial rebellion sneaking into her voice. "She wouldn't want power given to just anyone. She's personally approving every name on the list."

"She wouldn't need to know," Lilly whispered with defiant glee. She knew it was wrong, she knew people wouldn't like them experimenting with something so significant alone, but she didn't care. She needed to know if she was the catalyst and she needed to get Saffron power, and this was the only way she could see it happening.

Tereska hesitated for a moment, looking at Lilly in a way that made her feel a bit queasy, then nodded slowly. "I'm in."

"If I get Saffron here, today, can you get everything you need?" she asked.

"I can," Tereska confirmed.

"After lunch, in here," said Lilly, holding her hand out. "Deal?"

Tereska shook it. The deal was made.

~ƐӜƷ~

"You can't let her," Emma insisted. "She's getting too far in. If that is what Keren's doing this is going to have dire consequences."

"We should have pulled her out sooner!" snapped Jeffrey angrily. "I wanted to! I ignored my better judgment, on your command, and this is what's happened! So many times I've wanted to tell her and I didn't because of you!"

"We pull her out now," said Emma. "We know what's going on, as per the plan, and now we can get her out."

"How?" shouted the rabbit and stamped his foot angrily. He felt frustrated and afraid, both with her and with himself. "She's there! Why didn't you answer last night? I could have done something then!"

"Is Saffron still there?"

"Yes," said Jeffrey, sighing.

"I'll speak to Lori," she said, running her hands through her grey hair and looking old. "Whatever you do, don't let her take Saffron anywhere. We have a chance to stop this before it starts."

As Emma's face disappeared from the mirror, Jeffrey let out a cry of anguish and kicked his hind legs into the bottle of perfume on Lilly's chest of drawers, sending it flying across the room where the glass shattered against the wall, the scent of vanilla filling the room.

~ƐӜƷ~

Lilly didn't listen much during Loriana's session that morning, she was too busy watching Owen, wondering how to ask him about Billy. The fear Amy and Ashya had obviously felt made her doubt him, but he was so nice, and so gentle, she couldn't believe he would do anything to hurt anyone. Not deliberately anyway. He'd never mean to hurt people even when it happened by accident. She had to speak to him, she knew she'd feel better once he explained. Catching her watching him, the young Irishman smiled at her, his blue eyes twinkling, then turned back to listen to Caroline.

"So, how about that lemonade then?" asked Owen, approaching Lilly at the end of the session as everyone started to file out. "You've not forgotten have ye?"

"No, of course not," insisted Lilly. "Actually, I wanted to ask you something anyway, if that's okay?"

"Hit me," he said as they started to walk.

"It's about Billy Dawkins," she said nervously, watching his face for a reaction but there was none. "I just need to know if he's okay."

"Ye saw him with ye own eyes, no?"

"Of course," she said sheepishly. "It's just... some people were looking for him... and they said his mind has been *taken*. It sounded bad."

"I guess these friends of yours are those balance obsessed types?" asked Owen. "Terrified of upsetting the status quo? Scared of their own powers, but still want to use them against us?"

"Balance?" asked Lilly, confused. "I dunno. Yeah, I guess so."

"Lilly," he said, stopping and turning to face her, putting a hand gently on her shoulder. "We'll try and help ye mate Billy. We're getting there. He's in better shape than many of them, I can promise ye that." Lilly's skin started to crawl. "The more we do, the better we get, the more we achieve. The price will always be there, but we're figuring a way to pay it more cheaply."

"By sacrificing Billy?" she asked faintly, her voice cracking.

"You've got ye self a lot to learn, Lilly Prospero." He said, in a patronising voice, taking his hand away from her shoulder and looking disappointed. "Maybe I'll be passing on that lemonade again today. I forgot ye only a wee girl. I let ye power get to my head, and that's my fault. Come back to me when you've done a little growing."

Lilly watched him walk away then ran to her room, locked the door, and threw up copiously in the bathroom.

~ƐЖ3~

"Here," said Tereska, knocking on Lilly's door and handing her an empty fabric shopping bag before Lilly left on her quest to smuggle Saffron into Adamantine.

"What's this for?" she asked, allowing Tereska in and shutting the door behind her.

"It's not empty," explained Tereska. "I stole it from Lori's room. There's a coat she enchanted in there. It makes the wearer invisible. Get Saffron to wear it and she can come straight in"

"Wow," said Lilly, staring into the bag.

"I shall return in two hours," said Tereska formally, then left without a goodbye.

Lilly watched her leave then put her hand into the bag and felt a silky fabric inside it. Impressed, she stuffed the bag into her own backpack and hurried out, locking the door carefully. She left her room and closed the door behind her, her mind racing. It all suddenly felt wrong. The conversation with Owen had left her doubting both herself and everyone there. What would the price be? Would Saffron be hurt in the process? She hadn't followed Jeffrey's advice, she hadn't found everything out, and now she was going to step through that door without knowing what was on the other side. It felt wrong. But she had promised Saffron, and she couldn't let her down again. Not after everything she had been through, not when she had caused so much of her pain in the first place. Not getting power to Saffron seemed like a far greater price than anything she would have to pay just for doing the spell, but still, her gut seemed to be arguing with her. Her skin felt cold and her stomach churned, but she stepped out into the carpark without looking back.

~ƐӜƷ~

Watching Lilly walk away, Fawn stepped out from a doorway with a smile on her face, then turned and headed for Keren Archer's office.

Chapter Eighteen

When Lilly got home she climbed the stairs quietly, not wanting to alert Saffron to the fact that she was home before she had spoken to Jeffrey. She still couldn't decide what the right thing to do was, the turmoil inside her only intensifying on the way home, and the rabbit was the only person she could trust. The only voice of reason she had in her life. As she approached her bedroom door, carefully stepping around the creaky floorboards and holding her breath, she heard quiet voices speaking inside. For a moment assumed Saffron was in there with Jeffrey but then, as she listened, she realised she didn't recognise the female voice.

"Does she still trust you? Will she listen?" asked the woman she didn't know.

"Of course," came Jeffrey's voice. "She has no idea and I would like to keep it that way."

"You're not planning on staying on after the job has ended, are you?" asked the woman. "You don't actually intend to live the rest of your life as a pet rabbit."

"Actually…" started Jeffrey, then suddenly turned in surprise as Lilly had pushed the door open.

"What's going on?" she demanded, then saw the woman in the mirror and blanched. "And who's that?"

"Ah…" said the woman. "Lilly. I had hoped we wouldn't be meeting under these circumstances."

"I'm a job?" she asked Jeffrey, turning away from the woman in the mirror.

"Lilly," started the rabbit, hopping tentatively towards her. "I can explain."

"Explain what? That I'm a job?" Lilly asked, stepping back from him, her eyes burning. "That this woman sent you? That you sit around talking about me and how you try to trick me into trusting you?"

"It's not like that," Jeffrey insisted, sitting on his haunches and starting to tremble. "We couldn't tell you what was going on. We needed you to see what they're like on your own, see how manipulative and controlling they are so you wanted to work against them!"

"*They're* manipulative?" she cried, her arms out in exasperation. "*They're* controlling?"

"Maybe I can interject?" interrupted the woman in the mirror. "Lilly you need to understand you have provided information so significant we could bring down Keren and her team before they bring about this disaster. We could save the world because of you."

"They're using you," said Jeffrey sadly. "And now we can stop them."

"*They* are using me?" she cried. "*They* are manipulating me? *They* are controlling me? Are you seriously not even kidding me right now?"

"Lilly... please..." begged Jeffrey.

"No! No!" she screamed. "You don't get to say please to me! You've been lying to me from the day we met! You've been using me! You've been manipulating me! Do you know who has *always* been honest with me? THEM! Keren Archer and everyone at Adamantine, who by the way want me to save the world by actually doing something! *And* they have never once hidden that from me, they've never hidden anything from me. Not once! You tell me you want me to save the world but you couldn't even tell me why you were here."

"Lilly!" protested Jeffrey, tears matting the soft brown fur of his face. "I'm sorry!"

"I do not forgive you," she spat, and stepped out of the bedroom slamming the door behind her. She stood on the landing breathing hard, her face in her hands.

"Are you okay?" Saffron asked, standing in the doorway of the spare room looking frightened.

"Let's go," said Lilly, looking up at her, then heading down the stairs as Saffron scuttled behind her.

"Lilly! Wait!" Jeffrey called as Lilly reached the front door. She turned to watch as he came running down the stairs so fast he tripped over his feet and rolled down, landing heavily on his back at the bottom. "Lilly please don't go!" he wept, struggling to stand. "Lilly it's not safe! You can't go back!"

"Screw you," said Lilly and stepped outside, leaving the rabbit crying on the floor, awkwardly twisted in pain.

~ɛЖ3~

Lilly walked fast in furious silence, Saffron hurrying behind her. When they reached the end of the road that Adamantine Power was on, Lilly stopped and dropped her backpack to the floor. She pulled out the bag from Tereska and felt inside for the silky coat.

"What's going on?" asked Saffron nervously. "What was Jeffrey talking about? What's dangerous? What's happening?"

"Ignore him," she said and handed the invisible fabric to Saffron. "Put this on."

"Put what on?"

"Just take it," Lilly said through gritted teeth.

Saffron nervously held her hands out and gasped as she felt what it was, then took it and pulled it on. As soon as it was fastened she vanished. "Oh my god," she cried out. "I can't see me."

"That's the point," said Lilly fiercely. "Let's go."

They walked past the guard, Saffron's hand invisibly held in Lilly's, then straight up the ramp into the building. Few people were around during lunch, but those who could see her weren't aware of Saffron. She quickly made her way to her room, fished out her key, and let them in. Once the door was locked, Saffron took off her coat and looked around in amazement.

"This is awesome," she said, staring.

"I know," said Lilly, grimly. "Tereska will be here soon."

"Tereska?" asked Saffron, confused. "From school?"

"Yes."

"I'm scared," said Saffron, trembling. "Will it hurt?"

"I don't know."

"Jeffrey said magic has a price," Saffron went on, tucking her hair behind her ear and looking at the floor. "What will the price be for this?"

"Erm," Lilly hesitated, unease starting to replace the rage that had been clouding her. "I don't actually know."

"I guess just that someone else doesn't get theirs anymore, right?" she asked, twiddling at a strand of red hair.

"Keren said the powers are pulled from people who don't want them or want to hurt people with them," said Lilly, trying to sound confident but feeling incredibly anxious all over again.

"Why would someone not want their power?" asked Saffron, frowning. "Power is amazing."

"Well… I think it has something to do with this balance thing," said Lilly realising she hadn't really thought about it and feeling foolish. "Like, if you have a lot of power you'll mess up the balance of nature or something."

"That's not so bad. If it means I get magic pretty much anything is worth it."

"Amy, Ashya and Billy believe in balance…" said Lilly, thoughtfully. "And Mr Stubbs. And Jeffrey."

"So?"

"They use their powers."

"So?"

"I don't know… I'm just…" Lilly paused and sat on the sofa, a sick feeling starting to fall over her. It didn't add up. Something wasn't right and she couldn't make her brain process everything to figure out what it was. "Something doesn't feel right. Maybe we shouldn't do this."

"But Lilly!" protested Saffron. "You can't take *this* from me too! You just can't!"

A knock came at the door. Lilly looked nervously at Saffron for a moment then opened it. Tereska stepped inside, a bag over her shoulder, and nodded a cold nod at Lilly.

"Sit," she said to Saffron, pointing at the floor.

Saffron sat.

"Lilly, sit beside her."

Lilly obeyed, suddenly too overwhelmed to protest.

Tereska knelt and started pulling seemingly random objects out of the bag. She placed a box full of sand on the floor to the left of them, and a colourful blue and green marble on their right. A crystal vase of water went in front and a pale blue candle behind. She carefully lit the candle then stepped back.

"Whose power are we taking?" Lilly asked Tereska, her voice trembling.

"I don't know. All I have is a name. I stole this from Keren's department." Said Tereska without emotion. She held up a peculiarly textured piece of paper with purple ink deeply soaked into it and read, "Shana O'Neil."

"What will happen to her?" asked Lilly, wondering who Shana O'Neil was, what her power was, and whether she had any idea what was coming. Was she old or young, was she kind or cruel? Lilly was about to rip something so fundamental to who she was from her, and she had no idea who she was.

"We've never been successful before. We've never had the catalyst," said Tereska. "So I don't know. When the powers have been sucked out before it's always failed. Died. And so has the subject it was pulled from."

"They died?" demanded Lilly, standing up in horror.

"Yes. Please sit back down," said Tereska, pulling a heavy, leather bound book from her bag and placing it on the floor in front of her.

"But they died?" Lilly asked incredulously. "Every time?"

"Yes," said Tereska again, looking up at her. "Sit."

"What happened to the person the power was going to?" asked Saffron as Lilly remained standing, her head pounding and her knees feeling weak.

"Only the one whose power was taken died," said Tereska. "The receiver remained unharmed. We realised pretty quickly that we needed the Ultimate Power and there was no bypass."

"Saffron, please," Lilly begged, dropping on to her knees and taking Saffron's hands. "We need to stop this right now."

"But she said it only didn't work because they didn't have you! This will work fine!" insisted Saffron. "You said yourself, Shana O'Neil doesn't want her power."

"But she wants her life!" protested Lilly.

"Yeah?" asked Saffron, taking her hands from Lilly and giving her a cold look. "Well so did I."

"I'm ready to start," said Tereska, sitting cross legged and carefully opening the book, smoothing the pages flat.

"Wait!" Lilly cried. "Saffron we need to talk about this!"

Tereska started to speak. Her voice so quiet they could barely hear that sound was coming from her mouth at all.

"You promised me," said Saffron. "You promised me you'd fix this."

"But someone could die!"

"But they might not!"

"Is that a risk you're really happy taking?" Lilly wailed, looking from Tereska to Saffron in panic. She felt desperate. Suddenly she became aware of a strange swirling gold mist that was starting to spiral out of the enchanted objects. Nobody spoke and then, without warning, the mists swooped in on Lilly, straight into her chest. She screamed, feeling a burning heat and an icy chill simultaneously stabbing her with such agonising violence she was certain it would kill her.

"LIFE AND DEATH!" Tereska suddenly shouted. "LIFE AND DEATH. LIFE AND DEATH. LIFE AND DEATH."

Lilly felt her body being torn at, her brain screaming in agony, her skin burning and her flesh freezing. She turned in panic and agony to Saffron, trying to beg her for help but couldn't make any words form. Saffron stared at her with terrified eyes as invisible forces dragged at Lilly's body making her shake and stretch out like she was being pulled in every direction by violent horses.

Above Lilly's head, a huge ball of liquid fire started spinning and growing. Tereska stood, her eyes not leaving the ball of fire, a look of frenzied power driven joy on her face. As the ball grew brighter, Lilly felt all the pain and energy rush from her in a flood. She dropped to the ground, completely drained, and the ball of fire slammed into Saffron's heart, knocking her backwards onto the floor.

"It worked," whispered Tereska, as the golden mist that had engulfed Lilly started to trickle away from her, back into the objects it had escaped from.

"Saffron!" Lilly wept, forcing her aching body to move towards her collapsed friend, every movement searing with agony, tearing at her flesh and begging her to stop. But she forced herself on and leaned over Saffron, terror filling her as she looked at Saffron's pale face, so reminiscent of the last time Lilly had been the cause of her pain.

"Lilly?" Saffron whimpered, her eyes slowly opening, forcing herself to sit up and holding out a hand to touch Lilly's face. "Are you okay?"

"What did we do?" Lilly whispered, looking at Saffron, feeling sick with disgust both with Saffron and herself.

"It worked," said Tereska again. "We did it."

"I have magic?" asked Saffron, looking at her arms as if evidence could be seen on her skin.

"Whatever Shana O'Neil could do, you can do," said Tereska, in a matter of fact voice.

"This shouldn't have happened," Lilly said faintly.

"What can I do?" asked Saffron excitedly, taking Lilly's hand.

The moment their hands touched, a flurry of butterflies shot out of Lilly's fingers, hundreds and hundreds, filling the room with bright swirling colours. Saffron gasped and let go of Lilly, and immediately the butterflies stopped coming. Lilly stared in bewilderment around the room, butterflies everywhere spiralling and dancing on the air.

"What just happened?" gasped Lilly, ducking down and rushing to the window, throwing it open. Obediently the butterflies began to drift out into the cloudy, grey sky. "I was thinking about how when I first started getting magic I found out by making butterflies… then you held my hand and suddenly…"

"Enhancing is a rare power," muttered Tereska nervously. "Oh Keren is not going to be pleased if she knows I took it."

"What's Enhancing?" asked Saffron, examining her hands with fascination.

"Power boosting," Tereska explained. "Enhancers are greatly sought after."

"I'm sought after?" asked Saffron with pride, beaming.

"No, your *power* is," said Tereska disdainfully, wrinkling up her nose in disgust. Saffron looked down, embarrassed.

"This wasn't right," whispered Lilly, her head spinning and her body weak. "I don't feel right."

"It'll get easier," said Tereska, gathering the objects. "You're weak because your power is still too much for you to handle, your power controls you rather than you controlling it, but you did well. You held that much power in you and the transfer completed. That would have killed you if you weren't strong enough."

"I felt so much," Lilly muttered, shaking her head to try and stop the ringing in her ears. "That wasn't right"

Tereska ignored her, "Hopefully Keren will forgive the waste of such a power on a mortal, and see what we have accomplished for what it truly means."

"I'm not a mortal anymore," said Saffron.

"You're a mongrel Halfling," said Tereska, looking Saffron up and down with revulsion, then left, closing the door behind her.

"We need to leave," said Lilly, breathing hard and trying to force herself to stop shaking. "We need to go. Now. We can't stay."

"I want to stay!" insisted Saffron. "I want to learn! I want to do stuff!"

"I was wrong," Lilly sobbed, pulling at Saffron's hands. "That was wrong. Please. We need to go. Come on."

Saffron hesitated, looking at Lilly's face then nodded. "Okay," she said. They stepped out into the corridor, Lilly trembling as she fumbled with the key in the lock.

"Lilly, Saffron, come with me," came a voice. They spun around and saw Keren Archer, their mouths falling open. "Now."

The two girls watched the woman turn and leave, her heels clacking down the corridor. Lilly looked at Saffron, wondering if they could escape before she noticed. Just run, and get away from there and everything they had done.

"Come on, Lilly, you know that's not smart," came Fawn's voice behind them. Lilly tried to speak, but Fawn's delicate features were set so firmly that she knew it was pointless.

"Let's go," Lilly whispered to Saffron, and together they started to follow in Keren's wake.

Whilst Fawn followed, she didn't offer the same tour guide experience to Saffron that she had previously given Lilly, so Saffron stared around in wonder, taking it all in and looking totally overwhelmed and confused. They walked up the stairs to the carpeted corridor, then towards the door at the end with Keren's name etched in gold.

Keren pushed open the door and gestured for the girls, flanked by Fawn, to follow them in. They walked into the waiting room where Fawn took her seat, then, as Keren signalled to them to follow, they walked through into her office. Side by side, they anxiously walked across the white carpet, and sat in the seats, hands in their laps, eyes down.

"I am not sure where to start," Keren said, resting her elbows on the desk and looking at them thoughtfully. "Firstly, Saffron, welcome to our group. You were not born to this power but, for some reason, your mortal body has survived and accepted a power it was never designed to have. We are proud to have you amongst us."

"Oh, thank you," said Saffron sounding surprised.

"I assume that when Lilly used her power to save you, she infused you with her own life and that has saved you once again," said Keren. "Lilly's life force has given you the strength to withstand the force of power. It's quite amazing really," she paused and looked a little wistful, then looked serious again. "However, I need to speak about certain issues alone with

Lilly now, so if you would like to step back into the waiting room, Fawn will take care of you."

"I'd rather she stayed, actually," said Lilly boldly. However much standing up to Keren scared her, being left alone scared her more.

"Very well," said Keren, not arguing much to Lilly's surprise. "Lilly, there is something serious you need to be made aware of. I know you're having doubts about our team, I know you're full of questions and worries, maybe fear you don't truly belong here."

"Yes," said Lilly, deciding there was no point in protesting, they were already down the rabbit hole.

"The thing is," she said, gazing at Lilly with a look on her face that Lilly couldn't quite place. "You belong here. More than anywhere. More than anyone else does."

"Why?" asked Lilly. She felt her heart banging, she wanted to run. Something about her face and her tone frightened her more than anything else she had experienced since gaining her power.

"I'm your mother."

Chapter Nineteen

"It's too late," Loriana said, miserably. "She took my enchanted coat, she's smuggled Saffron in. I have just spoken to the Speaker and the transfer was completed. The mortal girl even survived it."

"Keren's got her," said Emma, her head in her hands. "We've lost."

"Surely we can find a way to stop this," Loriana insisted. "What can we do?"

"How?" asked Emma, despair in her voice. "There's nothing we can do. With the Ultimate Power they've won. We've lost."

~ƐЖЗ~

"No, you're wrong," said Lilly, staring at the Keren Archer in horror. "You can't be my mother. I have a mother."

"You were abducted as a baby," said Keren gently, her grey eyes staring into Lilly's. "We knew you were coming; an Oracle spoke of you. We were going to have the power to save the world because you. You, the Ultimate Power, the baby who held the fabric of life itself in her hands, were going to usher in that change."

"No!" Lilly insisted, shaking her head, refusing to believe it. It had to be lies. "No, no no."

"You had a bracelet," said Keren, folding her arms and leaning back, her voice calm. "A bracelet with a crystal. Do you remember?"

Lilly instinctively put her hand to her arm, "My charm bracelet."

"It was cursed," said Keren. "An enchanter put a power suppressing curse on that crystal, attached it to a bracelet, and attached the bracelet to you. You were taken from me and hidden, given a new name and a new family. But we found you. It took years, but we finally found you."

"It fell off…" Lilly murmured. She forced her mind back, trying to focus on the reality of the first day of school that seemed now like a lifetime ago. "No. No it was pulled. Someone pulled at me so hard I fell!"

"Alex," explained Keren. "I employed your adoptive mother, she does low level immaterial accounting for me, and recommended the school. She's malleable and complied easily. Alex was ready to save you. Ready to free you from the curse."

"But why not just tell me?" she Lilly asked, rubbing her head and feeling totally overwhelmed. "Why does everyone want to lie to me? Why does nobody trust me? I'm not stupid! I can handle the truth!"

"I didn't want to force you to join me out of biological obligation," said Keren, firmly. "I wanted to allow you the freedom to come because you believe in us. Because we make sense. Because not using your powers, not pushing yourself to develop to the best you can be, doesn't make sense. Because you want to achieve everything you can."

"I thought you were the only person who had been honest with me!" said Lilly, standing up angrily. "I thought you were the only person who had respected me enough to tell me what was going on. I was wrong. You're just as bad as everyone else. You just see me as a power. A tool. From the moment I was born you saw me as an Ultimate Power not your baby, not your daughter! Do you know the only people in the whole world who see me as someone in my own right? Who have never treated me with anything but love? You may have given birth to me but you are not my mother."

Lilly turned to leave, but Keren called out to her. "Lilly, I have the power to stop you. I will not lose this now."

"Do you?" she demanded, furiously, turning on Keren with rage on her face. "I could kill you in half a second if I wanted to. So go on, try and stop me," she stood still, daring the woman to move. Keren stayed seated so Lilly turned away again. "Come on, Saffron, let's go."

"Saffron," said Keren, standing and looking intently at Saffron, her voice like silk. "If you leave you will be giving up a chance to matter. If Lilly's life is truly in you, there's a chance you could replace her."

"What?" Saffron asked.

"She's right, of course, I cannot yet force her to join us," said Keren, smiling at her with a knowing look in her eyes. "But with you by my side, we could achieve the Ultimate Power through you. You, Saffron, could save the world."

"Saffron, don't listen to her," insisted Lilly, reaching out to pull her away. "She's lying to you. There's too much at stake. There's too big a price. I see that now, I was wrong to bring you here. This is my fault, please come with me."

"Go with Lilly and your life will be spent as her slave," said Keren casually, walking around the edge of the desk and perching on it in front of Saffron, putting a hand on her shoulder and speaking with sympathy and seduction. "You're an Enhancer now, and Lilly is The Life Giver. You'll dedicate your life to increasing her value, pushing the light further onto her. You will be nothing but her maid. Her lap dog. A pointless Halfling with no life of her own."

"Saffron!" Lilly begged, starting to panic. She was losing Saffron and she didn't know how to stop it. "Please?"

"No. No I can't," Saffron said, stepping away from Lilly and standing at Keren's side. "I lost everything because of you. This is my only chance. This is my chance to matter."

"But you matter to me!" Lilly wept.

"Maybe you should have thought of that before," she said coolly, her beautiful green eyes looking so full of pain and bitterness that Lilly knew she had lost her.

Keren slipped off the desk and stood beside Saffron, a maternal look on her face as she put an arm around Saffron's shoulders.

"If you walk out of this office," Keren said, staring at Lilly. "You will never be welcome back."

"Good," said Lilly, glaring at Keren. She looked at Saffron one last time, desperately hoping for a glimmer of regret in her choice but there was none. Turning, she left the room, slamming the door behind her. She stormed past Fawn, who didn't bother trying to stop her, and hurried through the corridors, feeling dizzy. She hoped nobody would try and stop her. She didn't know if she really could control her power enough to use it against them. She didn't know if she would use it even if she could. But she knew she needed to escape, and was desperate enough to try anything. She ran straight past the room she loved so much, past faces that stared after her, and out into the carpark without looking back. Nobody stood in her way.

She hurried through the carpark, out of the gates passed the guard who pointedly ignored her, and onto the road. As she ran down the path, she noticed a car with blacked out windows parked on the roadside. As she went to pass it, a window buzzed down and a voice called out, "Lilly?"

She stopped. Breathing hard. Terrified, she forced herself to turn and look to see whom had called to her. The back door opened and a woman she vaguely recognised stepped out.

"I know you," Lilly whispered, staring at her, trying to place her.

"Have you really left?" she asked faintly, surprise and joy on her face.

"Who are you?" asked Lilly suspiciously, racking her brain. She knew her face, she knew her voice.

"My name's Emma Bahman," said Emma. "Jeffrey works for me."

"You're the woman in my mirror" Lilly exclaimed, stepping back from her. "You were spying on me! Why are you here?"

"Come quickly," the woman said, stepping aside and gesturing to the car. "You need to get away from here right now. Get in."

"No!" Lilly said, backing away further and looking down the road, wanting to run. "No. I need to go home. I want my mum."

"Then let me give you a ride at least," insisted Emma.

"I don't think that's a good idea," said Lilly, shaking her head, feeling sick and dizzy and frightened and confused and desperate to get home and hide.

"I know who cursed you and I know why," said Emma, a look on her face that seemed to beg for trust. She looked almost afraid. "I can explain everything if you'll just give me a chance."

Lilly looked back at Adamantine, then at the car, then at Emma. "You know what my power is?"

"Yes."

"And you know I can use it?"

"Yes."

"If you try anything, do anything, I will use it against you," Lilly said, meaning every word. "Do you understand?"

Emma smiled a sad smile. "Yes, Lilly, I understand."

"Fine," said Lilly, and got into the dark car. Emma followed her in, and shut the door behind them. In the front of the car, a man in a hat started the engine and pulled away.

"I didn't expect to see you." Said Emma, leaning back, breathing a sigh of relief.

"Why are you here?" asked Lilly, in no mood for pleasantries and fed up of not being told the truth from the start.

"I haven't been in Adamantine for many years," said Emma, her voice quiet and heavy. "I haven't seen nor spoken to Keren in longer. I wanted to take a last look before… well. That's irrelevant now. You're here. It's over."

"Take me home, now please," said Lilly, looking out of the window.

"Gordon," Emma said, the man in the driver's seat glanced into the rear view mirror and nodded obediently.

"You were going to tell me who cursed me," said Lilly, looking back at Emma. "So Keren's story is true? She really is my mother?"

"Yes, she is," said Emma regretfully. "In as much as she gave birth to you. Your real name is Lilliana Archer and you were six months old when your aunt Lori abducted you, put the bracelet holding the crystal she had enchanted on you, and brought you to me."

"This doesn't make any sense," said Lilly, feeling lost. "Loriana is loyal to Keren, she told me so. She supports Owen's work that's taking people's minds. She wants me to use my power."

"Whilst reality is split between those who believe in the quest for power, and those who believe in maintaining the balance of nature, things are not as simple as that. Some, such as Keren, believe the quest for power comes above all else. That accumulating power, growing and developing your power, should matter more than the lives of those you trample to do so. Especially those without any power. Mortals are seen as immaterial. Rodents. But she is to the extreme. There are shades of grey, as with everything in life."

"And you?" asked Lilly. "What do you want?"

"I'm not as far in the other direction as many, some believe that using any power elevates us above the mortals inappropriately. We are all born equal, and to use a power you didn't choose to be born with makes you feel superior. I sympathise with that view but I'm not convinced. I believe that powers are part of us, and we need them, but we should never put the use of them above the wellbeing of those around us, never allow ourselves to feel superior or benefit artificially from them. To me, pushing to grow and develop them victimises those who cannot. Focusing on power and what we can do with it damages both ourselves and those around us. It is a utility, not the meaning of life, and should be used to benefit all including the mortals, rather than just those who have it."

"Right," said Lilly, not certain she was following it all but trying. A lot of Emma's words reminded her of Jeffrey and his attitude towards her power. It explained a lot. "You've not explained why my aunt abducted me. I was a baby! I couldn't have possibly done any harm."

"Loriana is not as devoted to the quest for power as your mother," said Emma, her voice softening. "She saw what the Oracles reported. She saw that you, your energy, your power, would bring about devastation if your mother were able to use it. At that time they didn't know exactly how they could utilise you, but they knew they could. You had been spoken of for too many generations of Seers. Whilst The Oracles are private and not inclined to give out exact details of people's lives, they are willing to share certain amounts and on you they were clear. You are power itself. Whilst Loriana believes power requires sacrifice, and pushing to improve is essential, she does not want to witness someone like Keren Archer at the helm of our planet."

"But my mum, my mum…" Lilly whispered, her mother's face in her head, the smell of her, the way she had always hugged her when she was sad. "She's my mummy."

"She is," agreed Emma emphatically. "She is a good woman who desperately wanted a child but couldn't have one. Both your parents have enough magic in their ancestry that they accepted your arrival without question, and we knew you'd be loved. You'd be safe."

"Why should I trust you? You took my magic from me," said Lilly, angrily. "I've never felt right, I've always felt like something's wrong with me and now I know why! You did it. You started the massive lie that turned into my whole life!"

"It was for the greater good," Emma insisted. "When we realised the curse had been broken we sent Jeffrey. He's an experienced Guardian and we knew we could trust him with you. We wanted you to be guided, to learn about your power safely, without trying to force you to do anything. We felt forcing you would push you away. We needed your trust. Your power is immense. Without trust we'd have nothing."

"So to get my trust you decided to lie to me. You put someone in my home claiming to care when he was just spying on me, and you used me to spy on your enemy," Lilly said. She hurt. She hurt so deeply inside that she didn't know how to handle it. "You're no better than them."

"Be that as it may, you are here not there," said Emma, rubbing her eyes. "I accept you're not happy with how it came about, but it worked. Keren's plan has failed, and that was what we needed from the start."

"Keren's plan hasn't failed," said Lilly miserably, picking at her thumb nail.

"What?" asked Emma, sitting upright and staring at her in panic.

"She has Saffron," said Lilly, looking down and picking at her thumb.

"But, but, what?" asked Emma looking flustered. "Saffron? Why would Saffron affect anything?"

"I didn't want to but we put power into her," Lilly said miserably, slumping back on the seat. "Keren said she has enough of my life energy in her that they could use her as the catalyst. She agreed."

"Oh my god," breathed Emma. "Gordon, put your foot down. We need to get to Lilly's right now."

"Why?" asked Lilly, as the driver skipped a red light and sped round a corner.

"Do you understand what's going to happen? Keren is going to be doubling the powers of herself and however many others she's got on side. Not just boosting, doubling. They will be invincible."

"Oh my god."

"And your friend will die in the process," said Emma, gripping the seat as the car skidded round another bend.

"Why?" cried Lilly. "I didn't die! I survived it! It hurt but I'm still here!"

"You are the Ultimate Power, Lilly!" said Emma. "Your power is intrinsic to you, it is your whole life force and it hurt you with just one power! How many people is Keren going to transfer powers to at once? How many life forces will be surging through Saffron in one hit?"

"A thousand," said Lilly, hopelessly.

"A thousand?" groaned Emma, her eyes wide and her face falling. "The deaths of a thousand will rest on her shoulders. Their lives will rip through her. Your essence may be in her, but it's not enough to sustain her. They will sacrifice her along with the thousand others who will die in the process. And however many more they take out when the rite is completed."

"Then we need to stop her!" insisted Lilly. "We can't let Saffron die!"

The car pulled up outside Lilly's house and Emma pulled a small, silver mirror from her pocket. "We need to make a plan. Right now. And we need reinforcements."

Chapter Twenty

"Hello, I'm Emma," said Emma, smiling at Lilly's mum. "I met you fifteen years ago."

"Erm, yes," said Lilly's mum, looking confused, but smiling welcomingly. "I think I remember."

"May I come in?"

Lilly's mum stepped back and allowed Emma to step into her warm kitchen. Lilly followed, with Amy, Ashya, Mr Stubbs, and several people Lilly didn't know.

"Erm, tea or coffee?" asked Lilly's mum gesturing vaguely towards the kettle whilst eyeing the crowd before her in confusion.

"No, but thank you," said Emma politely. "Would we be able to have the privacy of your living room, Mrs Prospero?"

"Oh… yes." Lilly's mum looked confused. "Lilly, what's going on?"

"I'll explain later mum," Lilly said.

A slow thud came down the stairs as Jeffrey awkwardly hopped into view. Lilly watched him, emotions flooding her. He looked in so much pain and she wanted to pick him up, kiss him and tell him she loved him. But she was hurting and angry, she felt betrayed. She stopped herself going to him, looking away sadly when he tried to catch her eye, her chest stabbing with pain.

"Jeffrey," Emma greeted him with a respectful nod.

The rabbit winced a little as he nodded back. Lilly's mum balked but shook her head, dismissing it. Emma led the group into the cosy living room where they filled the sofa and scattered across the floor. Lilly pushed the door shut with a click.

"Right," Emma said, seriously. "I have gathered you specifically because you're our only chance to stop Archer and restore the balance of Nature."

Around the room everyone watched her. Men and women of different ages and races, hanging on her every word. Except Jeffrey. Jeffrey watched Lilly. He caught Lilly's eye but she looked away again, though she could tell he was still watching her. She forced herself to listen to Emma, her mind too conflicted to deal with her emotions and thoughts about the rabbit yet. She needed to focus on the task at hand, Jeffrey could wait.

"First, Amy, I need you to stick to Lilly. If you See anything relevant, you tell her. I do understand the limitations, truly I do, but you could save us if things start going wrong before it happens."

"I'll try," Amy promised, nervously.

"The guard on the gate is a Freezer," Emma continued. "Ashya, you're going to need to use everything you've got to keep him hot. When he's hot he won't be able to move, he won't be able to alert anyone. He's advanced and capable. It will be hard. Can you do it?"

"Yes," said Ashya, grim determination etched across her face.

"Ariella," Emma said, turning to a woman in her thirties with a pierced nose and blue dreadlocks. "Look through the walls, make sure nobody is waiting and see if you can find the gathering. I expect them to be shielded but it is worth a shot."

"Sure thing boss," said Ariella.

"Beth, you work with Ariella," Emma said, to a curvy brunette in her twenties who was sitting cross legged on the floor. "Sense where power strongholds are within the building."

"Yep," agreed Beth, looking up to Ariella who nodded to her.

Emma went round the room, issuing instructions which were agreed to immediately, until she got to Lilly. "You, Lilly, have the hardest job of all. You will need to take down Saffron."

"What?" asked Lilly, sitting upright and looking horrified. "No! I'm not hurting Saffron!"

"Without her they can do nothing," Emma said firmly. "The lives won't be taken, the powers won't be transferred."

"Take her down how?" Lilly asked, shaking her head. There was no way she could agree to hurt her.

"Saffron's the weak link," Emma said. "We don't know what powers she will have in there but we know Saffron is new. She is vulnerable. She has no real power of her own and she is in a reality not designed for her. You can stop her quickly and efficiently. End it all."

"I can't!" protested Lilly, she knew what Emma wanted and she knew why she wasn't saying it explicitly. But she was fed up of being used and sick of not being trusted with the truth. "You tell me right now if you expect me to kill her!"

"This is dangerous work, Lilly. You could die, do you understand me? I would never ask you to kill, ever… but at the same time, if it came to that, if that was your only choice, then so be it. Once Saffron is taken out, Jordyn, Alyssa, Matthew, Gloria and Bo can deal with those left. Then, it will be up to you to take down Keren. She is stronger than us all. Except you. And she will have no hesitation in killing you if you do not do it fast."

Lilly looked around the room in panic. Everyone was watching her, eyes around the room stared at her and she felt sick to her stomach. She looked for Jeffrey, looked to see if he would defend her, tell her she didn't have to do anything she didn't want to. But she couldn't see him. He had left her.

~ƐӜӠ~

There are not many Guardians in the world. They're a rare being and they take on varying forms, and whilst they do not have much power,

there are certain abilities they are blessed with. Unfortunately, the
Guardian form is weak, and Jeffrey's was particularly vulnerable as he
teleported from Lilly's kitchen to the door of Adamantine. As he appeared
with a pop in the doorway, he felt his aching body flop to his side. He
struggled to breathe, the effort expelled in moving such a distance had
taken the last of his energy.

As the door opened and a man stepped out, distracted by lighting a
cigarette, Jeffrey forced his body to move and slipped inside. He pushed
himself back against the wall of the corridor and looked around, trying to
figure out where to go. He breathed hard, trying to ignore the pain in his
back and sides that stabbed him as his ribs scraped together. He felt
frightened and weak, but determined. Gritting his teeth and taking a deep
breath, the rabbit hopped slowly down the corridor ahead of him,
listening intently, and ducking into doorways when he heard anyone
approach.

"We have the Halfling secluded," said a man approaching down the
corridor then turning left, speaking to an elderly woman with grey flecks
speckled through her black curls. "She's in our department but could be
moved if necessary."

"How many are we waiting for?" asked the woman as they walked
away, Jeffrey following them quietly.

"Just two," said the man, stopping at a door painted white. "A new
name for Gwendoline the Enhancer to drain, and the Tomson woman is
yet to arrive. Then we are complete."

Jeffrey desperately wondered where Saffron was secluded and how to
find her. If he could get to her, free her, then Lilly would be saved and
none of this would have to go ahead.

~ƐӜӠ~

"Right, is everyone ready?" asked Emma, standing up.

"Where's Jeffrey?" asked Lilly.

"You don't need him, you'll be fine," Emma said, reassuringly.

"No I need him!" Insisted Lilly. "Where is he? He was here a minute ago."

Priscilla crept in and looked up at Lilly. "He's gone."

"He left me," Lilly murmured, her eyes filling with tears. "He promised. He promised he'd never leave me. I can't do this without Jeffrey."

"Listen to me, Lilly, you can do this, "Emma said, taking Lilly's hands and looking into her eyes fiercely. "You need to do this. Jeffrey's work is done. He knows that. You don't need him anymore."

"He promised he'd never leave me," she said again, tears running down her cheeks. "He promised! He promised!"

"You can do this." Emma said again.

~ƐӜƷ~

The woman disappeared through the white door, closing it behind her. So Jeffrey cautiously tailed the man down several corridors before he disappeared through a purple door. He looked around at the mass of purple doors, then saw another white one and it was slightly ajar. No other option was available to him, so he slipped inside.

The room was empty. The large windows looked out across a field, the sky a dull grey with speckles of rain starting to spit down. On the coffee table, by a green sofa, a book was open and Jeffrey hopped over to look at it. The effort to put his front paws up to the edge of table made him cry out in pain, everything inside him aching as if he had been stamped on.

"Is someone there?" came a girl's voice. "Hello? Please let me out. Please!"

"Saffron?" he called out, looking around.

"Who's there?" came the girl's voice again, she sounded terrified and weak.

"Is that you, Saffron? It's Jeffrey!" he called out, forcing his voice louder, despite the pain it caused his chest. He looked around then noticed, hidden from view behind a long bookcase, a door set back in the wall. He hopped over to it, putting his paw against the wood and pushing. It didn't move. "Saffron, please, you must not help Keren!"

"I don't have a choice!" she cried.

"You do have a choice! You always have a choice!" he insisted, looking around for a key or a button, anything he might be able to use to get the door open.

"Please get me out!"

"I'll try," he promised, then went back into the room. He opened a cupboard door and started poking around, the pain in his back worsening so much he felt like he would faint if he moved too suddenly, when a bag was forced over him and everything plunged into darkness. He was lifted in a sudden and agonising movement, and tumbled back into the darkness of the bag, his body contorted and broken. He screamed. He screamed a brutal scream as he lay helpless in the bottom of the bag, completely trapped.

Jeffrey was carried from the room, the bag swinging by his kidnappers' side, bumping roughly against legs and corners as he was moved through corridors. His piteous yelps of pain and whimpers of fear and despair achieving nothing except occasional tuts of disdain from his abductor.

He heard a knock, then a door opened and a female voice said, "Una? You have the Guardian I hear?"

"I hate it when you do that," came a young voice that Jeffrey assumed to be Una, the one carrying him. "But yes. I caught him poking around in the room where the Halfling is contained."

"Keren's busy. Can you dispose of it yourself?"

"Oh yes," Una said, with a wicked chuckle so callous that Jeffrey's whole body froze in fear. "I would enjoy it."

The door was closed again and Jeffrey was roughly carted back down the corridor in the bag that was his prison.

"Una?" Jeffrey called out. "Please let me go, Una, please let me go!"

"Let you go?" she asked with a laugh. "Well, if you insist."

Jeffrey couldn't believe what he had heard, certain he must be delirious with pain. But, minutes later, he heard the outer door open and close, then cold grey light entered the top of the bag, cold spots of rain landing on his face. Una tipped the bag up and Jeffrey landed with a crunching thud on the ground, a vicious crack sounding from his broken body.

"Go on then," she said, jutting her hip out. "Leave."

He looked up at her, terror on his face, rain landing on his eyes and making him blink frantically. Shocked and frightened, he nodded with gratitude and started to move, everything in his body begging him to stop and rest as he heard horrible scraping sounds that splintered at his flesh every time he stepped. But he kept going.

As he moved, slowly and awkwardly, he started to cry. He thought of Lilly, and how he had failed her. How hard he had tried to save her from what she now must face, but how he had let her down. He wanted to tell her how sorry he was; how sorry he was for everything.

He heard laughter from the doorway behind him, then a strange pressure started building in his lungs. He coughed, panic filling him as water suddenly gushed from his mouth. She was drowning him. He forced himself forward, his lungs pressing on his body, his head blinding him with pain and horror. He needed to get to Lilly, he needed to get to her and tell he was sorry, he needed to tell her he loved her and would never leave her. She needed him.

He vomited more water as the rain got heavier, bouncing from the tarmac around him and soaking into his body. Behind him Una's laughter increased maniacally as the water she moved in his body filled his lungs to the point he could no longer move. He fell to the ground, surrounded by the cars and concrete of the Adamantine carpark.

"Lilly!" he wept, fear and despair overwhelming him. "Please forgive me!"

Behind him the door shut as Una stepped out of the rain and into the building.

The rabbit lay alone, watching the rain fall above him as the water inside him took control. His eyes glazed over. And then he was gone.

~ƐӜƷ~

Four cars pulled up to the pavement outside the Adamantine gates, Lilly in the back of the first car feeling sick and terrified, wishing she could be anywhere else, and certain she wasn't strong enough to do this. Ashya stepped out into the rain, and approached the guard station with a smile. As he leaned out to ask her for ID, she blasted heat at him with such ferocity that the edge of the booth he sat in began to smoulder in seconds.

"Go!" she screamed out. "I've got him!"

Leaping from the car, Lilly followed Emma with everyone else as they raced through the gates and into the carpark. Everyone seemed so competent, so professional and determined. Then there was Lilly. Fifteen year old Lilly who was too afraid, too in experienced to achieve anything. She was going to let them down. She wanted to run. She wanted to get away and let them sort it out because she wasn't going to be able to do anything.

"Beth, Ariella, go ahead," Emma shouted through the rain. "Jordyn take up the flank and prepare to slow anyone down who tries to stop us."

They ran through the rain towards the doors when suddenly Lilly stopped and pointed at a brown heap of fur on the ground, soaked through and matted with blood. "What's that?"

"Just a dead animal, ignore it," said someone behind her, though Lilly wasn't listening.

"Jeffrey?" Lilly whispered, creeping forward and holding out a hand. She dropped to her knees, pushed the rabbit's ear back and saw his face. His eyes were open and soaked in tears and rain, his mouth still wide from screaming her name. "Jeffrey!" she cried. "Oh my God, Jeffrey. They killed you. They killed you!"

She felt herself falling apart, pain like she had never experienced stabbing through her body and filling her head. Tears flooded down her cheeks, her chest raking in sobs, as she gently stroked the dead rabbit's fur. She cried out in despair, tugging at her face and her hair, too horrified and heartbroken to stand or speak. After a moment, she leaned down and gently closed the rabbit's soft broken eyes to protect them from the rain.

"Oh Lilly," said Emma, crouching down and putting an arm around her. "I understand. He was an important part of your life, a Guardian becomes so much more than just a companion."

"He wasn't my Guardian!" Lilly shouted, standing up and turning on Emma with rage, her wet hair clinging to her cheeks. "He wasn't a Guide or a Teacher or anything you told him to be! He was my pet rabbit and they killed him!" she stopped, panting hard, then felt herself start to sob again. "And I didn't even get to tell him I forgive him."

"What do you want to do?" asked Emma.

Lilly turned away, staring that looming building and feeling a steely, cold determination taking hold of her. "Destroy them."

Chapter Twenty-One

"I've found one!" Keren Archer heard a male voice shouting from behind her office door. "I've found an Enhancer!"

"Wait right there," she heard Fawn say, in an effort to do her job correctly.

"No time!" the voice shouted, full of excitement. The door of her office was flung open and Paul Lockwood appeared, panting, and rushed over. Fawn stood apologetically behind him then silently closed the door. "Ms Archer, I've found an Enhancer. Everyone is assembled. We are ready for you."

"Are you not aware of the rules, Mr Lockwood?" asked Keren Archer, standing and casually walking around the desk.

"I… I'm sorry Ms Archer…" he stammered, a look of terror suddenly washing over his face. "I wanted to…"

Keren flicked her wrist absentmindedly towards him, lightning shooting out of her finger tips and straight into his heart. He cried out in agony, writhed, and then dropped.

"Fawn!" she called out.

"I'm so sorry," Fawn said, pushing the door open and looking nervous. "He got past me."

"I noticed," she said coolly, pointing at the man's body on the floor. "Dispose of this will you?"

Fawn nodded and stepped aside as Keren Archer walked past.

~ƐℋƷ~

"Stay right here," instructed Una. "Or you'll meet the same fate as that rabbit."

Saffron trembled but agreed. She was in the centre of an enormous room, surrounded by the enchanted objects she recognised from earlier, and further out a crowd a thousand strong stood around her in a deep circle. Una walked away leaving Saffron staring around in terror, watching the whispering crowd staring back at her. The high arched ceiling seemed to echo everything around her, the light was so dim she could barely make out the first row of faces that stared at her. She felt incredibly small, and overwhelmingly alone.

Behind her she heard the clang of the door opening and turned to see Keren Archer walking towards her.

"Hello there, Saffron," Keren said, a sinister smile across her face.

"Please," Saffron whispered. "I don't want to do this. Please don't make me."

"Oh, my dear girl," she said with a cruel laugh, walking towards her. "You're not going to do anything. Surely you don't really believe a Halfling like yourself could accomplish something as great as this? We have worked for too many years to risk ruining it with something like you."

"But… why am I here?" she stuttered, looking around, the eyes of everyone on her, all of them looking at her with a mixture of curiosity and revulsion.

"Oh, we still need you," she said, gently caressing the tumble of red curls that fell from Saffron's head. "My daughter may have aligned herself with those weak and pathetic mortal lovers, but that makes her vulnerable. That makes her stupid."

"Lilly…" breathed Saffron.

"It won't be long now, dear," she said, stepping past Saffron and walking away, her voice staying audible despite the size of the room. "You just wait right there."

At the top of the room Tereska stepped into view from amongst the crowd, standing in front of a large stone table. Saffron stared at her, pleading with her eyes, hoping that somehow the girl would take pity and do something, anything, to help her. Keren stepped onto the table and turned, looking proudly around the room. Tereska looked away from Saffron, and like the rest of the audience, gazed up at Keren.

"Fifteen years ago I made you a promise and today it shall be realised," Keren's voice rang out around the room, clear, confident and with gravitas. Saffron found herself captivated by the woman, despite the terror that threatened to bring her to her knees. "Today your loyalty shall be rewarded. From now on there shall be no question of prioritising an imagined balance. There shall be no concern for those too pathetic to command respect. There shall be no time wasted. From today, we shall RULE." She flung her hands in the air, lightning blasting from her finger tips as the crowd cheered and clapped. Saffron cowered in horror as tears escaped from her eyes and wished she had been left to die in the river.

~ƐӜƷ~

"That way," said Beth pointing down a corridor. "It's hot. Very, very hot."

Ariella turned and faced where Beth pointed and closed her eyes. "I see people. There are hundreds of people, and lightning. Lots of lightning."

"Look out!" shouted Jordyn, stepping forwards and holding up his arms as a group of people came round a corner ahead. A force field shot out and Lilly looked in amazement as Owen and a group of his friends froze behind a glimmering arc of light, his eyes locked wide open, his face hanging mid-sentence. "Go!"

"This way," said Ariella, leading them past the frozen group. Lilly stared in horror at Owen as they eased past, careful not to touch them, but pushed it from her mind and kept up with Ariella.

"I see Saffron" said Amy, hurrying beside Lilly and pulling her to a stop. "I see her. She's crying. I see you." She suddenly rocked on the spot, Lilly grabbed at her to support her before she fell. "Lilly, this isn't a good idea. This will end in death. I can feel it. It's all over everything! Oh god so much death. So much death." Amy started sobbing, tearing at her face, her eyes filled with absolute terror.

"That's why we have to do it," insisted Emma, stepping up to Lilly and speaking to her quietly, a hand on her arm.

"No! Stop! Please stop!" begged Amy. "We need to leave right now. This is the wrong thing to do!"

"They killed Jeffrey," said Lilly, forcing herself to stand up straight, not letting the fear inside show, and starting to walk after Ariella. "I'm not letting them kill my best friend too."

"Una's there," whispered Amy, starting to shake. "She did it, Lilly, she drowned Jeffrey."

"What?" Lilly cried, spinning back and grabbing Amy's arms. "Are you certain?"

Amy nodded, tears running down her face. "I saw it. I didn't believe it, I didn't say anything, but then he was there. She did it. I'm so sorry, Lilly, I'm so sorry."

"Which way?" Lilly asked Ariella, turning away from Amy, all fear and uncertainty gone.

"This way," said Ariella. "Not far now."

A man stepped out of a door to their left but Alyssa stepped forward, her hand out, and raised him high above the floor. The man cried out, suspended above the floor, frantically flapping his arms and legs and shouting abuse at the woman who held him there. They kept going, Amy crying out as visions flashed in her head, she cried in fear, but didn't try to stop their progress.

"Here," said Ariella, stopping momentarily, then slowly approaching a set of grey double doors. "Behind here. Down a corridor."

"It burns," said Beth stepping back. "I'm sorry. I can't. It's too hot."

"Nobody needs go on but Lilly now," Said Emma. "Lilly, go. Save the world."

Amy looked in her eyes, her face pure fear. "You don't have to do this," she whispered. "You shouldn't do this."

"I don't have a choice," Lilly said bitterly.

"You always have a choice," said Amy quietly.

The words hit her, Jeffrey's face flashing before her, and the absolute devastation of his death ripping into her chest so deeply it felt as if she were literally being torn apart. She choked back tears and gritted her teeth.

"No," she said, determined. "Jeffrey didn't want them to win. I should have listened before then it would never have come to this. This is my fault. I'm going to stop them." She turned away, pushed the doors open, and stepped into the corridor alone, the doors closing behind her.

~ƐӜ3~

Saffron watched as Tereska started Speaking. Around the room, faces gazed at her, an excited murmur moving amongst the crowd. Very slowly a gold mist started to creep from the objects around her. Delicate golden particles of light crept gingerly into the air and Saffron knew what was coming. She dropped to her knees and cried. She wanted to escape, she wanted to run away, but she was paralysed by fear, too terrified of what they would do to her if she tried.

The mist kept rising and rising, then golden lights started appearing high above everyone's heads. Saffron curled into a ball, blocking it out with her arms over her eyes, all hope leaving her as she felt the eyes of a thousand locked to her trembling body.

Behind her, she heard the door open.

~ƐЖƺ~

Lilly stepped into the room and took everything in in moments. Her mother standing on a stone alter, Tereska kneeling before her Speaking. Saffron curled in the foetal position as golden mists swirled around her, lights piling above her. A thousand people staring in excitement at what was happening suddenly turned their faces towards her in surprise.

"NO!" screamed Lilly. She ran through the golden mist and crouched beside her friend. With a flash, the mist began spinning in golden waves, the lights glowed so bright they were blinding.

"Lilly! Leave! Now!" begged Saffron, scrambling to her knees and trying to push Lilly away from her.

"I won't leave you!" Lilly shouted as she stood, a roaring sounding above and around them so deafening she could barely hear herself.

"LIFE AND DEATH!" screamed Tereska, standing, her arms out wide. "LIFE AND DEATH! LIFE AND DEATH!"

Lilly felt herself start to burn. It was an agonising, soul destroying heat that ate at her flesh and made her brain scream in blinding agony. She fell to the ground and wept, her whole body shaking, the pain so severe she twitched and writhed uncontrollably. She lost her vision, everything fading into blackness as her senses started to give up. In the darkness she saw Jeffrey's face, concern and love across it as she burdened her issues onto him without concern for his own. Then she saw his body. Limp, broken, soaked in tears and rain.

"THE POWER IS OURS!" came Keren's voice above the terrified girls, loud and ferocious, so powerful it shocked Lilly into focus.

It was happening. A thousand people were about to die and her mother was about to create an unstoppable army. She was losing the fight; she was too weak to stop it. She was meaningless. She was pointless. She was everything she had always feared and she was letting down the rabbit who had believed in her.

"NO!" Lilly cried out, pushing herself to standing and flinging her arms out before her as a wave of energy burst from her body; an eruption of power driven by pain and fear, love and despair. Around her a thousand bodies fell to the ground. All except Keren Archer, who stepped forward with venom across her face and sent a blast of electricity so hard at Lilly that she was knocked off her feet and thrown six foot through the air, skidding across the ground and crying out in pain.

"YOU STUPID LITTLE BITCH!" Keren shouted, stepping from the stone platform and storming past the fallen bodies towards her daughter. "YOU THINK THAT WILL STOP ME?"

Lilly watched as her mother stepped into the centre of the swirling mists. She towered over Saffron who trembled at her feet, power mad lust in her eyes. Her usually obsessively neat hair wild and loose, her hands held aloft begging the power to fill her.

"Stop!" Lilly cried out weakly.

"I WILL TAKE THEM ALL FOR MYSELF!" Keren shrieked, her eyes burning with power mad lust. "I WILL RULE THE WORLD! AND THE FIRST THING I WILL DO IS RID IT OF MORTALS AND PATHETIC HALFLINGS LIKE YOU!" she brandished a long finger at Saffron.

Lilly dragged herself to her feet, everything aching from the searing heat of the lightning and the crash as she had landed on the ground. She looked up and saw Saffron was cowering on the floor, terrified and vulnerable, no hope of escape beside the malevolent power of Lilly's mother. She wouldn't let her die alone, if Saffron was to die then she would be by her side, and they would go out together. She ran forwards, back into the golden glowing circle. The beams of light above them began to spin frantically, suddenly shooting down towards Lilly. She screamed as the light beams blasted through her body with a scorching force, then funnelled out and into Keren.

The two girls looked at each other in horror as Keren howled in triumph.

Lilly felt her face crumple, tears falling. She had promised Jeffrey she wanted to do good, to use her power to help people, and she had failed him. She had failed him and helped set in motion everything he was against, everything he had warned her away from. She sobbed.

Saffron stood up beside her friend and they held each other's eye contact, fear, loss and sorrow burning between them. Saffron held out her hand and Lilly took it.

The moment their hands touched, a wave of energy blasted from their hands with such intensity they nearly fell to the ground. It catapulted into Keren's crowing form, ripping the light back out of her and back into Lilly who stumbled with the force. From Lilly it burst free again, shooting up towards the sky like glowing rockets. Lilly fell hard to the ground, the ferocity and strength of the powers that had passed through her too much to bare, their hands breaking apart and the power they had produced falling away.

"NO!" screamed Keren, turning on the two girls, venomous fury burning in her eyes. "You stupid, pathetic children!"

As she raised her hands, ready to fire the deadly lightning straight into Saffron's heart, Lilly grabbed Saffron's hand again and sent a devastating power from their entwined fingers and straight at the vengeful witch. It struck Keren in the gut, freezing her before the electricity could escape her fingers. She writhed in momentary agony before falling in a heap on the ground.

The mist collapsed like a fallen building. The lights above shot away in all directions like fireworks.

Keren Archer's body lay lifeless on the ground.

"You killed your mother," whispered Saffron.

"It was her or you," said Lilly, not letting go of Saffron's hand as they looked around the now dark room, bodies lying scattered everywhere.

"Are they dead too?" whispered Saffron, gripping Lilly's hand tightly.

"I don't know," admitted Lilly, terrified that they were. Someone coughed and the two girls jumped in shock. A man in the crowd sat up looking shaken and dazed. "I guess not."

More started to move and stir, drained and weak but not dead. Lilly breathed a sigh of relief. She felt pain deep through her body, the powers that had ripped through her seeming to tear holes in her very being with their force, but she hadn't caused the death of a thousand people. She felt tears of relief start to creep down her cheeks.

A voice suddenly cried out, "What did you do? Is she dead?"

They looked around and saw Una standing amongst the crowd of fallen people. With a face full of hatred she stormed towards them.

"You!" Lilly dropped Saffron's hand and turned on her with outrage. "You killed my rabbit!"

"I… I… Lilly I'm sorry…" Una stuttered, genuine fear taking over her face as she backed away with her hands up. "It was orders. I had no choice."

"You *always* have a choice." Lilly growled as she raised her hands and Una cowered before her.

"Lilly, wait," said Saffron, gently placing a hand on her arm and speaking softly. "He wouldn't want you to do that."

"You're right," Lilly said, her head dropping and shame and misery threatening to allow tears to escape from her eyes.

"Thank you," Una whimpered. "I mean, come on, it was just a rabbit!"

Saffron turned furiously on Una and swung her fist hard into the girl's face sending her flying to the floor. "There is no such thing as *just* a rabbit!"

The girls breathed hard, looking down at Una in disgust, when behind them the door opened again. They turned to see Loriana and Emma walking towards them, their eyes wide as they took in the devastation around the room as slowly people were starting to move, most too afraid to stand.

"Is she dead?" asked Lori, approaching her sister's body.

"Yes," said Lilly, her head dropping. "I'm sorry.

"I expected it," she said, sadly.

Emma looked around the room, disgust on her face as she took in the crowd of weakened people. "If your power had been that bit stronger then so would they all be."

"Perhaps that is reason enough for her to need training," said Lori, looking sternly at Emma. "And I would suggest she stays on at Adamantine, under my tutorage."

"You think a thousand dead would be something good for a fifteen year old girl to carry on her shoulders?" asked Emma, outraged. "Surely this is evidence for needing to curtail her powers before they get too strong."

"Excuse me?" said Lilly. "How about you let me decide what to do for myself for once?" The two women went to argue but then, on seeing her face, fell silent. "If Amy had been trained by Adamantine, she'd have Seen that me coming here was exactly what Keren wanted. I could have been prepared long ago for what I was about to face. If I had been trained from earlier then I wouldn't have been so easily manipulated by Alex."

"Exactly" said Lori, glaring at Emma.

"But, if balance had been prioritised then this would never have happened in the first place!" Lilly went on. "Owen wouldn't have taken Billy's mind, Alex and Keren wouldn't be dead. Jeffrey wouldn't be dead." Her voice strained and broke as she finished.

"Precisely," said Emma, looking smugly at Lori.

"Lilliana, you were such a beautiful baby," said Lori, her voice soft and coaxing. "Help me run Adamantine. We can ensure that people like your mother never get the chance to use you like that again."

"That woman is not my mother," Said Lilly, a hardness in her voice. "And I do not want to work here again."

"Good," smiled Emma. "Come on Lilly, let's get you home to your mum."

"I'm not going with you either," Lilly said.

"But…"

Lilly held up a hand. "I don't think either of you are right. The pursuit of power even when it ruins lives is evil, and neglecting powers that could do the world so much good if they were trained is foolish!"

"So what are you going to do?" asked Emma. "Who are you going to join?"

"I'm not picking either of your causes!" she said, exasperated. "I'm not joining anyone! Do you know what Jeffrey believed in? What Jeffrey taught me to always work for?"

"What?" asked Lori.

"The greater good," said Saffron, stepping up to Lilly's side.

"Come on, Saffron." Said Lilly, then looked around the room and spoke loudly and with authority. "And don't anyone even think about trying to stop us."

In front of them, people parted, allowing the two girls to walk side by side out of the cursed room. Silently, they walked down the corridors and out of the building into the now dry air, a soft summer breeze having washed the clouds away. In the carpark Lilly pulled off her sweater, crouched down and gently scooped Jeffrey's body into it. She wrapped him up tenderly, kissing his head and crying quietly into his fur.

"Goodnight Jeffrey" she whispered.

Together they walked away from Adamantine. Lilly tenderly held Jeffrey's body in her arms, and Saffron remained respectfully silent. That evening they gathered together, family and animals, and buried Jeffrey under a rose bush in the garden. As everyone dispersed to sit by the BBQ in the warm evening sun, tears shed and hugs exchanged, Lilly and Saffron sat together looking at the soft mound of dirt that covered the rabbit's body.

"You could just bring him back, you know?" said Saffron quietly. "You did it with me... he doesn't have to stay gone."

"No. He wouldn't want that," she said, tears trickling down her cheeks. "He wouldn't want the price to be paid. I have to respect that."

"He'd have been proud of you, Lilly," Saffron said, resting her head on Lilly's shoulder.

"Somewhere he is," she said, smiling, knowing it was true. "And I intend to make him prouder."

Saffron sat up and looked her in the eye, held her hand out to Lilly. "We both will."

Lilly nodded, reached out, and took her hand.

The End

Read More
Siren Stories: The Ultimate Bibliography

Lilly Prospero And The Magic Rabbit (The Lilly Prospero Series Book 1)
By J.J. Barnes

Lilly Prospero And The Magic Rabbit is a young adult urban fantasy exploring the corrupting effects of absolute power on a teenage girl. When the unpopular and lonely Lilly Prospero is given a talking pet rabbit, her life begins to change. She is thrust into a world of magic, mystery, and danger, and has to get control of a power she doesn't understand fast to make the difference between life and death. The first in a new series by J.J. Barnes, Lilly Prospero And The Magic Rabbit is a tale full of excitement, sorrow and mystery, as Lilly Prospero shows just how strong a girl can be.
Available in Paperback and for Kindle.

Alana: A Ghost Story
By Jonathan McKinney

Alana is a ghost, trapped in the New York Film Academy dorms, where she died. She has friends, fellow ghosts, with whom she haunts the students living there, passing her time watching whatever TV shows and movies the students watch.

But she is restless. She wants to move on. And when a medium moves into the dorms, Alana gets a nasty shock, which turns her mundane afterlife upside down.

Alana is a light yet moving short story about a miraculous love that travels many years and many miles to save a lost, trapped and hopeless soul.

Available in Paperback and for Kindle.

Emily the Master Enchantress: The First Schildmaids Novel (The Schildmaids Saga Book 1)
By Jonathan McKinney

Hidden, veiled behind the compressed wealth of New York City, is a dank underbelly of exploitation and slavery, which most people never see, or sense, or suffer. A cruel, expanding world.

And when Emily Hayes-Brennan, a proficient enchantress with a good heart and a tendency to overshare, is recruited to the world renowned crime fighters, the Schildmaids, she will find that that cruel world threatens to expand around her, and everyone she cares about.

She will be confronted by conflicts of fate and choice, as she seeks to find her place in the world.

Available in Paperback and for Kindle.

After the Mad Dog in the Fog: An Erotic Schildmaids Novelette
By Jonathan McKinney and J.J. Barnes

Emily Hayes-Brennan wants to get through a simple night out in her home city of New York, introducing her new boyfriend Teo to her friends, so she can get him home and have sex with him for the very first time. But when an obnoxious admirer and old flame shows up, she begins to fear that her plans are going awry.

After the Mad Dog in the Fog is a wild and energetic novelette about love and desire, and about the free joy that comes from prioritising the one you love before all others.

Available in Paperback and for Kindle.

Lilly Prospero And The Mermaid's Curse (The Lilly Prospero Series Book 2)
By J.J. Barnes

Lilly Prospero And The Mermaid's Curse is a young adult, urban fantasy following Lilly Prospero and her friend Saffron Jones on a magical adventure to Whitstable.

Whilst on a family holiday, Lilly and Saffron meet mermaids under attack from a mysterious and violent stranger, work with a powerful coven of witches, and fight to save not only the lives of the mermaids, but their own lives as well.

Available in Paperback and for Kindle.

The Inadequacy of Alice Anders: A Schildmaids Short Story
By Jonathan McKinney

Alice Anders can summon vision of the future, which guide her heroic friends through heroic acts. Sometimes she'll see vulnerable people in danger; sometimes she'll see her superhero friends in places where they can help those who can't help themselves.

But, for the last three and a half weeks, she's not been able to summon a single vision—and given that she started working for the superhero team of her dreams, the Schildmaids, exactly three and a half weeks ago, she's becoming anxious about her worth. And to figure out why her power has gone away, she'll have to push herself, and face some hard truths.

The Inadequacy of Alice Anders is a light and bittersweet short story about the pain of loss, and about facing that pain when it threatens to hold you down and hold you back.

Available in Paperback and for Kindle.

The Fundamental Miri Mnene: The Second Schildmaids Novel (The Schildmaids Saga Book 2)
By Jonathan McKinney

Miri Mnene is the Syncerus, a warrior, and the strongest of the Schildmaids, the New York team of legendary crime fighters. But she was not always the Syncerus. Once, she was the Xuét☐ N☐nrén Shashou, the final student of the man-hating, man-killing Guan-yin Cheh.

And when she is sent to South Dakota to investigate a mystical brothel, which has been kidnapping women, kidnapping girls, and forcing them to work, she is confronted by the darkness that lives within her when her past and present collide.

The Fundamental Miri Mnene is a powerful novel about the lengths to which you should go, the lengths to which you must go, in order to see justice in the world.

Available in Paperback and for Kindle.

The Relief of Aurelia Kite: A Schildmaids Novella
By Jonathan McKinney

Aurelia Kite is a young New Yorker at Christmas, trapped in an abusive relationship, dreaming of escape. And when her controlling boyfriend Trafford takes on a new job, her path crosses with two highly serious female crime fighters, causing her to make a big decision about what she will and will not tolerate.

The Relief of Aurelia Kite is a harsh novella with a soft centre, about hope in the face of toxic romance, and about the salvation that can be found just by talking to a sympathetic stranger.

Available in Paperback and for Kindle.

Not Even Stars: The Third Schildmaids Novel
By Jonathan McKinney

Teo Roqué is journeying through Europe with Emily Hayes-Brennan, the woman he loves, when ancient hostilities give way to a war between powerful, clandestine organisations. A war which puts the young couple's lives in danger, as well as all those they care about.

And as a new threat emerges, fanning the conflict's flames, Teo and Emily must work together to end the war before it leads to a disaster much, much worse than they'd imagined.

Not Even Stars is an incredibly intense novel about all-consuming love, about awe-inspiring heroism, and about the cost of making the right choice when the fate of the world hangs in the balance.

Available in Paperback and for Kindle.

The Mystery of Ms. Riley: a Schildmaids Novella

By Jonathan McKinney

Alice Anders and Rakesha McKenzie are members of the Schildmaids, the legendary New York crime fighters. And when Alice sees visions of Nina Riley, a young New Yorker carrying a deep, hidden pain, the two heroes fight to determine what has caused that pain, and how to save Ms. Riley from a prison she cannot even see.

The Mystery of Ms. Riley is a harsh yet hopeful story about self-doubt, about ordinary, everyday oppression, and about the kind of love that defies the testimonies of everyone around you.

Available in Paperback and for Kindle.

Unholy Water: A Halloween Novel

By Jonathan McKinney

In the misty Lancashire town of Ecclesburn, kids go missing. But no one talks about it. Everyone knows why, but they don't talk about it. The grown ups smear garlic and holy water over their necks and wrists while walking the dog after dark, but they never say the V word.

And when one of the local pubs is taken over by a group of undead monsters, and a trio of vampire hunters is called to clear them out, a terrible series of events begins to play out, which will change the way Ecclesburnians live forever.

Unholy Water is a dark and bloodthirsty novel about desire in wild excess, about whether you should defy your circumstances or adapt to them, and about the kind of inflexible determination that can save or destroy those that matter most.

Available in Paperback and for Kindle.

Emerald Wren and the Coven of Seven
By J.J. Barnes

As a child, Emerald's grandfather gives her a magic lamp with the promise that she can change the world. As an adult Emerald is working hard as a waitress by day, and as part of a crime fighting coven by night.

And when they get news of a man working his way across the country, burning women to death in his wake, Emerald's coven of seven must take on the biggest challenge of their lives, and risk everything to save the people they love.

Available in Paperback and for Kindle.

Printed in Great Britain
by Amazon